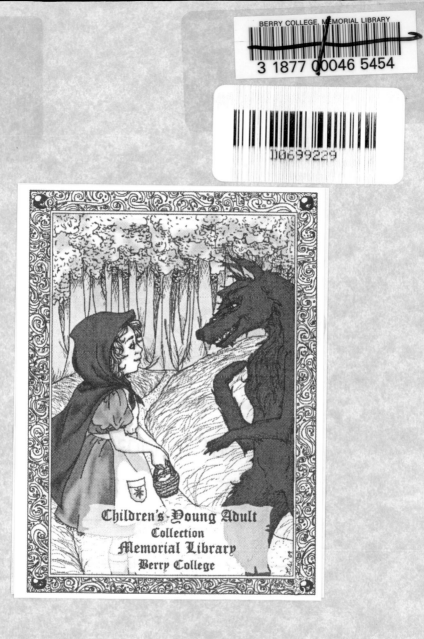

The Purple Heart

MARC TALBERT

The Purple Heart

Willa Perlman Books
An Imprint of HarperCollins*Publishers*

Library of Congress Cataloging-in-Publication Data
Talbert, Marc, 1953
    The purple heart / Marc Talbert.
        p.   cm.
    "Willa Perlman books."
    Summary: When his wounded father is sent home early from Vietnam, Luke finds it
difficult to adjust to the troubled, emotionally shaken man who seems so unlike the
fearless hero of his dreams.
    ISBN 0-06-020428-1. — ISBN 0-06-020429-X (lib. bdg.)
    [1. Fathers and sons—Fiction. 2. Interpersonal relations—Fiction. 3. Vietnamese
Conflict, 1961–1975—Fiction.] I. Title.
PZ7.T14145Pu 1992   91-23084
[Fic]—dc20   CIP
                                                                        AC

For
Captain Thomas Avey, USMC,
brother and friend
and
Edward A. Knapp,
friend and patron of science and art.

Spring 1967

CHAPTER

1

Luke couldn't sleep. He'd kicked off his covers, but he was still sweating. Luke never wore pajamas if he could help it. But tonight he'd worn them to bed in case a tornado was sighted and the town's sirens went off and he had to rush down to the safety of the basement. He didn't want to be naked if the house collapsed and rescue workers had to dig through the debris to save him and his picture was in the newspaper, on the front page.

Even so, he hated wearing pajamas. Tonight they clung to him like waxed paper left out in the sun. "Crud!" he mumbled, enjoying the way his father's favorite word scuffed along the back of his tongue. He lay as quietly as he could—spread-eagled, eyes closed—and tried to imagine himself floating on a layer of cool air.

Tornado season had come in May, a month early, with its greenish dusks in the middle of the day and its eerie stillness before storms. Luke wondered if a storm was approaching or if the night was simply breathless. Within the past week, Luke and his mother had spent three nights in the basement, staring wide-eyed at the floor joists above them, counting the nails that held them, praying that the boards would stay together. Luke and his mother had been in sleeping bags that they'd unrolled against the base of the cinder-block walls, their feet far apart and their heads almost bumping together in the southwest corner, close enough to share the light of a candle nubbin and hold hands across the clammy basement floor.

It should have been a treat to sleep in the cool of the basement, camping out with his mother, surrounded by an emergency stash of water, soda, crackers, peanut candies, extra candles, and plenty of matches. But sleeping in the basement meant that tornados or violent storms raged above, threatening to smash their house and everything in it.

Luke's fear and hatred of tornados was growing stronger all the time. He'd seen countless photos in the newspaper of smashed buildings and heard scores of stories about lengths of straw driven through trees, mobile homes turned on their heads, and horses carried for miles and laid gently on the ground, unscratched but dead. Luckily, the town of Clifton nestled in a wide valley created by two converging rivers, and so far tornados had always skipped from valley rim to valley rim, jumping over the town, never touching down. But several times in the past couple of years Luke had seen twisting, blurry, spinning tubes descend from the sky, not quite reaching the tops of trees, seeming like loose, wobbly, high-powered drills almost free of their bits, dangerous and unpredictable, whining and poking through boiling clouds the color of diesel exhaust.

Shuddering, Luke opened his eyes and looked out his bedroom window. Heat lightning flashed at irregular moments, not streaking down in crackling shafts but coming from beyond the horizon, as if the surrounding towns were being bombed by enemy troops or grain elevators were being blown up by roving bands of enemy guerrillas. Thunder followed each flash, faint and low, more a feeling than a sound, each time making Luke think that his ears were stuffed up. He stared at the patches of dim stars that barely shone through dark blotches of leaves of the ancient apple tree that grew outside his bedroom window. They disappeared with the heat lightning and reappeared moments before the thunder.

In his mind he heard his father's voice, brave and sure, the way he imagined him during combat: *We need mortar cover on Hill 33! Charlie is moving in . . . fast! More mortar! Alpha Company under attack! Get a move on! Get dancing 'fore the music stops! Don't waltz! Get Rocking 'n Rolling!*

Although he knew that his father couldn't make tornados go away or keep the house from flying apart, Luke remembered feeling safe before his father had left for Vietnam. But his father had returned home yesterday and Luke felt as unsafe in violent weather as he had when he and his mother were alone.

Sitting partway up, he reached above his shoulders, flipped over the pillow, and let his head sink into the fresh coolness of its newly exposed side. Closing his eyes, he tried to will himself asleep. But each time he heard the low rumble in the distance, he expected to feel the air shift, to feel it drop heavily to the ground and then silently bounce upward as a storm approached. And then his imagination took over and the thunder grew in his head, sounding like houses exploding or bullet-riddled, shrapnel-shredded barns collapsing, or mines popping off—sounds his father must have heard every day in Vietnam. Luke was certain that his father had been brave enough not to let these sounds bother him any more than the noise of a train in the distance. He wished he were as brave as his father.

Flipping onto his side, facing away from the window, Luke folded the pillow over his head so that it covered both ears. He could no longer hear the thunder but, in the silence he'd created, unwelcome images jarred his thoughts.

★

He saw her so clearly that she could have been standing in front of him: his mother, pregnant, her belly swelled to an enormous size, smiling from the kitchen door as he came home from school over a month ago. She'd hugged him so tightly Luke had been afraid her belly would split. And then she'd held him at arm's length—his belly button almost even with hers, almost kissing—and told him that his father was going to come home from Vietnam much earlier than they'd expected. Her cheeks were flushed with happiness as she spoke. "Your father will be here when the baby is born!" He knew his mother had been worried while his father was away, but it was then that Luke had realized that she'd thought that his father might not make it out of Vietnam alive, that he might be killed weeks, days, hours, *minutes* before he was supposed to come home—before the baby arrived, before he could see his second child.

"Go ahead," she'd said. "Tell your brother or sister." And she'd lifted the tails of his father's work shirt. It was a game they had played often, and Luke bent over and talked into his mother's earlike navel. "Dad's coming home!"

He was so excited that it wasn't until dinner that Luke thought to ask why his father was coming home so early. "He was wounded," his mother explained, dishing up mashed potatoes with her answer. "He's in a hospital in Tokyo . . . recuperating. But he's going to be all right."

"How? How was he wounded?" he asked, imagining his father clutching the round of his shoulder, his teeth bared, blackish blood oozing from between his fingers toward the pistol that spit steady fire.

"Well . . ." She avoided looking at him.

"Aw, come on," Luke pleaded. "Tell me."

His mother's lips tightened and she muttered, "I wish to God he hadn't up and joined the army." And then she looked at Luke. "I suspect you'd better ask your father about that," she said with unusual primness.

Luke stared at her in disbelief. He wanted to know so badly that it seemed cruel for her not to tell him. But Luke saw how her face had closed up.

He knew she'd made up her mind and that nothing he could say or do would change it.

He began to sulk—until it occurred to him that it would be a better story coming from his father, anyway.

Wounded. That must make my father a hero, Luke thought as he lay in bed.

★

But other feelings nibbled away at this thought as he pulled the pillow tighter around his head. Luke hated feeling that his father had come home early in the same way that tornados had come early this year.

Luke closed his eyes harder, hoping to squeeze this shameful thought from his head, but yet another image replaced the first. Again he pictured his mother, this time behind a chain-link fence at the Des Moines airport, holding her belly with one hand and waving with her other at a plane rolling to a stop. "There it is! There's your father's airplane!" she'd cried over the racket of the propellers that oddly enough grew louder as they slowed down. She'd grabbed Luke's upper arm with both hands and squeezed it tightly. Wincing, he'd searched for his father, his eyes frantically skimming over the people who were walking down the plane's rolling stairs and stepping onto the tarmac.

And then one figure caught his eye. Luke had squinted. This man was bent over sideways from the weight of the duffel bag hanging from a shoulder—he walked old, taking baby steps, as if something were wrong with his feet or his legs. One hand clutched a cane. But the closer he got, the faster Luke's heart beat.

His father had hobbled toward Luke and his mother and, to Luke's surprise, stopped a good ten or fifteen feet in front of them, far enough away so Luke could barely read "Canvin" in the squared letters on the plastic name tag pinned above the uniform's breast pocket. Luke looked up and saw his father's mouth quiver and read confusion in his eyes. Letting the duffel bag slide off his shoulder and drop to his feet, he looked from Luke to Luke's mother and back again, as if he couldn't believe what he saw.

His father's face reminded Luke of that of a kid who'd just scraped his knee and didn't know whether to cry or not. Finding his father's eyes too painful to look at, Luke lowered his gaze.

And then he heard his mother gasp and cry, "Patrick!" as she rushed toward his father. Luke saw his father wince as he bent over at the waist, his hips pushed away from Luke's mother by her stomach but his chin hooked over her shoulder.

10

And then Luke saw his father's eyes close as his arms reached around his wife's shoulders. The cane clattered onto the tarmac.

As Luke watched, his father's face pulled itself into a knot, gathering itself around his puckered mouth. Tears slicked down his cheeks and snot dripped from his nose. And then came the tortured sound of a winded horse—hollow and deep—as his father's mouth opened.

Luke wouldn't have been more shocked if the airplane behind his father had suddenly fallen apart piece by piece. He'd never seen his father cry before. Luke dropped his eyes again, this time staring at the scuffed tips of his dress shoes— shocked and ashamed.

He didn't know what to do or think or feel. Standing stock-still, he waited until his father and mother had stopped crying. Only then did he step forward, almost stepping up to his father—suddenly wanting to hug him—but at the last moment chickening out, veering away and picking up the duffel bag and cane at his feet.

He jumped as his father patted him on the back. "Luke, you've grown," he said in a choked and wavering voice. "Are . . . are you shaving yet?"

Luke knew that his father was trying to joke around, but the rough way his father then rubbed the top of his head with a row of knuckles took all the fun out of it. Luke hated having his head rubbed, and his father knew it. Maybe, Luke thought, he's so tired that he's forgotten.

He'd walked behind them—behind his father, who leaned on his mother for support—struggling as much with his feelings as with the heavy bag whose strap cut into his shoulder. His scalp crawled where his father had rubbed it.

★

"Crud," Luke mumbled to himself, wishing he wasn't remembering any of this. The way it should have been was so different. There should have been a brass band playing as his father walked down the rolling stairs, keeping time with his firm, measured steps. A cloud of balloons should have lifted from behind the airplane as he reached the tarmac, filling the sky with shrinking polka dots of red, white, and dark, dark blue. And as his father strode toward the fence, the sun should have sparkled from the rows of medals pinned to his chest, clanging bell-like against each other as they swaggered back and forth.

But it hadn't happened that way at all. It had happened so differently, so miserably.

Luke sat up in his bed, letting the pillow fall backward onto the mattress. The ride from Des

Moines had been quiet and his mother had driven—he couldn't remember another time when his mother had driven when his father was in the car. When they got home, his father, moving as if he were underwater and refusing any help, had hung up his uniform and jammed the cane and the contents of his duffel bag into a footlocker that Luke helped him drag from the basement to the hall closet. After that he'd choked down a sandwich, given Luke and his mother clumsy hugs, gone to bed, and slept through last night and most of today.

Luke stared out the window at the lightning, feeling queasy from remembering these things and from being so hot and sticky and being unable to sleep. Deciding that perhaps a little milk would calm his stomach and help him fall asleep, Luke slipped off the bed and quietly eased into the hallway. He went by memory rather than by sight in the hall's stifling darkness and almost ran into the opened door of the hallway closet. Stepping sideways just in time to avoid banging his head, Luke stopped and stared.

His father was kneeling on the hallway floor in his pajamas, probing his footlocker with the fading beam of a small flashlight. Medals and hats and boots and half-folded clothes sprawled on the floor beside him. Dog tags hung from a chain around his father's neck. There seemed to be too many of them.

"Huh?" his father grunted, shining the light into Luke's face, blinding him for a moment. "Oh," he said, sounding relieved as he lowered the flashlight's beam. Luke blinked away the blindness. His father looked embarrassed, as if he'd been caught stealing.

"Hi," Luke said softly, not knowing what else to say.

"What're you doing up so late?" his father asked, an unguarded gruffness in his voice.

"I . . . I couldn't sleep," Luke whispered, overcome by shyness. "I . . . I was going to get a glass of milk . . . to help me . . ."

His father's face softened as he considered Luke's answer. "It's hotter than a Saigon . . . lady," he finally said, his voice gentler than before. "Couldn't sleep, either. Seems that . . ." He closed his mouth and his eyes narrowed, as if in pain. "The thunder and lightning were . . . spooking me."

His father, afraid of the thunder and lightning? Naw! he thought. But his father did almost look scared, and Luke dropped his gaze to the littered floor. One medal caught his eye. It was purple and shaped like a heart. It was frightening and beautiful at the same time. In the darkened hallway, the golden profile of George Washington burned into the purple, almost seeming to glow. A Purple Heart? Luke had heard of them before, but he'd never seen one. *The* Purple Heart, awarded for wounds in battle?

"Is that . . . is that a Purple Heart?" he asked, pointing as he knelt.

He looked up after a few moments, surprised that his father didn't answer, wondering if his father had heard him.

His father had heard him, all right. And what Luke saw made him wish he'd never asked. His father had never looked at him like that before, and in the deep shadows cast by the flashlight he saw a strangeness in his father's eyes that he didn't recognize, an anger that was chilling.

"Yeah. It's a Purple Heart," said his father, grimacing. "They gave it to me after I was wounded . . . gave it to me in the hospital." His father reached out and touched the medal. "Crud," he muttered. Suddenly he grabbed it and threw it into the footlocker. With quick, choppy movements he grabbed a boot and threw it in also.

"Better get myself back to bed . . . before your ma wakes up," his father said, not looking at Luke. "Won't be any good in the morning if I don't. Won't be any good . . . at all."

"I . . . I'll just . . . I'll . . ." Luke stammered as he stepped around his father, keeping his back to the

15

darkness, facing his father but not looking at his face.

He rushed to the kitchen and slopped milk into a glass, drinking it so fast that each gulp choked down his throat like a handful of marbles. He was glad now that he'd worn pajamas tonight. His father had been like a stranger, and Luke would have felt embarrassed with nothing on.

Cautiously, he walked back to the hall. His father was gone and everything was back in the closet.

What's going on?

Numb, Luke crawled into bed, finally falling asleep to that question repeating itself over and over, echoing the sound of distant thunder.

C H A P T E R

2

Luke ran, leaning into every turn, hunched over and holding a textbook like a rifle against his chest. Feeling a breeze through his hair, he ducked and made a few low *chunka-chunka* sounds, pretending to sprint under the slow-moving blades of an idling helicopter.

Lifting his head—luckily, he remembered he was out in the open now, away from the drooping blades that carved a flattened umbrella shape in the air—he took a deep breath and sped up. He wanted to be home . . . now. After his restless night, Luke had felt tired all day. Finally school was over and he hadn't even stopped by Mike's house—he'd just yelled "Good-bye!" and kept on running as he passed Mike's driveway.

"Hey! Where ya going?" Mike had bellowed. He'd sounded surprised and maybe even a bit hurt. Luke almost always messed around with him after school, playing war games or watching television.

"Home!" Luke called over his shoulder. "See you tomorrow!"

That morning he'd waited and waited until the last possible minute, but he'd had to leave for school before his father got up. All day long he wished he'd seen his father sitting at the table wearing his battered construction worker's hard hat—the hat that perched on his head and jiggled every time he took a sip of coffee, jiggled as if it were delicately balanced on an egg that he'd hidden underneath. All day long Luke wished he'd seen his father that morning, all rested up and back to his old self. And now he wished he could run even faster—he wished he could *fly!*—so that he could be with his father at this very moment.

Luke had spent the whole school day remembering his father before he went off to Vietnam. He remembered his square face and the way his blue eyes twinkled and that his ears seemed to fold back, lying closer to his head, when he laughed. He remembered his father's thick arms, muscles bulging as he lifted his coffee cup, tense with being careful of such a tiny thing.

And, fidgeting at his desk, Luke remembered how much his father loved to tell stories, sitting on the edge of his bed with hair still stiff from cement dust and lime. And Luke remembered his father's hands, the skin fitting over his finger bones like mud-crusted garden gloves, rough from handling bricks and cement blocks in the heat of summer and the cold of winter, his fingernails thick and yellow as a horse's teeth.

When Luke realized that he couldn't remember any of his father's stories, he felt almost sick with despair. He'd strained to remember, staring at his math book, allowing the numbers to leapfrog over each other, to race toward the equal sign whether or not they were correct.

But it was no use. All he could remember was that his father's stories were funny and that he could make Luke laugh until it hurt and that then he would laugh, too, at his own cleverness. And Luke remembered the sweet smell of beer on his father's breath, almost as sweet as bread baking.

Luke rounded the last corner and charged down the sidewalk that led to the front of his house. Rushing up to the driveway, he slid to a stop and, suddenly shy, walked toward the kitchen door. What if his father was the way he'd been last night? What if he wasn't back to his old self? These questions exploded in his head as he walked to the kitchen door, each step heavier than the last. Luke wasn't sure he wanted to find out the answers.

The door opened just as he reached for the handle, and his mother beckoned him inside, a shushing finger to her lips. Luke followed her.

"Your dad's napping," she whispered, and then she gestured toward the kitchen table, on which sat a plate of chocolate-chip cookies. "I'll get you some milk."

Luke sat in his usual chair, placed his book on the table, and watched his mother pour a glass of milk and bring it over. She was wearing a long, loose, mud-colored maternity dress, which fell around her legs like a sun-faded curtain. It made her feet seem as if they had nothing to do with the way her stomach moved from side to side as she walked toward the table. The top part of her appeared to float, carrying the dress with it, and her feet seemed barely able to keep up.

She sat opposite him and stretched out her legs, her feet pointing toward the center of the kitchen. She rested her hands on the hill of her stomach, her finger tips touching. "Luke," she said, "I'd like for you to be especially quiet around the house for the next couple of weeks or so. Your father needs a lot of rest . . . a lot of peace and quiet." She tilted her head to one side and studied him.

Luke swallowed and his stomach filled with disappointment.

"With the baby coming and all . . . well, it's gonna be rough for a while, Luke," she continued, sitting up in her chair and reaching over the table toward his hands. "Babies take a lot of work . . . at least new babies do, and . . . and we'll be real short on sleep for a while. Your dad needs to get rested up before all that happens. I hope you understand . . . and I just know you'll do what you can to help, honey . . . so your father can get back on his feet. . . ."

She leaned into her chair, her face longer than usual. "Do you understand, Luke?"

"Sure," he said, so softly he could barely hear himself. "I understand." He understood that his father wasn't back to his old self after all, that his father was still the way he'd been last night. He understood that everything was messed up and that nothing was going to get better anytime soon.

Luke stuffed the rest of the cookie into his mouth. "I've got homework," he mumbled through the crumbs, getting up from the table and grabbing his book.

★

Luke sat on his bed, looking out his window at the gnarled limbs of the old apple tree. He'd half

21

expected his mother to call after him, asking him to come back into the kitchen so that she could find out about his day. She hadn't. Maybe she hadn't because she was trying to be as quiet as possible. Maybe she hadn't because she had other things to do that were more important—like seeing if his father was all right. Maybe she hadn't called after him because she understood that he needed to be alone. But no—it seemed as if his mother could think only of his father and of the baby that had taken over her body and their lives.

He held his breath and listened. The house was too quiet. It was like the quiet before a thunderstorm, before hail danced like popping corn on the lawn.

Luke sat in his bedroom for a long time, thinking and staring, trying not to feel his growing disappointment, sharp as hunger pains. He listened for any sounds of movement in the house. There were none. As he sat, he thought of his father getting off the plane and of his father in the hallway last night. His thoughts kept returning to the Purple Heart, its image burned into his mind, along with the way his father had thrown it into the footlocker.

And he thought of the questions Mike had asked him as they walked to school that morning.

"How many gooks did your dad kill?" Mike had

asked, as if Luke and his father had been up all night talking about the war like best buddies. And then before he'd had a chance to answer, Mike fired another question at him. "Did he see their brains splatter?"

Mike's questions bothered him. He'd barely seen his father since yesterday. He didn't even know how his father had been wounded. But Mike would have been disappointed to hear that, so Luke made up answers. "He killed two hundred gooks . . . you know, give or take." Mike didn't seem satisfied with this answer. "Sure he saw brains splatter . . . and guts and blood . . . and teeth, too." Mike had looked a little more satisfied, but not very.

Luke sat in his bedroom long enough so that the shadows of the apple tree outside had shifted noticeably, reminding him that it might almost be time for the television news to start. Maybe it already had.

Before his father had gone off to Vietnam, Luke had never really watched the television news. It had bored him. But for several months now, he'd been a television news fanatic.

Luke never admitted this to anybody, but the reason he'd never missed a night of news was because he secretly hoped to see his father talking to Morley Safer or some other hotshot reporter, telling them about a particularly brave thing that he'd done or a successful campaign that he'd just led.

Now, even with his father home, he craved the news. Luke got up off the bed and walked to his door, listened for a moment, and heard nothing. Being as quiet as possible, he walked out into the hallway—keeping close to the wall and its shadow—and then into the living room. He looked around. It was empty. He dropped to his knees in front of the television, turned the tiny knob on the far right of the set, and sat within an arm's length of the screen so that he could hear without turning the volume up above a murmur.

It took a while for the television set to warm up. As the screen grew brighter—an approaching headlight shining through a thick fog—Walter Cronkite's matter-of-fact voice became audible. And then a ghostly image appeared, flickering and growing stronger. As the screen's fog cleared, Luke saw Walter Cronkite in front of a large map of Vietnam that bent neatly around the curve of his head and down toward his shoulder. Luke had often marveled at how Vietnam fitted Walter Cronkite's shoulder.

These days, the Vietnam War was always the first thing on the news, and Luke was late but not too late.

". . . past nine days, an estimated eight thousand

24

North Vietnamese Regulars have tried to capture a key outpost that straddles a major enemy infiltration supply route to Da Nang," Walter Cronkite said, looking down as he shifted the top paper in his hands to the bottom of the stack. Looking up, he continued, almost smiling. "That siege finally ended today, but Allied soldiers pushing out from the base to secure the surrounding area found no trace of the enemy. Allied commanders now believe that the enemy troops have pulled back, possibly behind the border in Laos, to regroup for further attacks. We have a report today from Richard Threlkeld."

The screen seemed to blink, and Luke heard the *chunka-chunka* sound of helicopters before the next scene materialized: Men were rushing away from several helicopters through tall grass, hunched over and cradling rifles in their arms. It was then that he heard a loud moan coming from the doorway behind him. "In the aftermath of the siege, Allied soldiers have begun a mop-up campaign. . . ." Richard Threlkeld's urgent voice overpowered the sound of the helicopters as Luke's head snapped sideways to see what had made the moaning sound.

The light of the television flickered, making his father's face look as if it were twitching. Stubble softened his father's chin, and deep tired lines rumpled his cheeks. His father listed to one side, leaning against the side of the couch, his left hand gripping its back as if he were about to lose his balance.

"Dad . . ." Luke pushed himself up with his hands, swinging his knees under him and twisting around at the same time. He was certain that his father hadn't been there when he had crept into the living room.

". . . and according to field commanders these troops, walking in elephant grass taller than a man, encountered frequent signs of the enemy, but had little contact with them."

His father grimaced, not taking his eyes off the television, and Luke glanced at the screen to see what was the matter. There was a helmeted soldier, hunched under the weight of a plump backpack, pushing aside enormous blades of grass with the barrel of his rifle.

The scene suddenly flashed to a village, houses with thatched roofs and short peasants wearing loose pajama-like outfits and hats that looked like miniatures of the roofs. The peasants seemed bewildered as American soldiers lumbered around. Richard Threlkeld's voice droned on.

Luke had seen it all so many times before. Looking up, he saw that his father was staring at the screen as if Luke wasn't even in the room. His mouth was pulled back into a grimace and his teeth were bared, his eyes squinched tight.

Suddenly, Luke heard Walter Cronkite's voice again. "In the nation's capital, more than a dozen students were arrested today for burning draft cards on the steps of the Lincoln Memorial, protesting the war in Vietnam."

His father groaned again, louder this time, pain crumpling his face. He stood, covering his face with both hands, his shoulders shaking soundlessly, wagging his head back and forth.

Terrified, Luke spun on his heels and reached for the far right-hand knob on the television. His hand froze when he saw what was there.

Three shaggy-haired young men—hippies, his father had always called them, as if it were a dirty word—were being dragged down some white steps by policemen. One of them was shouting, "I will not burn women and children! I will not kill for my country!" *Coward*, Luke thought, wrenching the knob, killing the television screen. It was the worst insult he could think of.

Turning around, Luke faced the couch.

His father was no longer there.

CHAPTER

3

That night Luke crept down the hallway, clothed only in darkness, having finally discarded his pajamas in the unbearable heat. His stomach felt like a helium-filled balloon rising in his gut, shoving his heart and lungs aside. And his head seemed to shrink to the size of a pinhead. The pin's point was aimed at the rising balloon.

To clear his mind, Luke pretended he was a member of the Green Beret Special Forces, slinking through the jungles in search of Vietcong camps or trails. Mindful of booby traps, he felt the floor with his toes before he placed weight on his advancing foot—rocking backward from the ball behind his toes to the plumpness of his heels. Keeping watch, his head bobbed back and forth, his ears tuned to any kind of noise from the far end of the hall.

It was late, well past midnight. The last noise he'd heard from his parents' bedroom had been a couple of hours ago: deep, muffled cries followed by comforting sounds from his mother mingling with long, low sobs. A cry from his father had wakened Luke—he didn't know at first what it was—and had scared him more than anything he could remember. Goose bumps spread, rippling over his body. It had never occurred to him that his father might have nightmares. But what else could the bellowing and the choked cries and the sobs have been?

Luke paused in the hallway, waiting for his feelings to catch up with him. Ten minutes ago he'd been lying on his back, awake and feeling as naked inside as he was on the outside. He'd stared at the ceiling of his bedroom wondering what could have been chasing his father in his father's dream, or what dark and endless hole his father had been falling into. And then he'd stared out his window, at the dark blobs of leaves on the apple tree. No stars shone tonight. A layer of woolly clouds blanketed the sky, keeping in the heat soaked up by the earth during the day, sealing in moisture—thick as breath trapped in a sleeping bag.

As he lay awake, an image grew until it controlled his thoughts. It was as if the Purple Heart were pinned to the inside of his forehead, swinging from eye to eye, swinging so that he couldn't avoid seeing it no matter how much he struggled to look elsewhere. As it swung, it shimmered, just as it had when Luke had first seen it in the hallway, floating in the shallow pool of light.

Could the Purple Heart hold answers to the questions he'd hoped to ask his father? Luke couldn't shake the feeling that, maybe, to hold the Purple Heart was to hold the answers to why his father walked with a limp and why his father cried out in the night. Maybe.

Stopping in front of the hall closet, Luke crouched, listening with his entire body, each hair on his head tingling and alert. Carefully, he grasped the doorknob, twisting and pulling at the same time, slipped inside, and closed the door behind him.

It was as if he'd completely disappeared, melted into the darkness with the texture of coats and the smell of rubber boots. He closed his eyes, and for an instant the undersides of his eyelids seemed brighter than the closet's darkness. He wondered if the baby closed up inside his mother felt like this.

He groped in front of his shins, and his finger-tips seemed to buzz as they touched the hard front edge of the footlocker. Easing down onto his knees and resting his bottom on the chilly callus of his heels, Luke carefully lifted the lid, releasing musty air. He felt the floor next to him and found a rub ber boot to jam into the hinge of the lid's jaw.

Gently probing the footlocker, he tried to iden-tify what he felt: a hat, a shirt with a zillion buttons, papers rolled in tubes or folded, a round-cornered velvet-covered box. Slowly, he reached down—he wouldn't have reached down a booby-trapped tunnel more carefully—moving toward the side of the footlocker where he had seen the Pur-ple Heart strike when his father threw it in. The thin skin covering his knuckles brushed against the side, and he spread his fingers wide. His little fin-ger bumped something hard, right where the side met the bottom. With that touch he knew he'd found what he'd been looking for.

Flipping the medal into his palm, he rubbed the pad of his thumb over it and felt its face.

Luke was amazed at the details he could feel with his thumb, how his thumb made the Purple Heart come alive. Perhaps it was being in com-

31

plete darkness. Perhaps it was being able to see it in his mind's eye as it lay on the floor spotlighted by the flashlight.

The texture was almost the same as that of a quarter but fancier somehow—and more definite. He pictured what he felt: a profile of George Washington—different from a quarter because the high collar of an old-fashioned military uniform stuck up where his neck should be and because it wasn't round, but shaped more like a first grader's drawing of a heart. He knew that it was gold, not silver, with a heart-shaped layer of icy purple frozen on top of that. George Washington's profile in gold was melted partway into the purple.

The edges of this thing weren't squared off and corrugated, as a quarter's would be, but tapered like the dull edge of a letter opener. And it had a ribbon—he remembered it was purple with a white edge.

His fingers began to tremble. His father had gotten this medal for being wounded. In the dark of the closet, his mind churned out scene after scene of how that might have happened. He imagined his father skulking through thick underbrush, silent as a jaguar. He imagined men trailing behind his father, eyes big and trusting, knowing that where his father went, they would be safe. And then the scene exploded into chaos—bombs went off and his mind suddenly filled with smoke that didn't allow him to see his father get wounded.

Part of Luke was glad—he didn't want to see his father get hurt. Even so, another part of Luke was disappointed. His father must have handled it bravely—gritted his teeth and shouted instructions for his own medical care to the horrified medic.

His hand tightened over the medal and his heart raced as he heard steps approaching, coming down the hall from his parents' bedroom. He held his breath and his ears lifted with straining to hear as the footsteps came up to the closet. His father? Come to rummage around in the footlocker again?

No. The footsteps were lumbering and heavy and he could picture his mother's widened gait, her feet flared outward more than usual. He began breathing again as she walked by and then into the bathroom. She didn't bother to close the door and he clearly heard the *clunk* as she lowered the seat onto the toilet bowl.

He wished that she'd closed the door as he tried not to listen to the other sounds and, finally, to the flush and sucking swirl of water. She walked past the closet again, and within moments the house was quiet again.

Slowly, carefully, quietly, Luke held the medal in his left hand as he maneuvered the pinched boot from the jaw of the footlocker. Easing the lid down, he turned and opened the door.

Slinking down the hall, Luke held the Purple Heart tightly in one hand and cupped the other over his crotch. Fear pulsed through his body, and he imagined himself as an escaped prisoner-of-war, stripped naked as he snuck through the jungle, protecting that part of him that he imagined would be shot at before anything else.

He closed his bedroom door and crawled onto his bed, sliding his hand with the medal under his pillow as he laid his head down, his ear resting on his fist. The lump of his fist was uncomfortable, but he lay that way as if listening—listening for whatever the Purple Heart might tell him.

Luke heard nothing but blood pounding in his ears. And just as this drumbeat was about to lull him to sleep, the siren up the block began wailing, ordering people to seek shelter from an approaching storm.

Leaping from bed, Luke fumbled for his pajamas, which were in a pile by his bed, the top indistinguishable from the bottoms. He struggled to discover which was which.

His bedroom door opened and his mother's head popped in.

"You can put those on downstairs, honey. Come on, now, let's go."

"I'm coming," he said through his teeth, still

struggling. "I'll be there in a minute." He heard his father's footsteps approach. The door swung open.

His father shone the flashlight at him, the beam hitting Luke right where he didn't want to be hit. "Hey!" he cried out, blocking the light with a wad of pajamas.

Before Vietnam his father might have smiled and cried: "It's a boy!" Now there wasn't a trace of humor in his eyes.

"Tornados don't care what you're wearing," his father said in a grim voice. His face looked as if he hadn't slept for several days. "You're better off buck naked and alive than dead and wearing your Sunday best. Get a move on!" he barked.

Wide-eyed, Luke did as his father said. He got a move on. Naked, he stumbled down the stairs in front of his parents, only then realizing that in his haste he'd left the Purple Heart under his pillow.

The storm hit moments later, just as Luke finished pulling on his pajamas, and just before he wriggled into his sleeping bag. The house shook, and Luke imagined it being pulled up as if it were a rotten tooth, basement and all.

He turned toward the wall, partly to avoid the light of his father's trembling flashlight and partly to avoid looking at him sitting with his back against the wall, staring straight ahead as if he were seeing ghosts. It gave Luke the creeps. He hadn't realized until now how thin and gaunt his father was, how drawn and sickly. He looked like the pictures of prisoners-of-war in *Life* magazine—men with raccoon eyes and cheekbones that were as sharp as their chins.

And now they were all—his mother, his father, himself—prisoners in this basement.

Luke silently cursed himself for his stupidity and hoped that the Purple Heart would be safe under his pillow upstairs, that it would still be there in the morning . . . along with the rest of the house.

"Get a move on, Private!" Mike called over his shoulder to Luke. "They're gaining on us!" This afternoon it was Mike's turn to be sergeant.

As Mike darted down the sidewalk, zigging right and zagging left, he made a whistling noise and the ragged sound of a messy explosion. Luke, running behind, wouldn't have been surprised to see the sound rip through Mike's head, lifting its hairy top like a shag of grass blown skyward by a land mine.

"And watch for booby traps!" Mike barked, holding his arms crooked at the elbows, as if he were cradling a rifle or a machine gun. From half a block away, Mike looked as if he didn't have a neck, as if his head were rolling from rim to rim in the valley between his shoulders.

Luke ran as fast as he could, which wasn't as fast as Mike but fast enough, considering. For one thing he'd been awake most of the night, afraid to fall asleep because of the storm.

For another thing his right hand was jammed into the front pocket of his jeans, holding the Purple Heart. He wanted to be sure the medal didn't slowly work its way out of his pocket and then get dented or chipped by falling onto the sidewalk. Luke punched the air with his other fist, trying to catch up to Mike, without much luck.

Mike disappeared around the corner at the end of the block and was hidden by a tall, thick, shaggy hedge that grew over half the sidewalk. A few branches stuck out like threatening arms, poised to grab whatever ran by, as if warning passersby to steer clear of Mrs. Pederson's yard. Everybody steered clear of Mrs. Pederson regardless. Kids in the neighborhood grew up believing she was a witch.

Having a hand stuffed into his pocket made Luke's right shoulder curl forward and caused him to twist and lurch as he ran. His left leg reached out longer than his right leg, jarring him with each step. Luke ran as if he were wounded.

Wounded. *They got me!* he groaned to himself,

the voice in his head deep and breathless, a voice he hoped sounded like his father's. "Dirty commies!" he coughed. Scrunching his face, he hoped it was like his father's during the heat of a pitched battle—creased and puckered around his eyes and mouth. Instead, without warning, he remembered his father's face at the airport, tears slicking down.

"Crud!" he muttered, shaking his head to rid it of what he was picturing.

He saw the chunk of broken cement on the sidewalk just before he stepped on it, but it was too late—he rolled over onto his right ankle, almost falling. Pain shot up his leg, growing enormous. Tears sprang to his eyes, almost spilling.

"Mike! Hey, Mike!" he cried out, his voice cracking, hoping that Mike hadn't already gotten so far ahead that he couldn't hear. "Wait up!"

Mike's head popped out from the hedge's corner. "What's keeping you, soldier?" he bellowed, sounding as much like a drill sergeant as he possibly could.

"I twisted my ankle . . . bad." Luke groaned in spite of himself. Mike narrowed his eyes and watched as Luke took several halting steps. He crossed his arms over his chest. "It's because you were running with your stupid hand in your stupid pocket. You've had your hand in there the whole ding-dang day and *now*"—Mike took a step toward Luke—"you'd better tell me what it is this time or . . ."

Great, thought Luke. Mike had been pestering him all day about what he had in his pocket and he'd refused to tell. And now that he was hurt, Mike was going to try to bully it out of him.

Let him try, Luke thought. He had his reasons for not telling. He knew how excited Mike would be to see and hold his father's medal. But he also knew that Mike would ask about how his father was wounded. Luke was embarrassed that he still didn't know any details.

"I told you already," Luke said. "I don't have *anything* in my pocket . . . except my hand." He jammed his hand deeper into the pocket and his shoulder slumped, causing his head to tip.

"You do so," Mike said. "And if you don't show me what it is, I'll *make* you show me."

Luke spoke slowly, measuring each word. "I don't have anything . . . that you should see."

"Oh yeah?" Mike's voice grew hard as he became Sergeant Trainer once more. "Atten-hut!" he shouted, squaring his shoulders and snapping his feet together.

If there had been any doubt in Luke's mind, Mike's attitude vaporized it. He didn't care how much Mike wanted to see the Purple Heart, he'd *never* see it if Luke could help it. Luke knew by the look on Mike's "Sergeant Trainer" face that Mike was determined and that he could not be trusted. But for right now, Luke decided it would be wisest to play along—to play for time.

He drew himself up and obeyed Mike's command.

"Salute your commanding officer, Private Canvin," Mike ordered.

Luke almost smiled. Mike could be tricky.

"Yes, sir!" Luke said. Because his right hand was in its pocket, he saluted Mike with his left hand (almost hitting himself in the eye), at the same time knocking the heels of his sneakers together and making a loud click with the back of his tongue against the roof of his mouth. Renewed pain from moving his ankle burned up his leg. "Private Canvin reporting for duty, sir!" he said through clenched teeth.

Mike's face hardened. "That wasn't a proper salute, soldier! What arm do you salute with? Huh, Private? Huh?" He took a step closer and Luke's legs tightened and, keeping his head in one place, he searched for a way to escape. Even if he pulled his hand out of his pocket, it would be difficult to move quickly with a sore ankle, but he had to try.

Before Luke could answer, Mike's face suddenly softened. He was about to pounce—Luke could feel it in his bones.

"Hey, look, Luke," Mike said, smiling in a way that wasn't friendly, his words wheedling. "I won't tell anybody what you have in your pocket. Come on. I promise . . . honest. Cross my heart and hope to die."

Luke noticed that Mike's head was facing him, but that his eyes were looking off to the side, toward the hedge. From experience, Luke now knew from which direction Mike would attack.

Luke yanked his hand from his pocket, but before he could take a step Mike was all over him, grabbing his shoulders and pushing down with all his weight.

"Ow!" Luke bellowed, feeling his ankle melt into a puddle of pain. His knees buckled. Before he hit the sidewalk, Mike was grappling, trying to pull his right arm around his back into a hammerlock.

Luke squirmed and twisted and suddenly found himself facing Mike, who held his right hand in both of his.

"Let me see what you got," Mike grunted, trying to jam Luke's hand into the vise of his knees so he could pry it open.

"No!" Luke strained. Just as Mike got his right wrist between his legs, Luke realized that he'd been concentrating so much on the Purple Heart that he'd forgotten to use his left hand. He grabbed

Mike's shirt collar and twisted.

Mike looked up at him in surprise and then in anger. He grunted and fell over onto his side, keeping Luke's hand between his knees, pulling Luke with him. Luke tipped over and Mike scrambled on top. Luke glared at Mike, who was sitting on his chest, his teeth bared in his effort to pry open his hand.

"No!" Luke screamed. He closed his eyes and strained to keep his hand closed, to make it as hard as a walnut.

And then, with a feeling like a nut cracking, his hand popped open and Mike scampered away. "Crud!" Luke spat, hating himself for not being able to win against Mike when it was so important.

He heard Mike's gasp. "Wow! Is this your dad's?"

Luke rubbed his hand and his forearm, sullen and angry, but oddly relieved that he no longer had to keep the Purple Heart a secret from his closest friend. Reluctantly, he looked up.

"It isn't President Johnson's. Yeah, it's my dad's."

Mike came over to him, holding his hand out, palm up. The medal lay backside up. The light was such that it appeared to be a tiny, cupped pool of liquid gold. Mike held it out to him, and Luke gazed at the words etched onto the back: FOR MILITARY MERIT. And right below that: Patrick Canvin.

"A Purple Heart," Mike whispered, awestruck.

Luke took the medal by its ribbon from Mike's hand. "So," Mike continued whispering, "he got wounded, huh?"

Luke nodded, dreading the question he knew was coming next.

"How?"

Luke thought for a moment. "A bullet in the shoulder."

"Did he kill the guy that got him?"

Luke nodded and then sighed. "Yeah." He saw the hungry, curious look on Mike's face. "He shot him at close range and then popped off a bunch of other guys too . . . while he was waiting for the medic."

Mike nodded, turning shy, inspecting his own hand, which he'd scraped on the sidewalk from wrestling with Luke. And then he looked up, grinning. "Look. I'm wounded. Why don't you let me hold on to the Purple Heart for a while. I earned it."

Luke could feel anger buzzing around in his brain. He looked away from Mike, toward the hedge. "Sure," he said, "after I throw you into Mrs. Pederson's yard so she can make fertilizer out of you." His voice was tight.

He'd meant to sound awful. He'd meant to sound mean. But when he heard Mike's laugh, he realized how silly his threat had sounded. He looked at Mike, feeling more irritated than angry.

"Remember all those stories about Mrs. Pederson? You know, the ones Jake and his friends used to tell us?" Mike asked.

A tight smile slowly, almost painfully, grew on Luke's pinched face. He felt the texture of the Purple Heart with the pad of his thumb. "Yeah."

"Remember the one when she would rush out of her house with a butcher knife if we stepped on even one blade of her grass?" Mike laughed again. "And he told us that she fertilized her lawn with pets that she ground up so fast that their pieces were still alive when they hit the grass."

It was now Luke's turn to laugh, grudgingly.

"And how about her snatching bodies from the cemetery after they'd rotted for exactly a year? And then she'd bury them in her flower gardens and it didn't matter what color her flowers were supposed to be, they were red when they blossomed?"

Mike reached for Luke's hand, and Luke let Mike help him to his feet. Taking a cautious step, Luke found that his ankle wasn't as sore as he expected. In fact, it felt almost normal. Together, they rounded the corner of the block and Luke stared down the stretch of sidewalk that had always terrified him as a first grader walking to and from school. He and Mike had often held hands and run down this sidewalk, stealing glances at the opening to Mrs. Pederson's front yard, careful not to step on even the grass that grew between the squares of cement.

Luke looked at Mike. "And remember when I asked Jake why the police or the FBI or the marines or *somebody* didn't get her for doing those things? Remember what he said?"

Luke was embarrassed to think of that now and wondered if Mike felt the same way. "Yeah. The bell."

Mike whispered now, just as Jake had whispered when he'd told them this story. "Yeah. He said that she would ring her bell to call the ghosts of people who are still alive and that those ghosts would leave their bodies and *come* to her."

Luke stopped walking. "And he said that she hypnotized those ghosts and made the people they came from do anything she wanted."

Mike turned to Luke, covering his mouth with his hand to hold laughter in.

Luke's eyes narrowed. "I wonder," he said under his breath, "what would happen if *I* rang that bell. . . ."

Mike took his hand from his smiling mouth. "Cool." And then he frowned. "But *I* should be the one because *I'm* the sergeant today," he said.

"But *I* should be the one because it was *my* idea," Luke argued. He hated it when Mike pulled rank on him.

"I know what we're going to do," Mike said. "Draw sticks. The person with the shortest stick gets the honor." He broke two twigs from the hedge and stripped off the leaves. Turning his back to Luke, he arranged them in his fist so they both stuck up evenly, turned to face Luke, and held them practically under his nose.

Squeezing the Purple Heart extra hard for luck, Luke plucked a twig from Mike's fist and held it up to the one that remained in Mike's hand. He smiled.

Mike frowned. "Two out of three. . . ."

"No way! You stand guard out here and I'll go . . . go call for some ghosts."

Luke's ankle ached as he started toward the gap in the hedge leading to Mrs. Pederson's yard. But the pain lessened with each step and finally disappeared.

He veered left and slipped through the narrow opening.

CHAPTER

5

Light, sound—even air—seemed to disappear inside Mrs. Pederson's yard. Looking quickly to his left, Luke saw yellow, blue, purple, and orange flowers mixed with a sprinkling of red. He thought of how silly that story about the red flowers was.

The bell was supposed to be somewhere near the front porch, so he ran past two old, gnarled apple trees, one on either side of the sidewalk. The house appeared, seeming to cringe. Its front porch gaped, and the windows on either side were two glazed eyes. An image of Mrs. Pederson with a butcher knife cut through his thoughts.

To his left he spied an old bell hanging from a rusty metal arch that was mounted atop a wooden post stuck crookedly into the ground. A length of frazzled rope dangled from the side. Luke took two steps over the grass, slipped the Purple Heart into his pocket, and grabbed the rope.

Blood pumped in his ears as he yanked on the rope, which stretched slightly but didn't move. Tightening his grip on it, he drew himself up and threw his whole weight downward . . . leaning, grunting.

The rope groaned and Luke eased up, fearing that it would snap in two. Just then the bell broke free of its rust and clanged—tinny and rough—without an ounce of authority in its sound. Luke found himself looking up into the mouth of the bell, the clapper sitting in the darkness like a shriveled tongue.

He would have rung it again, but the bell froze where it was. It remained sideways, but the sound of its single, weak clang echoed in his head and set his teeth on edge.

Mission accomplished! he announced to himself, conjuring up his father's voice.

Letting go of the rope, Luke spun around and leaped toward the sidewalk. He began to run and then skidded to a halt.

It was as if she'd appeared out of thin air or had risen from the ground. She stood in the grass next to the sidewalk, facing him. He'd seen her from a distance many times before, but never this close. Her skin was stretched long with wrinkles and was so much like tissue paper that Luke would not have been surprised to be able to see through her to the flowers and hedge beyond. And her hair was a fuzzy white frost. Her feet were rooted in the grass and she leaned to his right, toward the sidewalk, crooked almost to the point of falling over, blocking his way. The only things about her that seemed alive were her dark eyes, which twitched in their sockets.

He shivered, knowing that she'd probably seen him struggle with her bell, knowing that while he'd struggled she'd been able to position herself so as to block his way out of the yard.

And then he saw that she held a knife, its blade thin and delicate from too much sharpening. And in her other hand she clutched flowers of various sizes and shapes—all of them red.

A black hole erupted across her face. Her mouth! He panicked, feeling surrounded, trapped, *haunted*. All of those childhood fears that he'd thought were gone came alive, groping and sliding through his slimy innards. His heart ticked like a bomb set to explode at any moment, and before he could stop himself, he bellowed and ran across the yard, away from this apparition who was Mrs. Pederson. He didn't even slow down as he approached the towering wall of green but instead turned his shoulder to the hedge and rammed into it. Tucking his chin so as to protect his face, he fought through branches that grabbed and poked at him. The hedge seemed to lift him up—his feet no longer touched the ground.

Luke thrashed and kicked, grunting as he forced his way through the hedge. In his fury he thought he heard Mrs. Pederson yell with a voice that crackled—or was it the twigs and branches snapping off so close to his ears? It sounded like the word "Stop!" but he couldn't be sure, and even if it had been, he wouldn't have stopped for anybody or anything.

Suddenly Luke was through the hedge and on the sidewalk, running harder than he'd ever run before.

From behind he heard Mike call his name, but he kept on running, feeling as if his heart were bursting and his lungs were shredding.

Luke squinted as he ran. Visions of Mrs. Pederson flashed in his mind like a nightmare slide show: *(click)* Mrs. Pederson leaning over the sidewalk, blocking his way—*(click)* Mrs. Pederson's face opening up into a black hole—*(click)* Mrs. Pederson's knife and the red flowers in her other hand—*(click)* the bell's mouth open as if to scream, its clapper a mummified tongue, but no

51

sound coming out.

Luke opened his eyes wide to let daylight blind him to these images, and he ran until his fear was almost spent, until he could run no farther.

"Crud!" he muttered. He couldn't believe he'd been so scared of her, that he'd actually screamed and then run. As he slowed to a walk, he heard Mike's heavy breathing grow louder even before he heard the sound of his approaching footsteps. *What had gotten into him?* Luke felt as if somebody else—or *something*—had controlled his body for a moment.

The bell? Mrs. Pederson? He shuddered.

"Hey, Luke!" Mike gasped, stumbling up next to Luke. "What happened? Did you . . . did you see . . . see Mrs. Pederson?" he asked, gulping air. "Did she try . . . try to get you?"

Gulping air also, Luke thought of the knife, its blade so sharp and slim, and nodded.

"Whoo-eee!" Mike shouted, pushing himself upright and throwing back his head. He was breathing easier now. "I heard the bell and . . . and then I heard a yell," he said. "Or a scream . . . like swearing or something! Geeze, she sounded like a cat getting run over. I almost went in . . . in after you but then you came out . . . out of the *hedge*!" His eyes were full of admiration. "You were running so

fast, I couldn't keep up with you!"

Luke stared back at Mike. Mike didn't know that Mrs. Pederson wasn't the one who screamed, didn't know how scared he'd been, didn't know that he hadn't been brave—that he'd run for his life, that *he'd* screamed, for cripe's sake. Mike had a dopey expression on his face and was looking at him as if he were some kind of hero, was looking at him as if he expected to hear all about the brave thing he'd just done.

"You did it!" Mike laughed, slapping Luke on the shoulder. "You rang her ding-dang, ding-dong bell!"

"Yeah," Luke said uncertainly.

"All *right!*" Mike slapped him again, almost knocking him over. "What happened? Come on. I gotta know! I gotta!"

Luke groaned before he could stop himself. He didn't feel up to inventing a fantastic story for Mike. He'd already told Mike lies about his father and Vietnam, and it was getting hard to keep them all straight. His eyes soured with tears as he looked at Mike, angry that Mike was making him feel as if he had to lie—again.

"Nothing," he mumbled. "Nothing much." He looked at Mike, expecting to see disappointment, expecting to have to tell Mike to bug off. Instead, he saw more intense admiration in Mike's face.

"Oh, come on," Mike said, encouragement in his voice. "You can tell me. It's not like you're *bragging* or something. . . ."

Bragging? Mike couldn't have gotten it more wrong if he'd tried.

"I just ran in and rang the bell and . . ." Luke began to explain, but Mike was too excited to let him finish.

"And she just happened to be waiting—right?— to get you and you rang her bell anyway—right?— and you escaped. You got out of her yard . . . *alive!*"

Luke shut his mouth. Mike didn't want to know what really happened. Anyway, he wouldn't believe Luke now even if he told the truth on a stack of Bibles.

As they approached his driveway, Mike stopped and turned to Luke. "Wanna come in and watch TV?"

Luke was tempted. And he felt uneasy about going home, about having to be so quiet and careful around his father. But right now, more than anything, he wanted to be alone. He wanted to get home, go to his room, and sort out his feelings. "Naw," he said. "I need to, you know . . . help my mom with stuff."

"Aw, come on," Mike wheedled. "Just for a little while. I bet I could sneak us a few potato chips."

"No," Luke said, stubbornness pushing his jaw out.

Mike studied him for a moment. He nodded and stood at attention. "Permission for leave granted, Private!" he said in his sergeant's voice. "Report for duty tomorrow at oh eight hundred." And then he gave Luke a smart salute, spun on his heel, and marched up his own driveway.

★

Luke walked into the kitchen as quietly as he could. He paused to listen and didn't hear anything. The house felt empty—empty of people but filled with uneasiness.

Still he heard nothing as he sneaked through the kitchen and then through the living room—no groans or snores or creaking of floors—no water running or thump-thump of iron on ironing board. He sniffed, trying to detect the faint telltale smells of perfume or after-shave or the moist scent of soap that has just been used. He smelled nothing and should have begun to relax. But he couldn't. Something didn't feel right.

Quietly, barely breathing, he eased shut his bedroom door. He felt like such a sissy, being scared in his own house, and he thought of the way he'd

55

been in Mrs. Pederson's yard. His heart quickened and he felt a shadow of the panic that had caused him to scream and run.

His gut crumpled as he doubled over to sit on the edge of his bed, propping his head on his hands, elbows wedged behind his kneecaps. His ankle pulsed in a dull way, a faint echo of the ache in his heart. Why had he acted that way? Why had he lost his head like that? She's just an old lady, he scolded himself. It's just an old, rusty bell.

His father would never have acted like that. His father would have stood his ground—would have been brave enough to stick around, to take his lumps from Mrs. Pederson. Luke thought of the knife she'd held. Now, sitting in his room, it seemed ridiculous to think of Mrs. Pederson trying to stab him. His father would have known that.

Luke's hand moved toward the pocket with the Purple Heart. It was time to put it back where it belonged. Besides, after what had happened in Mrs. Pederson's yard, he didn't deserve to have it. He drew his hand away from the pocket. He knew that if he touched it now, took comfort in its feel, he wouldn't take it back.

Luke stood and walked to his bedroom door. He listened again for sounds of his parents but still he heard nothing. The silence yawned larger as he opened the door and glided down the hallway.

Pulling open the closet door, he dropped to his knees in front of the footlocker, leaned to the left, and slipped his right hand into the right pocket of his jeans. His fingers spread apart, filling out the pocket, smoothing the cloth inside.

His eyes widened and his body went rigid. His fingertips touched nothing but lint-crusted cloth.

The Purple Heart was gone!

6

The Purple Heart!

Luke's fingers wriggled, desperate to feel what was no longer in his pocket. He felt for holes through which the medal might have slipped, but there were no holes, only the tail of knotted thread that held together the pointed bottom of the pocket.

Where could it be? He swore he'd put it in his pocket before he rang the bell. His thoughts tripped over each other, stumbling backward, reeling, trying to remember when he'd last felt it, trying to think of where it might have fallen out.

The sidewalk? As he ran from Mrs. Pederson's yard? Maybe.

But he wasn't convinced, didn't *want* to be convinced. If it had fallen out on the sidewalk, somebody might have picked it up by now. Squeezing his eyes tighter, he tried to think of less horrible possibilities.

The hedge as he wrestled with the branches? He pictured a branch snatching the medal from where it had eased up from his pocket.

And then he thought of Mrs. Pederson's yard.

Groaning, he remembered putting the medal back into his pocket before he rang the bell. But he hadn't checked to make sure it was safe inside.

In his mind, Luke saw in slow motion what must have happened. He saw the Purple Heart dangle from his fingers as his hand moved toward his pocket. He saw his fingers release the medal and he saw the medal slide, skidding down the outside of his jeans, falling, sinking, disappearing into the grass.

Luke's head jerked sideways at the sound of a car door slamming shut next to the house. Scrambling to his feet, he closed the closet door just as he heard the creak of the kitchen door opening and his mother's voice call, "Yoo-hoo! Luke? We're home!"

He turned, his heart tripping over itself, just as his mother appeared in the hallway, a smile connecting her ears.

"Oh, I'm so glad you're here!" she said, coming up to him and taking him in her arms. "I was afraid that maybe you were at Mike's, watching television or . . . or whatever!" Holding his face in her hands, she took a step from him and patted one of his cheeks. "If I'd had to wait to tell you the news, I would have just . . . just gone crazy!"

"Hey." Luke looked over his mother's shoulder and saw his father, bent slightly at the waist, half in and half out of the shadow that cut slantwise across the hallway from the kitchen. "Howdy."

Luke's mother stepped aside, and Luke didn't know if he dared believe what he was seeing. His father stood with a smile on his face that almost matched his mother's. Even in the half-and-half light Luke saw a twinkle in his eyes, which made his sunken cheeks seem less grim.

"Come on in and let's have us a party." His father tipped his head toward the kitchen. "Come on! We've got somethin' to celebrate!"

Luke's mother took his arm in both of hers and whispered in his ear, "It's great to see him happy!" Luke swallowed and nodded.

This is what he'd been dreaming of since his mother had told him that his father was coming home. But what would happen to his father's happiness when he found out that the Purple Heart was gone? Luke cringed, knowing that his father's

60

happiness would be blown to smithereens. And it would be Luke's fault. All Luke's fault.

His father was sitting in his usual chair at the table holding a beer can as Luke and his mother walked into the room's brightness. Helping his mother into her chair, Luke then sat in his own chair, not knowing what else to do. His father took a swig from the can in his hand, sucking instead of sipping, swallowing noisily, and then smiled at him.

"I'm signed up," his father began, "only this time it ain't the army. It's college! Can you believe it? Your old man's going to college." Luke jumped as his father slapped the table with his open hand. Luke's father laughed, but his laughter was uneasy. "Gonna be a college student! Maybe I should just grow out my hair and not wash it and maybe wear me a few beads and let a little mold grow on my face and call it a beard. Maybe I should get me some exercise marching in demonstrations and ..."

"Your dad can't work as a bricklayer anymore," his mother interrupted, "because of his . . . because of his injury. So we decided to take advantage of the GI Bill and see what there was for him to study at the community college."

"Yeah," his father said, sucking again at his beer. "What do you think of your old man being in television?" His father looked and sounded less grim as he tipped another slug of beer into his mouth.

Luke's eyes widened. "Television?"

His father threw back his head and his Adam's apple bobbed as if he were drinking his own laughter. "You are the limit, Luke. I won't be *on* TV, you silly. I'll *fix* 'em. What with color television taking over, why we'll *never* have enough people to fix the danged things." His smile relaxed as he sat back in his chair. "Your mom and I went through the 'Help Wanted' section of the paper this morning, and the jobs that caught my eye were for auto mechanics and for TV repairmen. And the closest I want to get to grease is your mother's fried chicken." He winked at Luke's mother and then looked back at Luke. "Well, what do you think?"

"I . . . it's great." Luke forced up the corners of his mouth, even though, inside, he felt more like the sunken middle part of a smile. Making televisions work seemed more like magic than anything else. But the missing Purple Heart took all the joy from his father's news. Luke had to find it before his father discovered it was gone. He had to find it before all this happiness was destroyed. "Well," he said, trying to sound cheerful, "I've got some homework to do."

"Good for you!" His father leaned back in his chair, winced, and quickly sat up as he rekindled his smile. "We'll both have to do homework from now on. Maybe you can help me with mine . . . especially the math."

Luke forced himself to grin, thinking of those times when his father had tried to help him with his math. It always ended with his father stomping off.

As he turned to leave, his mother reached out and stopped him. "You're a good kid, Luke. You know that?" She smiled.

His mother's words should have made Luke feel wonderful. But he felt now like a total fraud. If she only knew, he thought: knew that he'd stolen his father's medal—and lost it.

★

Feeling betrayed by the world, he sat on his bed and tried to think of what he should do. He knew that he should search for the medal—the sooner the better. He realized he'd boxed himself into a corner by telling his parents he had homework. But he couldn't wait.

Closing his bedroom door, he walked past his bed, lifted the window, unhooked the screen, and then lowered himself feetfirst to the ground.

Scampering around the house and down the sidewalk, he slowed to a half walk, half run and tried to calm himself. He had to keep his wits about him. *What would Dad do?* As he went, he tried to take his mind off his growing fear by pretending he was his father, out on patrol in Vietnam.

There was danger at every turn. His heart pounded and he imagined himself carrying a rifle—an M-16. He was alone in the jungle, separated from the rest of his patrol and surrounded by the enemy. He walked with his knees bent and his shoulders hunched. His eyes shifted back and forth, looking for unblinking eyes in every bush and for heads to appear and disappear from the sides of every tree.

His ears tingled. The sound of cars became the distant droning of airplanes on bombing missions. The faint sound of a power mower became that of a helicopter, evacuating wounded soldiers from a battlefield. Luke reminded himself that these were friendly sounds—the enemy didn't have airplanes or helicopters.

It was the occasional silence that made the hair on the back of his neck prickly. The enemy was extremely silent. He began to sweat. The Vietcong could be anywhere. They *were* everywhere. Suddenly the danger seemed real. Pretending was no longer fun.

He imagined mines and booby traps—things called Toe Poppers and Bouncing Betties. He stepped carefully. The cracks between the blocks of sidewalk were trip wires, and exhaust pipes from parked cars were gun barrels, aimed to shoot him when he snagged his foot on a wire. Painted crosswalks, faint and delicate where cars ran over them, were swinging rope bridges stretched between rice paddy irrigation ditches, bridges that were built to break in two at the thin parts.

Nothing could be trusted.

And then, before he felt ready, he rounded a corner and Mrs. Pederson's hedge stretched away from him. Vietnam disappeared and he was suddenly back in Iowa. His eyes roved up and down the scraggly row of bushes, searching for the place from which he'd emerged onto the sidewalk. He walked toward a likely spot, marked with a broken branch that stuck out over the sidewalk, its leaves wilted. Grabbing this branch, he elbowed his way into the thicket.

He strained to be silent, but twigs snapped and leaves rustled. He bowed his head to protect his face and also to search the gaps between the stalks for the medal. Just in case.

Before he stepped from the protection of the hedge, Luke scoped out the yard and tiny house. The ridge of the house sagged in the middle, and the white paint on its sides was flaking off, showing dark wood underneath, reminding Luke of peeling gray patches of dead skin. Shadowy white lace curtains fringed the tops and sides of the windows—the kind of curtains that you can look through from the inside without being seen from the outside.

And there were more old apple trees in the yard than he remembered—old and gnarled and covered with patches of small leaves that didn't look healthy. Even though apple blossoms had come and gone, Luke saw no apples.

Tensing, he heard the drone of voices to his left. He turned his head and saw several heavy bumblebees dive-bombing Mrs. Pederson's flowers. He relaxed—the bees were making the voice sounds.

He crouched to prepare himself and sucked in the kind of deep breath he took before jumping into a swimming pool. He eased himself out of the hedge and slowly crawled on his elbows to the nearest apple tree. He tried to pretend he was in Vietnam, on patrol, trying to locate an enemy camp. For once, his imagination failed him.

Peering around the trunk, he studied the house. He felt he was being watched—from where, he couldn't tell. He snaked around the tree and across the lawn, dragging his legs to keep his butt low, and glanced up at the house every few seconds as he searched the grass with his eyes and the flat of his hands.

From a distance the lawn looked smooth. But as

Luke searched, he saw that it was sparse and cut too short. The dirt between the blades of grass felt lumpy and uneven, with shiny piles of the thin, stringy dirt that comes from burrowing worms.

As he approached the base of the bell post, the feeling that he was being watched grew stronger. Luke looked up to the house, and the corner of his eye caught a motion that looked as if a side curtain had just fallen back into place. He lunged toward the spot where he'd stood to ring the bell and frantically searched the area, scampering empty-handed to the safety of the nearest apple tree. His heart beat and his breath came in little wheezing gasps.

Had she seen him? Luke waited . . . and listened. *Was it a cat playing with the curtain? Or were his eyes tricking him?*

Luke waited, willing his breath to be normal. With each breath he thought about the only other place the Purple Heart might be. Mrs. Pederson could have found it and taken it inside. And if she had it inside, he would have to ask her for it—go up to her door and knock and ask her for it. He would have to do this thing like a soldier. That's what his dad would have done.

Luke got up, brushed off the knees of his jeans, and stood at attention. As he marched to the porch, he tried not to look at the bell, but he noticed that it still lay sideways, its mouth open in a silent scream. Snapping his eyes forward, he clomped up the porch stairs to the warped screen door.

He reached out and rapped, so hard that his knuckles smarted. Still standing at attention, Luke kept his eyes forward and his shoulders square. He listened for footsteps, heard only silence, and rapped again.

CHAPTER

7

Luke stood in front of the door, feeling taunted by the silence.

"Mrs. Pederson!" he cried, and banged on the door with the flat of his hand.

He could hear faint noises outside the hedge—cars mostly, and birds. But the house seemed to exist in a bubble that somehow mixed sound with light so that they became the same sensation—a sensation he felt with his whole body, not just his ears and eyes. He was certain that Mrs. Pederson heard him knock as she held the Purple Heart in her hands, gloating as she stroked George Washington's cheek with her fingers.

He kicked the door and screamed, "Hey! I know

you're in there." Again he waited. Still, nothing happened and Luke let an enormous grunt of frustration explode from his gut.

He reached out and tried the doorknob with a jerk of his wrist. It didn't budge. "Come on!" he half cried and half moaned.

He kept his hand on the knob, leaned forward, and rested the top of his head on the door. Maybe she's deaf and has turned off her hearing aid, he thought. Maybe she's napping. Or maybe she's hurt inside and can't come to the door.

And then the worst possibility of all occurred to him: Maybe Mrs. Pederson had somehow died since he'd seen her and was in a heap on the floor, the Purple Heart imprisoned in her hand.

He snapped upright and let go of the knob. Hunched over and careful, Luke peered into the windows on either side of the door. The house was dark inside, and the glass of each window seemed coated with an oily layer of grime. He crept around the house but the darkness and the grime made it impossible to see inside.

He tested each window and found them all either locked, painted, or swollen shut. As he made his way around the house, the fear within him grew. Something had happened to Mrs. Pederson. If she was hurt or dead, the Purple Heart might be lost and never returned.

Trying the last window, he decided that he should call Mrs. Pederson on the telephone and if she didn't answer that he should call the police and tell them to check on her. He wouldn't have to give them his name. And if they asked how he knew something was wrong, he would tell them that he could smell something dead from outside her house.

Luke didn't dare leave Mrs. Pederson's yard by the front walk—he didn't want anybody to see him leave and think that he'd had anything to do with her being hurt or dead. He went to a far corner to push his way through the hedge and ran home.

★

Just as he opened the kitchen door, he remembered that he'd left the house from his bedroom window and that he should have come into the house that way. But it was too late. Three pairs of eyes turned to look at him as he stood in the doorway. And one pair was the dark, twitching eyes of Mrs. Pederson herself.

How did she know where to come? Maybe she *is* a witch, Luke thought.

His mother's eyes grew large and she began to get up from her chair.

His father reached out a hand from where he

sat, gesturing her to stay where she was. "I told you he'd be back . . . in his own sweet time." His father was smiling but in his eyes Luke saw the stranger he'd bumped into in the hallway on the night his father came home. And, just as he had that night, Luke dropped his gaze from his father's face. It was then he saw the Purple Heart, looking small and fragile in the middle of the table.

Luke leaned into the doorframe for balance. He looked up as his mother spoke. "We were just talking about you," she said. "Mrs. Pederson said that you . . . that this afternoon you . . . that you ran into her yard and rang the bell she has by her front porch."

Fearfully, Luke looked from his mother's carefully polite face to his father's. He found no comfort there. His father's face was struggling to keep from looking angry, but anger bubbled up in his face—in his eyes, in his mouth, in a tic in his cheek—bubbled up and disappeared and bubbled up again, like the surface of slowly boiling water.

He felt cast out by his parents. As if commanded, his eyes turned toward Mrs. Pederson. The old woman stared back at him, her shocking white eyebrows bristling.

"I had half a mind to keep it." Her voice didn't sound at all like the voice he'd heard this afternoon. It was old and thin, but it was also smooth.

She glanced at the table, at the Purple Heart. "I knew what it was the moment I laid eyes on it. My Elijah had one from the Second World War."

Luke's father cleared his throat. "I believe you have some apologizing to do . . . to Mrs. Pederson here . . . for what you did this afternoon."

Luke felt a tightness in his throat that almost cut off his breath. "I'm sorry," he said, looking down at his feet.

"That's a poor excuse for an apology." His father seemed to sift his words through his teeth, letting the polite words out, keeping the hot, angry words inside his mouth where they appeared to be burning his tongue.

Luke's mother reached out and tried to soothe the back of his father's hand, which lay open next to the Purple Heart. "Luke," she said quietly, "you gave Mrs. Pederson quite a shock, and we've decided . . . the three of us have decided that . . ." She looked at Luke, closed her mouth, and tried to smile. Nodding toward the wall, next to Luke, she said, "Luke, grab that chair and sit down. Tell us what you were doing in her yard . . . why you did that."

Luke didn't trust his body. Keeping a hand on the wall for support, he eased himself into the chair.

He forced his head up and faced Mrs. Pederson.

In his head he heard a mocking voice: *Name, rank, serial number. Name, rank, serial number.* He cleared his throat to silence this voice. "I . . . Mike and I heard stories . . . and I just wanted to ring the bell!" he blurted out, the anger with himself mixed up with his words to Mrs. Pederson.

Mrs. Pederson's eyes flashed, mistaking his anger for defiance. "If you were my boy . . ." she said in a voice that rose with each word.

"I'm sure Luke will be happy to help you out . . . just as we agreed," Luke's mother said, quickly.

Mrs. Pederson ignored Luke's mother. "Don't think I don't know about the stories people tell. Don't think I don't know what people say." Her words were clear, even though her voice wavered.

Luke was startled by the crab quickness of her hands as she reached for the Purple Heart. The knuckles of her fingers were swollen, and each segment of each finger grew out at an odd angle. "If I hadn't found *this*," she said, lifting it up from its ribbon, "I wouldn't have known whose parents to talk to. If you were my boy . . ." she repeated, dropping the medal to the table. Luke winced, fearful that the purple plastic would chip.

"We're glad you came to see us." Luke was surprised to hear such calm words come from his father's stormy face. "We're truly sorry for the trouble Luke caused you, but we're grateful you let us

74

know . . . so we could nip this thing in the bud."

Mrs. Pederson nodded and looked from Luke to Luke's father. "I should expect to see Luke tomorrow?"

"Yes," Luke's father said. "First thing, seeing as how it's Saturday. And every day after school next week too. And I'll come over sometime around noon to see to it that he's working hard enough."

Mrs. Pederson nodded. "Good."

"Luke, would you help Mrs. Pederson home . . . make sure she gets there okay?" His father was giving an order, barely disguised in politeness.

Luke nodded and leaned forward, preparing to stand.

"I can make my own way home." Mrs. Pederson stepped toward the kitchen door and paused before she pushed it open. "I will see you tomorrow, Luke Canvin, at eight o'clock," she said, looking at Luke. "And you can't call saying you're sick. I don't have a telephone."

★

Luke stared at the clasped hands in his lap, waiting for the silence to break, getting more tense the longer it lasted. It was as if he were in the kitchen alone—he couldn't even hear his parents breathing. When he looked up, he felt shot down by the

75

four eyes that stared at him.

His mother spoke first.

"We've always expected better of you . . ." she began, and then quickly closed her mouth, sucking in her bottom lip and frowning. "I mean . . . Luke, we . . . I just don't know *what* to think. When Mrs. Pederson came here and asked for you, I thought you were in your room doing homework and then . . . we saw you'd slipped out the window. And then Mrs. Pederson showed us your father's Purple Heart and we . . . I just couldn't *believe* it. And *then* she told us how she got it. Well . . ." Luke felt his chest tighten as he watched his mother struggle to remain calm. She was trying too hard to make it easier for them all. He wished that she would just yell, get it out, get it over with.

But his father's anger changed all that.

He picked up the Purple Heart. "You stole this from me." He spoke in a hoarse near-whisper. "You stole it and then you shamed me." Luke's throat tightened as he watched his father shift his weight in his chair and wince.

"How could you!" he shouted, and both Luke and his mother jumped. "You"—and his father pointed a shaking finger at Luke, aimed right for Luke's throat—"you have shamed me and hurt me. . . ." Spittle exploded from his mouth with each word. "You have *wounded* me"—he banged on his chest—"and I don't know *what* to think any-more."

Luke braced himself, too shocked to cry out. His father stumbled to his feet and walked to him.

"If you want to be a hero so much, *here!* Take it! *Take* it!" His father tossed the Purple Heart at Luke's chest. It bounced, stinging, and landed on top of his hands.

His father walked to the refrigerator, limping more now than Luke had seen before. He tore open the door and grabbed a beer and stormed into the living room.

Luke looked down at the medal in his lap. A sob rose from his core and he closed his eyes and strained to open his mouth wide enough to let it out. His jaw pushed against his swollen chest. And then he felt his mother's arms around him and her breath brushed his ear as she spoke.

"Luke, don't . . . don't . . . it's all right, Luke . . . we love you, Luke. Your father loves you." He felt the bulge of her belly press against him and wished he could crawl inside her. "You're a good boy, Luke. Your dad knows that . . . we know that."

Shaking his head, gasping for air, he felt tears falling on his hands.

CHAPTER

8

"I don't want to go," Luke said, under his breath but loud enough for his mother to hear as she worked at the stove, her back to him.

"I don't imagine you do," she said, her words clipped. She turned around, bringing him a plate of scrambled eggs and toast. "But I think it's only fair."

"All I did was run in to her yard and ring her stupid bell." He stared at the plate. Sometimes he thought of golden yolks as the brains spilled from head-shaped shells.

"Luke," his mother said as she sat across the table from him, "I know you don't want to go, but I hope you understand why you're going. What you did . . ." Her eyes were impatient, and she let out her breath with a sigh. "You really did it up in a big way . . . when you decided to stir things up . . . make a little excitement." She made her voice goofy, trying to transform what she said into a joke.

Luke wasn't fooled. He turned his head toward the window but continued looking at his mother from the corner of his eye. She was more tired than usual. Luke knew that she'd had a bad night—he had too. After Mrs. Pederson left, his father had continued drinking can after can of beer, until he passed out on the living room couch. Luke had never seen his father this way before. Before Vietnam, it seemed to Luke that his father grew more lively and cheerful when he had a few beers. But last night his father had grown quieter. His eyes had seemed to retreat into his head, peering at the world like those of a wild animal from the shadows of a cave, peering from under the ledge of his brow at his mother and at him as if they were somehow dangerous. He growled his words, as if warning them to keep their distance but to stay where he could see them.

Finally, Luke and his mother had half carried, half helped his father to his parents' bedroom. He'd been surprised at how light his father was. Before Vietnam, Luke wouldn't have been able to help lift him any more than he could help his mother pick up a car.

When he'd helped his mother take off his father's shoes, he had seen a dark stain growing from the fly of his father's pants. Luke had watched in horror as his father made a huge puddle on the floor. His father must have peed for thirty seconds, maybe a minute, and not even known it. His mother had tried to laugh about it, saying she needed practice changing diapers, what with the baby coming. But her laughter came out as hiccuping sobs.

Luke had gone to bed with an anxious, fearful buzzing in his head. He'd caused his father to act the way he had, and he was scared that his father would never be the same again. Once more, in the middle of the night, he was awakened by his father's bellowing, louder than ever.

★

His mother shifted her weight on the chair and looked out the kitchen window. "Your father had a rough night, Luke. I'm sorry you had to be there when . . ." She sat up straighter, trying to look strong but sounding wrung out. "But, you know, healing takes time. He's going to be all right."

"Sure," Luke muttered, picking up a fork and poking at his eggs without looking at them. She'd said that once before, the day she'd told him his father was coming home from a hospital in Tokyo. It hadn't been true then and it wasn't true now.

"What did you say, Luke?"

Startled, Luke looked up to his mother's blazing eyes. As he struggled to find words to take back what he'd said, the fire in her eyes died and she sighed. "I know you didn't mean to do anything hurtful," she said, sitting back in her chair and resting her hands on her stomach. "I . . . I know you weren't trying to hurt any of us on purpose, Luke. But . . ." She rubbed one of her eyes in the way of a tired little kid. "Do you see what I meant when I asked you to be careful . . . to be quiet?"

Luke nodded, feeling miserable—about what he'd done to his father, about what he'd done to his mother, about how his father was acting. This misery was heaped upon the misery he already felt about having to go to Mrs. Pederson's house.

"Oh, Luke," his mother said, leaning forward as if over a barrel, reaching across the table, almost sticking her elbow into the eggs. She cupped his chin in one hand, lifting his face so that his eyes looked directly into hers. "It's a raw deal for all of us. It just isn't fair . . . what your dad is going through, what we're going through. But that's life . . . it's just one of those things." She was now close to tears. "I'm sorry . . . sorry as I can be." She let go of his chin. "You'd better eat those before

81

they get cold," she added.

"I'm not hungry," Luke mumbled, not wanting to disappoint her further by being ungrateful, but knowing that he'd throw up if he tried to eat the eggs. He pushed the plate to the middle of the table.

"Luke," his mother said, sighing, "I want you to have enough zip to get through the day. There's no telling what Mrs. Pederson will have you do."

She looked behind him and he sensed a change in the room. "Good morning, honey," his mother said. She sounded uncertain.

Without a word, Luke's father walked toward the table and was just about to sit when a knock came from the kitchen door. Pausing for a moment, as if confused, Luke's father continued across the kitchen and opened the door.

"Is Luke here?" Mike's voice filled the room. "Sir," he added, sounding somewhat shy. From where he sat, Luke couldn't see Mike but he could picture him looking up at his father, his eyes bigger than normal, his mouth hanging open like a puppy's.

"Yes," his father said in a rasp, and then cleared his throat.

"Can he come out and . . . and play?"

Luke's father cleared his throat again. "No," he said in a flat voice. "He's busy today."

"Oh." In the silence that followed, Luke sensed

that Mike wanted to ask why. But if he did, he must have chickened out. "Okay. 'Bye," he said in a voice that faded, sounding as if Mike were already running down the driveway.

Luke's father closed the door and turned around. The puffy skin around his eyes was blackened, almost as if somebody had socked him in each eye. His hair was spiky with grease. Even his ears looked droopy—saggy and wrinkled and old. And his mouth didn't seem to know what to do with itself.

Easing himself down onto the chair next to Luke, he looked at him with red-rimmed, sleep-crusted eyes. "I must have been a barrel of laughs last night," he said, half whispering, squinting so that he could focus on Luke's face, which he was having trouble doing. "Crud! I haven't . . . haven't done that for . . . since . . . Saigon."

Luke's father blinked, long and hard, and opened his eyes to look down at the plate of eggs. "Those yours?" he asked.

Luke shook his head.

His father took hold of the plate, pulled it over, and began shoveling the eggs into his mouth, his hand trembling, chunks of egg tumbling off the fork with each bite. Luke watched his father chew and was disgusted to see bits of scrambled eggs clinging to a corner of his mouth. Pushing his chair back, Luke mumbled, "I gotta go."

"I'll come check on you . . . later this morning," his father said through the food in his mouth, his face only inches from the plate.

★

Luke took another, longer route to Mrs. Pederson's house. As he walked, he tried to make believe he was on a military patrol, making his way through the jungles of Vietnam. He tried to feel the way he'd felt yesterday, feeling the jungle air and hearing the sounds of battle.

But he wasn't a soldier in Vietnam. He wasn't his father. He was Luke Canvin, a stupid, scrawny boy in the middle of Iowa. His mouth was clamped so tight that the backs of his jaws ached. In his ears he heard a high-pitched hum.

He tried to relax and caught himself just before he thrust his hands into the pockets of his jeans. Letting his arms flop to his sides, he felt the Purple Heart each time he took a step. Each time he lifted his leg, it wedged itself deeper into the narrowing-widening crook where the base of his hip met the top of his leg. He didn't want to touch the Purple Heart, to be reminded of the crisis he'd created by taking it. In fact, he didn't want to have it with him at all. But he'd been afraid to give it back to his father—afraid of how his father would react. And he'd been reluctant to leave it in his bedroom, where it would have nagged him all day. Instead, he'd pinned it to the inside of his pocket so that it wouldn't work its way out and get lost.

The walk to Mrs. Pederson's house was over sooner than Luke would have liked. As he approached the gap in her hedge, his steps became stiffer, more hesitant.

He tried to push his feelings of misery aside along with an unruly branch from the hedge, but they followed him even as the branch snapped back to position. Luke turned up the sidewalk and walked toward the porch, stumbling over the first step. Taking a deep breath, he heard the humming in his ears grow louder. Raising his right hand almost in a salute, he rapped and waited, heard nothing inside the house, and rapped again.

After a few moments the faint sound of footsteps approached from the other side of the door. He was seized by a desire to turn and run, but his legs were locked in place. And then, level with his stomach, the knob in front of him twisted and the door opened a crack. Luke couldn't see anything in the narrow opening and he didn't know what to do. After a few moments the door opened wider, and Luke found himself looking into Mrs. Pederson's face.

Luke stared, suddenly not feeling any part of himself from the neck down. It was as if his head were filled with helium and floating in air anchored by a thin string that he himself was stepping on.

"Come in, Luke Canvin," she said, sounding almost shy. And then she disappeared. He heard her footsteps as she walked away from him.

Luke felt his body materialize, twice as heavy as before. He eased the door open and slipped inside. The hall was empty. Its hollow dimness seemed to push the ceiling and walls upward and away, making the house appear much larger on the inside than it looked from the outside. The hallway's musty smell reminded him of the air released from his father's opened footlocker. Trying not to make a sound, he walked toward the dim light at the end of the hallway and stepped into the kitchen.

The kitchen was hidden in shadows that seemed to shift toward whatever he looked at. Everything in the kitchen was old: the refrigerator, the small table next to the window—everything looked like black-and-white photos in yellowed *Life* magazines. Even the light coming from the window seemed somehow aged.

The kitchen also smelled old, as if the odor of

boiling potatoes had soaked into the walls and floor and ceiling and could never be scrubbed out.

But Mrs. Pederson looked older than anything in the kitchen. She stood by the little table in front of the window. Luke was surprised to see a large scrap of cloth—a scarf or a dishtowel—wrapped around her head like a turban. Over her dress she was wearing an apron with large ruffles sewn onto the straps, giving her big shoulders. And she leaned her hand on the table next to a squat, bluish carnival glass vase filled with flowers. The light in the room was such that he couldn't exactly tell what color they were.

Red, perhaps?

"I have some things for you to do . . . some lifting and cleaning," she said. "And I have some boxes under my bed that I want carried up to the attic and some things from the attic brought down here." She was all business but, unlike yesterday, she no longer seemed angry. Instead, she seemed somewhat ill at ease about having him in her house. He followed her from the dim kitchen to an even dimmer bedroom.

Not waiting for instructions, he dropped to his hands and knees and burrowed his head and shoulders under her bed. There was lots of dust— as he moved, it rippled almost like waves on a lake. He took little, quick breaths to avoid breathing it in. Even so, dust stiffened the inside of his nose, smelling faintly of talcum powder.

"There should be two small boxes on your right." Mrs. Pederson sounded as if she were in the next room. "Bring those out . . . if you would."

Carrying the two boxes, he followed her through the kitchen to the other side of the house where, in the middle of the ceiling, a trapdoor was flopped open. An old ladder stuck up into the darkness. Mrs. Pederson stopped at the base of the ladder and turned to look at Luke. "You go up the ladder first, and I'll be right behind—to tell you where to put them. Don't want to be at the top of the ladder with you down there peeking at my knickers." And then she laughed, a high nervous laugh, surprising Luke with its pleasantness.

The attic—really only a crawl space, with no room to stand up—was packed with things that seemed to take up the space where there should have been air for breathing. As Luke crouched near the trapdoor, Mrs. Pederson's head popped up next to him. She looked around her, squinting. "Sometimes my brain feels stuffed with junk, just like this attic," she said, a tiny smile playing with the corners of her mouth. "Why don't you take that box over there," she continued, pointing now, "and move it over here." Luke crawled toward the box, easing the weight of each hand and knee onto the boards in case they were rotted or split.

It seemed that Mrs. Pederson had him move everything in the attic at least once to make enough room for the boxes he'd carried up. The dust was thicker in the attic than under Mrs. Pederson's bed, in layers so thick that it looked almost as if he could pick it up and shake it like a heavy wool blanket. He sneezed frequently, and each time Mrs. Pederson said, "Bless you, Luke Canvin." Sometimes she barely got out that blessing before he sneezed again, and she'd repeat herself without pausing for breath.

"That's enough for now," she finally said, her tiny smile growing larger. "I'm afraid you'll blow the roof off with your next sneeze."

Luke looked at her, his eyebrows rising in surprise, and smiled. "I'm sneezing the floor clean . . . up here," he said, hesitantly, not knowing how Mrs. Pederson would take his little joke.

She laughed—a more confident laugh than he'd heard earlier. "That's enough for now," she repeated, and Luke didn't know for a moment if she meant joking or work. "Oh, one more thing," she said, squinting up at him. "That wooden box . . . the carved wooden box up there . . . the one about this big?" And she had her flattened hands apart a little more than a foot.

He peered around, spotted it close by, and nodded.

"Bring it down. And be careful of it, Luke Canvin," Mrs. Pederson called. "Be careful."

CHAPTER

9

Luke was careful, but even so he banged the edge of the box on several rungs of the ladder as he made his way down, fighting for balance with each step. The box was much heavier than he had expected it to be, and its varnished surfaces were slick in his dust-powdered hands. He dug his fingers into the crevices of the deep carvings that covered its sides and cringed each time the box hit a rung, expecting Mrs. Pederson to reprimand him. If she noticed, she didn't say a thing.

As he came down the stairs, Luke wrestled not only with the box but with his feelings about Mrs. Pederson. She was nothing like he thought she should be, and he felt tricked. She actually joked around, even poking fun at herself. It was this sense of humor that confused him the most.

The box seemed to grow heavier. His arms were more tired than he realized from shifting boxes in the attic, and they seemed to stretch longer with each step. By leaning backward he was able to keep from dropping what he held.

As he followed Mrs. Pederson to the kitchen, he wondered how the stories about her being a witch had gotten started. He couldn't imagine her being anybody's grandmother, but she didn't seem like witch material, either. She was birdlike—her head moved forward slightly with each step, reminding Luke of a pigeon walking.

Maybe, he thought, she had done something bloody and unspeakable in the past. Maybe she had an evil side that he hadn't seen yet. Or maybe she was nice until your guard was down and then . . . *wham-oh!* Would she now turn around and grab a knife and run after him?

She turned around and Luke tensed, expecting the worst. Instead of seeing crazy eyes and anger, he saw a smiling face. It was not an easy smile—her face didn't seem used to smiling—but it was nice enough.

"You can put the box on the table, Luke Canvin," she said, never taking her eyes off him.

Walking to the table, he eased the box onto its

Formica top, which appeared glassy in the kitchen's light, nicked and scratched in patterns that reminded him of the ice on a skating rink. As he sat, Luke saw that the carving on the box made a dense pattern of leaves and vines.

She sat across from him, and there was a stretch of uncomfortable silence as Luke stared at the box, wondering what was inside it.

Mrs. Pederson took a sharp, deep breath and looked at Luke. "I thought you'd be interested to see some things in this box." She nodded toward it. Pulling the box toward her, she lifted the lid. She reached in and bent so low over the open box that Luke wondered if she was trying to find something by its smell. Concentrating changed her face completely as thousands of tiny wrinkles appeared, making her ugly.

"My Elijah got several decorations in the war," she said in a soft voice that was hollow from speaking into the box. "He served his country well, Luke Canvin. He was a hero . . . to me." Her face suddenly relaxed, and most of the wrinkles disappeared. "Ah, here it is." She sighed. It was spooky, as if there were two Mrs. Pedersons in the same body—one more wrinkled than the other and each taking turns appearing on her face.

She sat up and pulled her hand from the box. "His Good Conduct Medal."

Luke stared, dumbstruck, as she laid it on the table and then began rooting around in the box again.

"How did he . . . what did he do to get it?" Luke asked, his hand inching toward the medal. He wanted to touch it but didn't know if he should.

"I don't know," she said, pausing in her rummaging to gaze at it.

The medal was gold colored and round. Circling it were the words EFFICIENCY, HONOR, FIDELITY. An eagle, wings spread, stood on a long sword laid across the cover of a closed book.

"He must have been a good soldier, though," she said, looking up at Luke.

Luke glanced at Mrs. Pederson and back down to the medal. It didn't look heroic—unlike his father's Purple Heart.

Mrs. Pederson plunged her hand into the box again. "There," she said, smiling, drawing out another medal.

Luke sucked in his breath. This medal was beautiful, a robed woman standing with a crown of light rays. She had wings and held a sword in one hand, pointing down as if she were ordering somebody to kneel. In the other hand she held a shield. "What is it?" he asked.

"A Victory Medal," Mrs. Pederson said. "Practically everybody got one for serving in the war."

"Oh." Luke was disappointed to hear that.

Once more Mrs. Pederson bent over the box. "Ah, here's the one I thought you'd like to see." She pulled her hand from the box, and Luke instantly recognized its heart shape. She held it above the table and stared at it herself. It twisted slowly on its ribbon, going first one way and then the other, showing both sides. It was like his father's but older-seeming, softer. It was the difference between a shining new quarter and a quarter that had spent years in hundreds of pockets, rubbing and clinking against other coins. "Here," she said, reaching toward Luke. He held out his hand, and she dropped it into his palm, backside up.

There, etched below the motto FOR MILITARY MERIT was a name that sounded as if it came from the Bible: Elijah Pederson.

He looked from the medal to Mrs. Pederson and found she was looking at him, her chin almost resting on her chest, her eyes steady and calm. He wanted to ask her how her husband had been wounded. He wanted to know the story. He wanted to know because it seemed that knowing the story of Elijah Pederson would bring him closer to knowing what had happened to his father.

It was as if she'd read his thoughts. "Elijah never told me much about the War. I learned more from the newspaper and the newsreels than I ever learned from him. All I know is that it must have been terrible . . . the bombing, the marching, the rain, the mud, the barbed wire . . . the stink of death." She pulled her shoulders back and her face tightened, becoming more stern. "He was a quiet man, my Elijah . . . a peaceful, quiet man. He kept his thoughts to himself . . . and his feelings. And I never pried. I never pestered him the way some women do."

Luke nodded and swallowed his disappointment.

Mrs. Pederson nodded along with him. "I wondered too, Luke Canvin. Often, as I watched Elijah go into the orchard in the morning, a little hitch in his step, I wondered what dreadful things he carried in his heart. I only know that he did what he had to do . . . he did his duty and he defended his country by risking his life. I only know that he didn't enjoy it . . . it brought him no joy, the killing. But he must have done it, and it must have made him hurt fearsomely each time he killed another man."

She looked down at the wooden box. "I loved him for his quietness. But I do wish that he'd unburdened himself . . . a little. He might have lived longer. . . ." She looked up, and Luke saw a glistening in her eyes and embarrassment hardening her mouth.

"Well, I suppose we'd better get back to work,"

she said briskly. "I would like you to do some cleaning"—she smiled, as if she were telling a joke on herself—"dusting under things . . . where I can no longer reach."

Luke held out the Purple Heart, and just as she took it, they both froze, their arms stretched across the table, their fingers almost touching. The feeble sound of a bell drifted through the kitchen. It was followed by the rush of a clearer, brighter ring. And then another and another.

Mrs. Pederson gasped, and her hand thumped to the table. Horrified, Luke looked into Mrs. Pederson's face. As if in a remembered nightmare, he saw a hole open, swallowing her face. Her mouth! Her throat had tightened, but instead of a scream, a terrifying silence poured from her mouth followed by a wheezing rattle that formed the words "Stop them! Stop them!"

Luke leaped from his seat and ran through the hallway to the front door. While he ran, the ringing stopped. Gasping now, he threw open the door and grabbed the jamb to stop himself from tumbling outside. He stared, not believing what he saw.

Mike ran down the sidewalk, his shoulders hunched, his head swaying back and forth.

And just as he neared the end of Mrs. Pederson's sidewalk, Luke watched his father's frame step into the gap in the hedge, filling it right where Mike was aimed.

Suddenly Mike saw Luke's father. He pulled himself up, trying to keep from ramming the man's stomach. Luke's father's arms shot upward to fend off the body hurtling toward him.

Luke closed his eyes against their falling—but not seeing was worse than seeing. Opening his eyes, he saw his father falling, Mike sprawled on top of him. The moment his father hit the pavement, he scrambled to his feet, grabbing Mike's shirt collar, pulling him off the sidewalk with a strength that didn't match his shrunken body. His father held Mike by the nape of his neck, and Mike hung for a few startled moments, limp as a kitten, before trying to wrench himself free.

"Not so fast!" his father growled, taking hold of Mike's upper arm. Mike had gone suddenly rigid as Luke's father marched him onto the porch. As they got closer, Luke saw that his father's fingers dug into the tender flesh just under Mike's armpit, pressing the nerve against the bone. His father's face was hard and angry. Mike's face was about to shatter.

Something landed gently on Luke's shoulder, feeling for a moment like a settling bird searching for balance on the branch of a tree. He glanced behind him and saw Mrs. Pederson peering at Mike, her clawlike hand perched on his shoulder.

Her face had undergone yet another transformation—Luke saw no gentleness, no humor, no kindness there. Hers was the face of a witch. Anger had fanned her black-seeming eyes to glowing coals. And hatred had scorched her white skin a livid red.

"And who are you?" she asked, her voice a flattened low note.

Mike was so scared that he couldn't get out his own name. He looked from Mrs. Pederson to Luke, his eyes begging for help. Luke stood, frozen in place, staring blankly at Mike, who began to cry.

Surprised, Luke's father let go of Mike's arm. Mike swallowed a sob and spun around, running down the sidewalk in a sloppy zigzag, as if he couldn't see straight.

"Well," his father said. "Maybe that'll teach him." He reached out and took Mrs. Pederson's elbow in his hand. "Are you all right, ma'am?"

Mrs. Pederson's mouth trembled and the fire in her eyes had turned to ash. She nodded and then whispered, "Let's go inside."

Silently, Luke followed his father and Mrs. Pederson into the house. They walked to the kitchen and sat around the table. Mrs. Pederson looked out the window and cleared her throat.

"Elijah and I owned an apple orchard . . . bought

it after the war . . . a large orchard . . . where this part of town is now." Her voice sounded as if it were lost and she was struggling to find it. "Elijah set up the bell . . . that bell by the porch . . . for me to call him to dinner and . . . to call him in case of fire or tornado. I could always feel bad weather coming . . . in my bones. I could always tell when tornadoes or hail or blizzards were coming. He trusted my gift."

Luke breathed in, filling his lungs completely, and pictured the apple tree outside his bedroom window.

"The town grew," Mrs. Pederson continued. "And people began to steal apples as if the apples didn't belong to anybody . . . as if we didn't make our living from those apples. Once Elijah caught some boys selling apples . . . *our* apples . . . Jonathans . . . alongside the road. He boxed some ears and tanned some hides. And then the pranks started.

"The worst one was when the boys sneaked in and rang the bell. Each time Elijah came a-runnin', fearful that something was terribly wrong . . . that maybe I'd cut off my finger with a carving knife or that the chimney had caught fire. And when he found out he'd been tricked, he'd be madder than a wet cat. He'd fly into a rage."

Luke closed his eyes. The look on her face was ferocious—wounded and sad at the same time.

With his eyes closed he seemed to feel her voice grow louder. He heard his father shifting his weight on his chair.

"One day I had a headache that grew until I thought my head would explode. I knew a bad storm was coming. I thought it might be a tornado. So, finally, when I couldn't stand it any longer, I rang the bell and Elijah came a-runnin'. He wanted to catch those boys red-handed as I rang and rang and he ran and ran, thinking it was those boys, and . . ." Mrs. Pederson breathed in sharply and Luke opened his eyes. Tears were streaking down her face and she began to sob. "He dropped *dead* . . . heart attack . . . died when . . . his heart exploded . . . and . . . and his face was . . . *purple* and he was . . . *dead* . . . and his face lay in the mud and . . . and the tornado skipped over the house."

Luke shuddered and Mrs. Pederson covered her face with her hands. Luke's father stared out the window, his face set as hard as a piece of stone.

Luke heard her whisper through her hands. "The bell . . . it was the . . . the last thing he . . . he ever heard." She uncovered her mouth and her voice gathered strength. "I never, *never* wanted to hear that bell again until it rang to let Elijah know I was coming . . . coming on the wings of Death himself . . . coming to join him."

CHAPTER

10

Luke was glad to be back home from school, and alone. His mother wasn't home and his father was at his first day of community college. Carrying his math book to his bedroom, he lay down on his bed and looked out the window.

He stared at the old apple tree, whose branches reached out, almost touching his room. Since Mrs. Pederson had told of Elijah's death, he found himself staring at this tree often. Even though he'd looked at it all his life, during every season and in all kinds of light, he'd never known that it had once belonged to the Pedersons. Knowing that now made it look different and gave him the creeps.

But he didn't want to think about all that, and he closed his eyes, trying to relax, trying not to think of the rotten Monday he'd barely survived.

All day long, Mike got more and more on Luke's nerves. Mike was pissed and Luke didn't blame him. What had happened after Mike ran into his father had been awful. But Luke didn't think that Mike should be angry at him. *He* hadn't done anything to Mike. It hadn't been *his* fault.

If Mike had heard that story and seen Mrs. Pederson's face as she told it—if Mike hadn't been caught by Luke's father and felt humiliated by his father's treatment—if Luke's father hadn't called up Mike's parents and reported what Mike had done—if Mike hadn't rung the bell in the first place!—then Mike would have acted differently today.

But none of those *ifs* were true, and all day long Mike had made it impossible for Luke to tell him Mrs. Pederson's story. Mike had gone out of his way to be ornery, letting Luke know that he was no longer Luke's best friend. All day long Luke had tried to ignore Mike, hoping that everything would turn back to normal. But that had been next to impossible.

From the moment he got to school, Luke found that everywhere he turned Mike was there, staring at him with eyes made into slits that were almost as thin as his tight-lipped mouth. As hard as he tried, Luke couldn't get away from him. And every once in a while, when he least expected it, Mike would saunter up to him, muttering "I thought so" or "Weird" or "Cripes" as he walked by. And then, just when Luke was angry enough to bop him, Mike stopped. That was almost as annoying to Luke as his pestering.

Quietly, even though he was alone in the house, Luke got up from the bed, went to the window, unhooked the screen, and slipped outside. He wanted to leave his anger inside. Walking up to the apple tree, he turned and sat in the V made by two roots that were as thick as his thighs. He leaned back against the trunk and closed his eyes. Underneath his thighs and bottom he felt smaller roots that formed ropy webs between the larger roots. He tried to ignore the discomfort they caused. But it was as hard to ignore as Mike had been, and his anger at Mike's unfairness flared.

The way the roots felt merged with the trapped feeling he'd endured all day, and Luke flashed to the image of a tiger cage. He'd seen photographs in magazines—cubelike cages the Vietcong made of bamboo bars on all sides—barely big enough for an American prisoner-of-war to crouch inside. He wished he could stick Mike in one.

His eyes still closed, Luke pulled his legs under him and squatted. He pressed his elbows to his sides and imagined how Mike would feel, bound hand and foot, squatting on bamboo poles spaced several inches apart. Ropes looped around his neck, tying him to the top four corners of the bamboo cage. As he grimaced, his neck muscles tightened, and he pretended he was Mike, testing the ropes by leaning a little to his left and a little to his right.

He couldn't move far. When he moved left, the right ropes choked him. It was all so cleverly done that if Mike fell asleep, he would hang himself. And regardless of which direction he moved, the ropes were placed so that they tugged, disciplining him, making him stay perfectly, painfully still.

He wanted Mike to be in pain. And already, after just a few minutes in this make-believe tiger cage, Luke ached to move. He couldn't imagine how men lived for weeks, sometimes months, inside these boxes of torture. He wondered how long Mike would last. Two minutes, he decided—tops.

His neck ached from holding it in one position. Opening his eyes, he immediately wanted to melt into the ground.

His father stood off to his left, books under one arm, his sports jacket draped over the other, the knot of his tie pulled down, his shirt collar unbuttoned. He stared at Luke, puzzled.

Luke hoped his father hadn't figured out what

he was doing under this tree. But if he had, he didn't let on. And then, to Luke's surprise, his father walked to the tree and sat one root over, grunting as he did so.

They didn't say anything for several minutes. Luke looked up as his father cleared his throat. "Had a hard day at school, too?" he asked.

Luke nodded. "Yeah," he said.

"I don't know." His father sighed, setting his books on his thighs and covering them with his jacket. "I just don't know. Guess I didn't remember how awful school can be . . . being cooped up in a classroom. I stand out like a sore thumb." He looked at Luke and Luke admired his father's clean-shaven face. "I don't have long hair and . . . Cripes! When I was a bricklayer . . . even at the end of a friggin' hot day . . . my clothes didn't stink like some of theirs do."

The question sprang from Luke's mouth, sounding to Luke like his mother when he got home from school. "What happened today . . . at school?"

His father looked at him, as if deciding whether or not he should tell him. "Well. I just . . . There were some things I heard today that . . ." He squinted at remembering. "Crud! They made me angry and I . . . I blew it. I mean, these two punks, they were sitting next to me and one of them—he

106

had a beard—trying to look like Jesus Christ, for crissake! . . . was talking about the war and talking some garbage about American soldiers being war criminals. And this guy was talking that trash loud enough for me to hear. He goshdarn *wanted* me to hear! It was like I had a sign pinned to my backside that said: 'Vietnam Vet. Please kick!'"

Luke looked down from his father's face and saw his hands clasped on top of his jacket, the knuckles whitened. "He *wanted* me to hear," his father continued, his voice lower now. "He was baiting me and I almost acted like a large-mouthed bass . . . I almost took his bait. I almost knocked his friggin' head . . ."

The catch in his father's voice caused Luke to look up. His father was looking down at him, his eyes wide, as if he'd just realized something important. "What does he know, anyway! *Nothing*, that's what. I could've told him so much . . . about being there . . . about being in Vietnam. I could've told him how it *felt*. But, crud! He'd've just laughed in my face. He wouldn't've understood squat."

Luke saw tears building in his father's eyes and suddenly, more than anything, he didn't want his father to cry. "He's just a hippie . . . you know, a draft dodger," he said, trying to sound brave but his voice coming out small and thin. In his hand

107

he felt the Purple Heart and it startled him—he didn't remember putting his hand in his pocket.

His father nodded and kept looking at him. His Adam's apple bobbed as he swallowed. "I haven't known what to tell your mother . . . or you. There's so *much*! You just couldn't understand. Couldn't."

He glanced at Luke and saw Luke was staring at him. His eyes bounced away, shy and embarrassed. "Crud," he continued. "When I joined up, I knew it wasn't like World War Two. Now, *that* was a war *everybody* thought was right. Maybe in Vietnam it wasn't a *good* war, but it was *my* war . . . the war for *my* generation . . . and I didn't think it could be a bad war . . . not with President Johnson and everybody else over in Washington for it. Crud. I guess now I just didn't know *what* kind of war it was . . . in Vietnam."

Luke sensed his father's body relaxing as he talked. He noticed his fingers playing with the lapel of the sports jacket in his lap as he continued. "Did a lot of thinking in that hospital . . . in Tokyo . . . about why I joined, why I left you and your mother to go. I didn't have to join up but I . . . I guess I was just cocky enough to think I was being a brave son-of-a-buck . . . like my old man in World War Two." He squinted, as if in pain. "Maybe some men are brave . . . better men than me, anyway. But the more I thought about it, the more I felt

108

that I went over to that stinkin' hole because I *wasn't* brave . . . 'cause I told too many people what I thought about those protesters . . . 'cause I told too many people that those lousy creeps were *cowards* and that they didn't deserve to be Americans if they didn't lay it on the line . . . if they didn't fight for their country. Lord! It got so that I thought people would think *I* was a coward if I didn't go. . . ."

Luke tensed. He didn't want to hear what his father was saying. He didn't want it to be true.

"Everybody wants to be a hero . . . 'specially to their son . . . but I . . . I just don't want to lie to you, Luke. Not now." Luke didn't want to look at the pain he saw in his father's face, but he couldn't tear his eyes away. His father glanced down. "Luke, what're you fiddling with in your pocket?"

Luke's heart almost skipped a beat, and he looked down to where he held the Purple Heart. "Nothing," he mumbled.

"Come on, Luke. I ain't blind."

Slowly, fearfully, Luke pulled his hand out, and because the Purple Heart was pinned inside, the pocket came with it. Turning it palm side up, he uncurled his fingers. The Purple Heart lay in his hand, George Washington's face showing.

His father grunted. "It's a dandy, isn't it," he said. "But you know something, Luke? Nobody *wants* to get a Purple Heart. You don't go out of your *way* to get one. You have to get *wounded*." Luke's fingers closed over the medal.

"Don't get me wrong," his father continued. "It was nice of them to give it to me, but it's not something that helps you remember anything . . . anything especially *wonderful*."

And then his father began to laugh—a tense, unhappy laugh.

"You know where I was wounded?" His father's voice was sharp, had an angry edge to it.

Luke held his breath. Now that his father was going to tell him, he didn't know if he wanted to hear.

"Well, I'll tell you. My butt. My rear end. My *ass!* Couldn't sit for a month. Couldn't lie on my back. The bandages filled my pants like diapers, and that stinking cream they dressed it with stained my pants all the way through so that . . ." He leaned back against the tree. "That's not important," he said, closing his eyes and tipping his head back.

No! Luke cried inside. *No, no, no!* He didn't want to hear any more.

But his father continued. "We were on patrol . . . seven of us. We were supposed to be in a secured area so, as usual, we weren't being especially quiet . . . you know, we were horsing around. We knew better, but it felt so good to let off steam . . . you know? My buddy, Dick . . . Remember Dick? The one I wrote you about from New Mexico?" He reached into his shirt from the top button and pulled out the dog tags. Fumbling with them for a moment, he held one out for Luke to see. "This one was Dick's."

Luke stared at the name punched with raised letters into the metal: Dick North. His father let the tags drop, and they landed on top of his tie. "Well, Dick was walking in front of me and was turning around to make some smart-ass joke. I heard something and the—" His father's head snapped toward Luke. "You sure you want to hear this?"

Stunned, Luke swallowed. He'd been wanting to know since he found out his father was wounded. Until now.

"I'm gonna tell you anyway," his father said, before Luke could answer. "I gotta." Tears welled up and he brushed them away angrily. "Dick was walking in front of me . . . and I heard something . . . a crack, maybe a stick breaking . . . maybe something else . . . and close, too . . . real close . . . and . . . and Dick's face disappeared. It just . . . just up and disappeared. There was *nothing* where his face had been. I mean, just a big . . . a *big* hole . . . and a sound came out and blood spurted and bubbled . . . like he was *trying* to say something only his mouth . . . his *face*, for crissake! . . . it wasn't there!" He was fighting his own breath,

111

trying to keep from sobbing. "I dropped to the ground and I crawled around behind where Dick fell. I hid behind him and I . . . I listened to his last breath. Crud! And then they started firing at *me*. I tucked down and hid behind Dick . . . like he was a bunch of sandbags or something . . . and I popped up every once in a while, my gun on rock'n'roll, firing over his chest. And I felt his body jerk every time a bullet hit him instead of me. And when everything got quiet, I felt something wet and I reached back and I grabbed . . . all I grabbed was a handful of . . . of blood and cloth . . . and . . ."

Luke stared at his father, his mouth open, his eyes wide, his heart beating in his throat. Tears poured down his father's face.

"I was . . . I was so *pissed* . . . *scared* . . . Hell, I'd messed my pants . . . right where I was shot . . . right in my wound. That's probably what caused the infection. And the guys used to joke around about diaper rash. . . ."

His father's face was slick. And the only thing Luke could think to do was to unpin the Purple Heart from his pocket and hold it out to his father. His fingers shook so hard, he pricked himself twice with the pin before he got it undone. His father's tears fell on the medal and on his hand for several minutes before he noticed what Luke was doing.

Taking the Purple Heart, his father said, "Crud!" Sniffling and trying to smile, he looked at Luke. "I'm sorry . . . I'm just a sorry ol' excuse for a father, Luke. I'm sorry. I *am!*"

And then he reached an arm around Luke's shoulder and pulled him close. Luke buried his face in his father's side and threw his arms around him, hugging as tightly as he could. He'd been longing to do this ever since his father had come home. He'd been longing so much it had hurt—he hadn't known how much until now.

And as he hugged his father, he fought his own tears. He fought and fought and fought.

But the tears won.

CHAPTER

11

Luke looked above the trees to the dark clouds that rose in the sky like a slow-motion wave about to break, about to crush the trees, about to crush him. Luke dawdled as he walked away from school. Occasional anger flashed through his body, as searing as lightning, and an aching disappointment grumbled in dark corners of his mind, wordless but as full of meaning as the strong, deep thunder coming from the clouds.

For the second day in a row, Mike had been ornery. Finally, at recess, when he couldn't take it anymore, Luke had walked up to Mike and stood in front of him, his hands on his hips, his elbows sharp and threatening.

"Hey, Mike," he'd said. "I'm sorry about my dad and all that . . . you know, at Mrs. Pederson's."

Mike had simply spun on his heel and stared in the opposite direction.

"Mike!" Luke pleaded. And Mike had walked away. Luke's face had wilted with the shock of Mike's meanness. His hands had slipped off his hips.

He looked at the dark clouds as he remembered this, and he wished that Mike was with him and that he was Mike's sergeant. It was his turn to be sergeant, after all. He thought of all the painful, humiliating things he could order Mike to do.

I could tie him to a tree and hose him down and wait for lightning to strike him, he thought, looking once more at the ominous wall of cloud.

Or better yet, Luke thought, I could make him do knuckle pushups . . . in gravel.

And then he pictured Mike marching up and down the sidewalk in front of his house, wearing only his underwear. And Luke pictured kids from school gathering in his front yard staring and laughing and pointing at Mike. He grinned, thinking of how he would stand next to the sidewalk and wait until Mike marched by and then yank down the underpants.

Just as he was picturing Mike struggling to march with his knees banded together, Luke heard the slap-slap of footsteps approaching from be-hind. He looked over his shoulder just in time to see Mike whizz by.

"Hey, Mike," Luke called. "Mike!" But Mike kept on running as if he hadn't heard a thing.

And then it struck him. This wasn't even the way to Mike's house. Mike had run past his own house so that he could run past Luke and ignore him on purpose one more time.

Clenching his jaw to keep from yelling again, to keep from begging Mike to stop, Luke dropped his gaze and stared at the sidewalk. He felt a hot rush of tears in his eyes. But before they could spill, a circle of sidewalk cement instantly darkened and he heard a splat. And then another and another. Each darkened circle was the size of a quarter.

They weren't his tears—they came from the sky. Faster now, huge raindrops sizzled as they hit the sidewalk, inches apart, looking like bullet holes following Mike, striking closer and closer but never quite close enough, as Mike ran down the side-walk and disappeared around a corner.

★

Luke couldn't believe it. His finger trembled as it reached toward the curled edge of the note taped to the refrigerator. Pencil scratches filled the piece

116

of paper, the letters written in such haste that he could barely make out what they said: "At hospital with your mom. Go to Mike's. Will call later. Dad."

It was happening! His mother was having a baby.

He felt an incredible rush of happiness. And right behind the happiness came a jolt of fear. He'd heard that sometimes women died giving birth.

He stood facing the refrigerator, staring at the note, as these feelings collided in the middle of his chest. He gasped as the wave of happiness swallowed the fear and he let his math book drop to the kitchen floor. Jumping as high as he could, he punched the air with one fist and yelled, "Yahoo!"

He was suddenly so happy that he felt as if somebody had pumped him full of the wonderful news. "All right!" he bellowed, using one whole breath. But as much happiness as he let out, even more rushed in to take its place.

And then he thought of Mike. It was as if he'd been punctured. His father wanted him to go to Mike's house. He was going to call at Mike's house. But that was the last place in the world Luke wanted to go. So, what if his father couldn't get him there? He'll call here, Luke reasoned.

Glancing at the window, he saw it had begun to rain fitfully. The rain made his decision to stay home feel even more right.

And then he thought of Mrs. Pederson. "Crud!"

he muttered. Mrs. Pederson was expecting him to help her this afternoon—had even paid him a little something in advance and then told him not to tell his father—that his father might not approve of his being paid at all for work that was supposed to be a punishment. But even with the money, Luke couldn't help her. Not now, not if his father was going to call at any minute from the hospital. Even so, he didn't feel right about not showing up. He wished she had a telephone.

It won't take long, he told himself, and he charged toward the door.

The rain had stopped, and the dark polka dots on the cement were fading as they dried, filling the air with the ripe smell of rain. He ran toward Mrs. Pederson's, so full of his news that it took him a half block for the silence to hit him.

He stumbled to a stop and looked around him, straining to hear. He heard nothing. It was as if he'd gone deaf. No birds sang. No wind rustled the leaves of the trees. No dogs barked. With relief, he heard the distant sound of a car.

And then, as his ears strained to hear anything more—it came to him, almost floating, as soft as a bubble popping.

He heard the sound of the bell ringing. The sound grew in his mind—a long-forgotten memory rising to the surface.

It was Mrs. Pederson's bell.

Why?

And the wind answered him with a roar, sounding like an enormous wave ready to crest, ready to smash into the top of the clouds and fall, churning, on top of him.

And then the sirens started to wail.

He began to run just as the wind struck, smacking his face like a swung pillow, knocking him off balance. The sound of the bell was drowned in the shrill of the wind. *She must feel it in her bones.* He ran toward Mrs. Pederson's house, butting his head against the wind.

Rain began to fall, stinging. The wind pulled the breath out of him and he struggled to hold some inside.

His only thought was of Mrs. Pederson. He pictured her standing by her bell, buffeted by the wind, holding on to the rope for balance as she rang the bell, her dress blowing behind her, shredding as it flapped.

A page of newspaper, held down on the sidewalk by the wind, leaped up. It pounced on Luke's face, pressing hard. Luke tore at it, ripping off hunks of paper, feeling as if he were tearing off hunks of his own skin.

119

Picking up his pace, he ran with only one thought in mind—that he had to get to Mrs. Pederson because she'd been calling for help.

The hedge loomed, the branches thrashing. Sand blasted his face and he ran through the gap in the hedge and into Mrs. Pederson's yard.

The wind continued to shriek, but its force was diminished. Luke grew dizzy in the relative stillness, as if he were floating round and round in an eddy of water. As he ran from the hedge, the eddy grew more powerful, swirling like flushed water—pulling him—sucking him—toward the porch. He looked up, expecting to see a funnel searching for him with its hoselike mouth. Instead, he saw shredded bits of blackened cloud and the shingles of Mrs. Pederson's house raised like the hair of a frightened cat.

Luke staggered up the steps and threw open the screen door and pushed his way inside. The house shuddered and he threw his weight backwards against the door, forcing it shut.

Turning around, looking down the throat of the hallway, he saw Mrs. Pederson standing, hugging her own shoulders, her face like that of a ghost. Her eyes were closed and she rocked back and forth, as if trying to comfort herself. "I'm coming, Elijah!" she wailed. "I'm a-coming!"

"Mrs. Pederson!" he yelled. She opened her eyes

and her mouth. She struggled to loosen her own grip on her shoulders and held out her arms to him. She looked like a terrified child.

He ran to her and grabbed both of her hands before she could throw her arms around him. He ran under her arms, pulling her toward the kitchen. She followed, as if they were part of an insane square dance, tugging at him so lightly that he felt he must be dragging a flag that was fluttering in a light breeze.

He spied the darkness under the table and stopped. Seeing fear in Mrs. Pederson's eyes, he tried to sound reassuring even as he yelled loudly enough to be heard. "Mrs. Pederson! Under there! We'll be safe . . . under there!"

Closing her mouth, she nodded and lowered herself stiffly to her knees and crawled underneath. He followed, and she huddled next to him and against the wall, which pulsed with the force of the wind that was beating against the house.

Luke reached for a chair, toppling it as he pulled it under the table. It lay sideways, a barrier against attack. He grabbed the other two chairs around the table for protection, making walls of the chairbacks and legs. He knew the chairs wouldn't do much against the storm's fury, but it was better than nothing.

He looked at Mrs. Pederson. Incredibly, her

knees were drawn up to her chest and she stared at him, forlorn and lost, pitiful and small. Leaning toward her, he reached around her shoulder and held her close, as if she were a child and he were the father. He wished he could whisper to her, tell her that everything was going to be all right. But the wind never took a breath, never let up in its howling. All he heard mixed in with the wind was the faint, musical sound of a window exploding.

Suddenly it was deafeningly silent, so silent it was hard to breathe, as if the wind had snatched away the air as well as sound.

As the silence hit, Mrs. Pederson began to shiver so hard he thought that she would fly apart.

CHAPTER

12

Luke scrambled over a huge branch that lay across the sidewalk, torn from a large elm tree during the storm. The walk was littered with debris—shingles and shredded leaves piled up against bushes and fences and bits of greasy paper and foil that had blown from tipped-over garbage cans.

Mike saw the jockey shorts first, lying in the middle of the sidewalk. Luke was surprised they were there—most everything of value had been picked up by now. Running to them, Mike plucked them off the cement as if they were soiled and grinned at Luke. "I wonder who lost these?"

Luke laughed, picturing a naked boy running around town, searching for the underwear that had been blown right off his body. "We'll know him when we see him," Luke said.

Mike dropped the shorts and scrambled over the crooked elbow of an arm-shaped branch, excited now about finding other treasures.

Luke was happy to be friends with Mike again. The day his baby sister had come home, Mike had come over to see her. Mike had acted as if nothing had happened between them, and Luke took that for an apology.

Looking around from where he stood, Luke found it was tempting to think that what he saw was the result of an enemy bombing raid. It was tempting to think of enemy bombers in formation, flying so low that you could almost see the pilots behind their glass bubbles—to imagine taking aim at these planes with a machine gun and riddling their sleek, fishlike underbellies with bullets, bringing them down in flames.

For five days now, the town had been a perfect place to play war, to imagine attacks and counterattacks. A couple of houses had lost their roofs, and most houses had at least one or two boarded-up windows. A few cars, looking like smashed bugs, remained parked alongside curbs, the trees or utility poles that had rested on top of them gone now. Large trees that had tipped over left craters where their roots had grown. From the right angle these craters looked as if they'd been created by mortar, lobbed into town from nearby cornfields.

Mike and Luke had played hard the past couple of days, using the destruction caused by the tornado as the most realistic battlefield on which they'd ever played. They had played so hard at war that, much to their amazement, they were all played out for now.

Mike's head popped up from behind the branch where he'd been stooped over, looking. He smiled. "Well, have you changed her diapers yet?"

"Sure," Luke said, even though he hadn't. He'd held his sister, Catherine, and watched her sleep. But that was about all. He couldn't say she was cute, but he found himself studying her, his eyes tracing the folds of skin on her face—especially under her chin and around her eyes. And he'd felt her fingers, which seemed so delicate that he was afraid they might snap off. When she'd grabbed one of his fingers, he was shocked at how strong her grip was.

"Pretty gross, huh?" Mike said. "Like great big gobs of greasy grimy gopher guts, huh?"

Instead of answering, instead of pretending that he knew, Luke leaned forward and shouted, "Race you!" And he started running, dodging garbage that still lay on the sidewalk.

He heard Mike close behind him and tried to

speed up, but there was too much stuff in his way. Not wanting Mike to hear how hard he was working, he forced himself to breathe through his nose. His nostrils drew air as well as a flattened straw.

And then Mike passed him.

"Hey!" Luke cried out, as if Mike were cheating.

He tried to catch up but just couldn't. Mike's driveway was right ahead and he kept his eyes on it, disappointed when Mike reached it first.

"Want to come in . . . watch something on TV?" Mike asked, trying to keep from panting. His chest heaved anyway and Luke was glad that Mike had to work plenty hard to beat him.

"Can't . . . gotta get home," Luke said. "Want to come over to see the baby?"

"Naw." Mike screwed up his face, as if disgusted. "I've already seen her once. Seen one baby, you've seen them all."

"Want to help me at Mrs. Pederson's later?" Luke asked. Yesterday both he and Mike had worked for her, cleaning up the yard from the storm. And trimming the hedge.

"Aw, I don't know." Mike looked down at his feet, tapping his right foot, the toe of his shoe fanning back and forth in an arc. Mrs. Pederson paid them hardly anything at all for their work. Luke didn't mind so much—he still felt guilty about the trouble he'd caused her. But Mike had been so disappointed that he'd barely remembered to thank her.

"Well, if you want to, I'll be there."

Mike looked up, his eyes sheepish. "Okay. I might," he said. "Or I might not." And then he laughed, turned, and walked up his driveway, waving a hand without bothering to turn around.

"See you tomorrow," Luke called after him.

★

Luke was careful going into the house, trying not to make any noise. Tiptoeing through the kitchen, he listened for telltale sounds of Catherine. He heard nothing but the drip-drip of the kitchen faucet.

Walking into the living room, he saw his mother lying on the sofa. Her bare feet poked out from a wildly colored crocheted afghan that was pulled up to her shoulders. Her eyes were closed, and Luke saw bumps under the afghan that made him think that her hands held each other, resting below her gently rising and falling chest—where her stomach had been so large only a few days before.

Since she had come back from the hospital, Luke had found himself looking at her as if something were wrong. He remembered how funny he had thought she looked with her beach-ball belly. But now she looked funny without it—flat and shrunken. Holding his breath to be extra quiet, Luke walked to the bedroom hallway. If his mother was asleep in the living room without Catherine, Luke knew that his father must be home from school and in their bedroom.

Luke sniffed. The house smelled more complicated these days. The air was heavy with the scent of curdled milk, sweetened. And mixed in was the smell of baby powder and a faint sourness that was strongest in the bathroom, where the diaper pail sat next to the stool.

Hesitating, Luke peeked inside his parents' bedroom. In the middle of the bed was Catherine, in a cocoon of pink baby blankets. On the edge of the bed sat his father, gazing down at the baby. His father looked tired, but not in the same way he'd looked when he'd come home from Vietnam. He looked tired and happy at the same time—as if he'd run a long race and won.

Luke stood for several minutes, until his father sensed he wasn't alone with Catherine and looked up. "Howdy," his father whispered, smiling. Quietly, Luke crossed over to his parents' bed and sat on the edge opposite his father. Leaning over, he peered into Catherine's face. She wasn't looking as puffy and red as she had been looking this morning. But he still couldn't decide if she looked more like his father or more like his mother. Or like him.

As he watched, Catherine's mouth moved and her eyes closed tighter and she sighed, a bubble of spit appearing in the corner of her mouth. And then she gave out a little squeak and her eyes opened a crack. Her mouth was closed but her jaws began to work, and suddenly her mouth gaped and she began to cry. For such a tiny thing she made a very large sound.

His father sighed. "Crud. I was afraid that would happen . . . while your mom was resting," he said, loud enough to be heard above Catherine's cry. "Time for another feeding, most likely. We'll just have to wake up your mother."

"No need to do that."

Luke and his father looked toward the bedroom door. There stood Luke's mother, her hair rumpled and her face tired, but her smile charged with energy, her cheeks fairly glowing.

"I swear I heard her cry in my head before she opened her mouth," she said, walking to the bed.

Luke's mother stared at Catherine as if she couldn't believe what she was seeing. And then she sat next to Luke's father and began pulling up the tails of her blouse and unbuttoning it at the same time. Luke knew there was nothing bad about Catherine sucking on his mother's breasts. But yesterday when he'd seen his mother take out a breast and offer it to Catherine, he'd felt giggly

129

nervous, as if he'd walked in on his mother while she was taking a bath. He'd also felt jealous, wanting to be close to his mother, to be cradled that way in her arms. And he'd felt curious, wondering how it all worked—the breast and the sucking and the milk.

He knew his mother didn't mind his being there. But it all seemed private—something just between his mother and Catherine. Before his mother finished unbuttoning her blouse, Luke turned his head and got to his feet. The crying stopped as suddenly as it had started. "Gotta help Mrs. Pederson for a while," he said.

His father cleared his throat. "I'll walk you there, maybe see what you've been working at so hard."

"I'll see you two later." Luke stole a glance at his mother as he walked out of the bedroom. She held Catherine against her opened blouse and her eyes were partly closed. She looked as if she were listening to the most beautiful music in the world.

Luke and his father walked through the house in silence. As they stepped outside, Luke's father paused for a moment and threw his head back, letting the sunlight smack him in the face. "Isn't this the berries!" he said, smiling. And then he looked down at Luke. "Makes *me* feel like a fifth wheel too, Luke. But isn't it a pretty sight, your mother feeding Catherine like that?"

Luke scuffed at the pavement with the toe of his right foot. "Yeah," he said, looking up and trying to smile. The smile came easier than he'd thought it would.

"Just like you used to do," his father added. Luke felt himself blushing.

His father held out a hand, and Luke looked at it for a moment. He couldn't remember the last time he'd held his father's hand. He felt too old for it but he didn't want to hurt his father's feelings—and the hand was tempting. Slipping his hand into his father's, he was surprised at how comfortable it felt as they walked down the driveway and turned onto the sidewalk. He liked the way his father's thumb stroked his knuckles and the backs of his fingers.

"Don't think I told you how proud I am of how you helped Mrs. Pederson the other day . . . during the storm." His father squeezed Luke's hand and let it go.

Luke looked down to hide his embarrassed smile. "I had to let her know and then . . ."

"Luke, I've been thinking . . . just a little bit and . . ." His father frowned. "What you did took courage . . . the kind of courage I saw a lot of in Vietnam. Now, I bet you anything you didn't get up that morning and say to yourself, 'I'm gonna act courageous today. Gonna do something to make 'em proud.'" He smiled. "You just did what you *had* to do, *when* you had to do it. Like helping her during the storm . . . and helping her now. *That's* courage, Luke. I don't know anything else that says it better . . . except what your ma went through at the hospital."

Luke ached with things that he wanted to say but that didn't have words. "Dad," he said quietly, trying anyway, "I'm sorry . . . about everything."

They turned a corner and Mrs. Pederson's hedge came into view. One flank of it was wild and shaggy, going off to their left. Running straight down the sidewalk away from them, the other flank was neat as a brick wall—at least as high as Luke could reach with the hedge trimmers.

"Looks like you could use a little help with the top there," his father said, stopping.

"Yeah." Luke had thought of borrowing somebody's ladder to help with the high parts.

His father cleared his throat. "Since everybody's apologizing all over the place . . . well, Luke, I've been wanting to do some apologizing myself . . . to you. I'm . . . I'm sorry about . . . about everything too and . . ." His eyebrows knocked together. "Crud!" he muttered and then smiled, reaching into his pocket.

Luke stared as his father handed him the Purple Heart.

"Here," his father said. "I'd be proud for you to help take care of this thing for me. You've earned it, what with the way I've been acting and all."

Luke took the medal with trembling fingers. George Washington looked off to the left, calm and unflustered, as he closed his hand over it.

"Thanks," he said, not trusting his voice to say anything more. And then he pinned it on his shirt.

His father placed a hand on Luke's shoulder and squeezed it gently.

On August 7, 1782, General George Washington established the first American military decoration. Called the Badge of Military Merit, it was made of purple cloth cut into the shape of a heart and edged with narrow lace. "The road to glory in a patriot army and a free country is opened to all," General Washington wrote, making it clear that this military decoration was to be the first ever awarded to deserving officers and enlisted men without regard to their rank. It soon became known as the Purple Heart. Nobody knows for certain why General Washington chose the shape of a heart or the color purple—but today it seems a perfect symbol of bravery while under fire.

Only three people are known to have been awarded General Washington's Badge of Military Merit. The first was Sergeant Elijah Churchill of the Fourth Troop, Second Regiment of Light Dragoons, for his gallantry, extraordinary fidelity, and essential service in the raids of Fort St. George on November 23, 1780, and Fort Slongo on October 2, 1781. After the Revolutionary War the decoration fell into disuse and was almost forgotten for one hundred fifty years.

In 1932, in part to commemorate the two hundredth anniversary of George Washington's birth (February 22, 1732), General Douglas MacArthur revived the Badge of Military Merit as an Army decoration to be officially called the Purple Heart Medal. It soon became the only military decoration to recognize soldiers in the Army who suffered wounds, injuries, or death while in combat action against an enemy of the United States.

In 1942 President Roosevelt extended the Purple Heart to members of the Navy, Marine Corps, and Coast Guard. In 1952 President Truman made the Purple Heart retroactive to April 5, 1917, which allowed World War One servicemen to receive the medal. In 1962 President Kennedy extended eligibility for the Purple Heart to any American civilian who served with a branch of the armed forces.

Tony Harrison

A bibliography
1957–1987

Tony Harrison

A bibliography
1957–1987

Compiled by
John R. Kaiser

MANSELL

LONDON AND NEW YORK

First published 1989 by Mansell Publishing Limited
A Cassell imprint
Artillery House, Artillery Row, London SW1P 1RT, England
125 East 23rd Street, Suite 300, New York 10010, U.S.A.

British Library Cataloguing in Publication Data

Kaiser, John R.
  Tony Harrison: a bibliography, 1957–1987.
  1. Poetry in English. Harrison, Tony, 1937—
  Bibliographies
  I. Title
  016.821'.914

  ISBN 0-7201-2024-1

Library of Congress Cataloging-in-Publication Data

Kaiser, John R. (John Robert)
  Tony Harrison: a bibliography, 1957–1987 / compiled by John R.
  Kaiser.
    p. cm.
  ISBN 0-7201-2024-1 : $45.00
  1. Harrison, Tony, 1937- —Bibliography. I. Title.
  Z8387.95.K35 1989
  [PR6058.A6943]
  016.822'914—dc20   89-36328
                                                          CIP

This book has been printed and bound in Great Britain.
Typeset in Plantin by Colset (Private) Ltd.,
Singapore, and printed and bound by
Billing and Sons Ltd., Worcester, on
Publisher's Antique Wove paper.

Contents

ACKNOWLEDGEMENTS

A great many people have helped in the preparation of this bibliography and I am most grateful to all of them.

Above all, I am indebted to Tony Harrison for his cooperation and generosity. I also wish to acknowledge the special help and services of Bernard Stone of the Turret Bookshop, without whom this work could not have been completed.

Many individuals, acting in an official or personal capacity, and unknown persons representing institutions, have gone out of their way to be helpful and I should like to express my gratitude to them. Mr. Neil Astley (Bloodaxe Books); Mr. Jonathan Barker; The British Library; Mr. William M. Colleran (University Edition); BBC Radio and Television; Professor John Barnard (University of Leeds); Ms. Constance Cruikshank (Faber and Faber); Miss Lesley Gordon (Special Collections, University of Newcastle upon Tyne Library); Mr. Curt Janota; Mr. Peter Jay (Anvil Press); Mrs. Margaret Leach (Poetry Book Society); Ms. Susan M'Carty (Poetry Library); Ms. Sarah Morgan (Publicity Officer, Book Trust); Mr. P.S. Morrish (Brotherton Library, The University of Leeds); Mr. Andrew Motion (Chatto and Windus); Northern House; Penguin Books Ltd.; Quartet Books, Ltd.; Mr. Ronald R. Reiner; Mr. Alan Ross (London Magazine Editions); Mr. David Roy (Century Hutchinson General Publishing); Mr. Keith Sagar; Mr. John Silkin (*Stand Magazine*); Ms. Helen Sprott (Faber and Faber); Mr. Stephen Tabor; Yoji Yamaguchi (Random House) and Mr. Robin Yapp (Yapp Brothers).

INTRODUCTION

Up until now there has been no full-scale bibliography of the work of Tony Harrison, undoubtedly one of the most important poets writing in English today. Thus it seems time to establish a beginning for an exhaustive bibliography of Harrison's work.

Although the format and most of the procedures followed in this bibliography are conventional and will be obvious to the user upon examination of the listings themselves, a few comments may be useful. As much as possible, I have followed the format of the excellent work of Jack W.C. Hagstrom and George Bixby in their *Thom Gunn: A Bibliography 1940–1978* (London: Bertram Rota, 1979). Each section of the bibliography is preceded by a separate introduction.

All of my citations and descriptions have been based, wherever possible, on examination of the items themselves. Any item which I have not personally examined is annotated, before the description, by the statement 'Not Seen' in square brackets.

Notes that add details or explanations are used throughout the bibliography and are inserted at points where they seem most appropriate. Information included in notes is generally based on examination of the item itself, but a variety of other sources have been used.

I have made no attempt to trace in any systematic manner the printing history of a given poem or prose piece, but this can easily be done by consulting the index. I have made no attempt to identify textual revisions of poems; however, parts of poems published separately and changes of titles are noted and included in the index.

Square brackets surrounding any data indicate that the information given does not appear as such. Thus square brackets are used with page numbers, dates and in transcriptions of title pages and descriptions of dust wrappers and covers to describe publishers' logos, decorative devices, etc., that cannot be adequately transcribed per se. Square brackets are also used to describe information that is not transcribed in the description, i.e. 'Pennsylvania State University Press / [5 lines of addresses].'

Accepted practice is observed when transcribing upper and lower case letters. Unless there is an indication otherwise, the type is roman, and I have made no attempt to indicate either size of the upper and lower case letters or the amount of space between individual letters or words. In the description of title pages and quasifacsimile material all printing is in black; colored printing is indicated before the relevant letters or words. A vertical rule marks the end of each line, and any type variation or specific color that continues on the following line is indicated again at the beginning of that line.

Designation of colors is perhaps one of the most difficult undertakings that a bibliographer faces. The color numbers for all colors (with a few exceptions when a color could not be reasonably matched) except black, white, gold and silver refer to the *ISCC-NBC* (Inter-Society Color Council-National Bureau of Standards) *Color-Name Charts Illustrated with Centroid Colors (Supplement to NBS Circular 553)*. I have not systematically attempted to distinguish among types of cloth or paper used for bindings and wrappers. Wove paper is distinguished from laid paper and, when identifiable, special papers are named. For dust wrappers and paper wrappers, the indicated color of the paper is that of the base (i.e. unprinted paper stock) and the color of the finished wrapper is given when it is not the same as the base color. The word 'shiny' has been used to describe the whole spectrum of coated papers and glossy printing.

The collation is given by signatures and by leaves for sewn books. Standard notations (numbers or letters) are used for signatures. In most cases, books are not actually signed on the sheets and therefore the signature marks are enclosed in square brackets. Books described as having 'perfect bindings' are those in which all pages have been cut and are held together by glue or some other adhesive material; since identifiable signatures are generally no longer present, only the total number of leaves are given.

The size of an individual leaf is given to the nearest tenth of a centimeter, height preceding width. This also applies to size descriptions of broadsheets, labels, etc.

In all sections and subsections all items are listed chronologically. In Section C, items within a given year are listed preferentially by season, month and specific date. When only the year of publication is known for any given items, it is placed at the end of the listing for the year in which it was published.

Prices of each item at the time of publication are given only for the country in which the book was published. The exception to this is for books where the publisher has indicated foreign prices.

Publication data are based on information supplied by publishers and supplemented, as required, from other sources. The phrase, 'Data unavailable from publisher,' indicates that the publisher either could not locate or preferred not to reveal the information requested.

The list of reviews and other works on Tony Harrison have been selected and in no way is exhaustive. Only one book containing translations was found; others may exist. The bibliography does not give a listing of manuscripts nor such miscellanies as blurbs on dust jackets and publicity releases which contain excerpts of Harrison's writings.

Unquestionably there are errors, omissions, and incorrect data in this book. My aim has been to be as thorough and accurate as is possible. Any additions and emendations would be welcome and should be sent to the publisher.

ABBREVIATIONS

Abbreviations for Tony Harrison's principal works, subsequently used
in this bibliography, are listed alphabetically below.

AKFJK	A KUMQUAT FOR JOHN KEATS
AM	AIKIN MATA
A42	ANNO 42
BD	BOW DOWN
C	CONTINUOUS
DV	DRAMATIC VERSE 1973-1985
E	EARTHWORKS
FTSOE	FROM THE SCHOOL OF ELOQUENCE
LU	LOOKING UP
NIP	NEWCASTLE IS PERU
PP	PALLADAS: POEMS
PB	PHAEDRA BRITANNICA
SP	SELECTED POEMS
TS	TEN SONNETS FROM THE SCHOOL OF ELOQUENCE
TBB	THE BARTERED BRIDE
TFG	THE FIRE GAP
TL	THE LOINERS
TM	THE MISANTHROPE
TMS	THE MYSTERIES
TO	THE ORESTEIA
TP	THE PASSION
TW	THEATRE WORKS 1973–1985
USM	U.S. MARTIAL
V	V
VR	VOORTREKKER

A

BOOKS, PAMPHLETS AND
BROADSHEETS BY
TONY HARRISON

In this section all books, pamphlets and broadsheets by Tony Harrison
are listed in chronological order. Data on reprints and new editions are
included. No attempt has been made to denote textual differences in a
poem when it is reprinted in a subsequent volume.

A1   EARTHWORKS   1964

a. *First edition:*

[cover title] [horizontal rule] / NORTHERN HOUSE PAMPHLET
POETS / [horizontal rule] / [in vivid red(11)] *Earthworks* / [in vivid red]
T.W. Harrison / [horizontal rule] / two shillings / fifty cents/ [horizontal
rule]

Collation: [1]^8 = 8 leaves; 20.4 × 13.4 cm.

Binding: Sewn into heavy white wove paper wrappers; heavy white wove
paper; all edges trimmed.

Publication date: 30 October 1964

Price: 2 shillings / 50 cents

Number of copies: The publisher reports "c. 1000?" copies.

Pagination: [1] title page; [2] Acknowledgements / [horizontal rule] /
[5 lines] / *Hand-set at the / School of English, University of Leeds* /
MCMLXIV / Copyright T.W. Harrison 1964; 3–15 text; [16] at the
lower left-hand corner] UNPS4096.

Contents: My Migratory Bird and the Divine — The Hybrid Growth
— The Flat Dweller's Revolt — The New Earth — The Promised Land
— The Pit of Perception — The Pathetic Fallacy — The Hands — A
Part of the Mainland: Bardsey Island

A2   AIKIN MATA   1966

a. *First edition*

Aikin Mata / *The Lysistrata of Aristophanes* / Translated and adapted /
by T.W. HARRISON / and / JAMES SIMMONS / 'The Greeks'/ *They
care for the outward show of this life, / but of the life to come they are
heeless.* / THE KORAN / IBADAN / OXFORD UNIVERSITY PRESS
/ 1966

Collation: [A]^{16} + B^8 + C^{16} = 40 leaves; 17.2 × 11 cm.

Binding: Bound in paper-covered boards printed in black and darkish
medium red (15) and lettered down the spine in white: AIKIN MATA
OXFORD; on the front cover an illustration of two figures, decorative
designs and letters in Arabic and Greek in black and white; on the upper
quarter of the cover in white: AIKIN / MATA; on the rear cover in
black : OXFORD UNIVERSITY PRESS / Translated and adapted / by
/ T.W. HARRISON / and / JAMES SIMMONS; white wove paper; all
edges trimmed; white wove endpapers.

Publication date: 1966.

Price: Data unavailable from publisher

Number of copies: Data unavailable from publisher

Pagination: [1] half-title; [2] blank; [3] title page; [4] *Oxford University Press, Ely House, London W.1* / [4 lines of city locations] / *Oxford House, Iddo Gate, P.M.B. 5095, Ibadan, Negeria* / Oxford University Press 1966 / [4 lines of rights information] / Cover designed by Shyam Varma / from an original idea by Allan Leary / *Printed and bound in England by / Cox & Wyman Ltd., London, Fakenham and Reading*; [5–6] THE LYSISTRATA OF ARISTOPHANES; [7] A NOTE ON THE TRANSLATION; [8] blank; [9]–12 FOREWORD; [13] *Characters*; [14] *The scene takes place somewhere in Hausaland at an indefinite time.* / *There is a prolonged, violent (imaginary) war in progress between / what is now (roughly) the Northern and what is now / (roughly) the East and Western Regions of Nigeria*; [15]–78 text; [79]–80 NOTES.

Contents: Aikin Mata.

A3   NEWCASTLE IS PERU   1969

a. *First edition*:

NEWCASTLE / IS / PERU/ [single rule] / Newcastle upon Tyne / 1969

Collation: [1]⁸ = 8 leaves; 23.9 × 14.5 cm.

Binding: [Not Seen]Sewn into a white card binding with a 'purplish' dust wrapper of paper different from that of the text; on the front of the wrapper: 'TONY HARRISON / [Woodcut of Newcastle city scene] / [in red] NEWCASTLE IS PERU'; on the rear wrapper: 'a woodcut of "the Tyne god" '; white 'Bulkrite' paper; all edges trimmed.

Publication date: 1969. Details were unavailable from the publisher.

Note: The book was probably published between January and May, 1969. The Library of Congress copy has a stamped receipt date of May 29, 1969.

Price: Data unavailable from publisher.

Number of copies: 200 (of which 26 copies were numbered and signed).

Pagination: [1] title-page; [2] FOR JUANITA DE MENA; [3] *Correct your maps: Newcastle is Peru!* / John Cleveland [woodcut of a geographer and a globe] / [5 line quote form the 'Medea' of Seneca in Latin]; [4] blank; [5–7] [Prose statement by Harrison]; on page [7]—(from a transcript of a recording made of the poetry reading, / NEWCASTLE

IS PERU, given at the University of Newcastle / upon Tyne, Friday, 10 May, 1968.); [8] [reproduction of a woodcut of two hippogriffs with a shield bearing a coat of arms]; [9–15] text; [16] The poem first appeared in the *London Magazine*. / The worksheets were given to the University / Library, Newcastle upon Tyne, by the author in / 1968, during his year as Northern Arts Fellow in / Poetry at the Universities of Newcastle upon / Tyne and Durham. / The woodcuts were collected by the Newcastle / printer Andrew Reid, and have been deposited / by his firm, Hindson, Reid, Jordison, in / Newcastle University Library. / Hand set in 12 pt Garamond by / Gale R. Owen Penelope Pickstone Barie Land / Marilyn Bjork Helen Henstridge Diana Sadler / R.K.R. Thornton Elizabeth Hodgkinson / Sylvia M. Berry Margaret Wright Ingrid Schick / and Tony Harrison. / The Paper is *Bulkrite*./ 200 copies printed on a Double Crown Columbian / by Tony Harrison and Alistair Elliot at the Eagle / Press, University Library, Newcastle upon the Tyne, / 26 copies numbered and signed by the author.

Contents: Newcastle is Peru

Note: On page [9] there is a woodcut of a chess rook in the center of the page directly above the text.

b. *Second edition*

NEWCASTLE / IS PERU / TONY HARRISON / [single rule] / Northern House / Newcastle upon Tyne / 1974.

Collation: [1]⁸ = 8 leaves; 21.2 × 15.2 cm.

Binding: Stapled three times in heavy white plain card wrapper; white wove paper; all edges trimmed; dust wrapper of textured light gray (264) wove paper; on the front wrapper: TONY HARRISON / [woodcut of the church of San Marco] / NEWCASTLE IS PERU; on the rear wrapper in the center: [a woodcut of the head of a northern god].

Publication date: 1974

Price: 40p ($1.20)

Number of copies: The publisher reports "c. 1000?" copies.

Pagination: [1] title page; [2–15] Same as A3a [The first 16 lines are the same as A3a] This second edition is printed by photolithography / from an edition handset on 12 pt Garamond at the / Eagle Press, University Library, Newcastle upon / Tyne 1969. / © 1974 Tony Harrison U.K. IFFN 0078–1738 / ISBN 0 900570 18 0 / Published 1974 by / Northern House, 58 Queens Road / Newcastle upon Tyne NE2 2PR, U.K. / 40p ($1.20) [Number 23].

Contents: Newcastle is Peru

a. *First edition*

THE LOINERS / Tony Harrison / LONDON MAGAZINE
EDITIONS LONDON 1970

Collation: [A]–F^8 = 48 leaves; 20.3 × 15.5 cm.

Binding: Bound in black paper covered boards and lettered down the spine in gold: THE LOINERS Tony Harrison / [across the base of the spine in gold the publisher's logo: a leaf]; white wove paper; all edges trimmed; white wove end papers; dust wrapper of white wove paper, shiny on the exterior and printed in bright red and vivid yellow (82).

Publication date: July 1970

Price: £1.25

Number of copies 1,000

Pagination: [1] half-title; [2] blank; [3] title page; [4] ACKNOWLEDGEMENTS / [7 lines] /; Published by London Magazine Editions / 30 Thurloe Place, London, SW7 / © London Magazine Editions, 1970 / SBN 900626 19 4 / Printed in Great Britain by / Billing & Sons Limited, Guildford and London; 5–6 CONTENTS : 7 [7 lines of quotations]; [8] blank; [9] PART ONE; [10] blank; 11–18 text; [19] PART TWO / [2 line quote and source]; 20–58 text; [59] PART THREE; [60] blank, 61–77 text; [78] blank; [79] PART FOUR; / *for / Juanita de Mena*; [80] blank; 81–87 text, [88] blank; [89] PART FIVE; [90] blank; 91–96 text.

Contents: Part One — Thomas Campney and the Copernican System — Ginger's Friday — The Pocket Wars of Peanuts Joe — Allotments — A Proper Caution; Part Two — The White Queen: 1. Satyrae — 2. The Railroad Heroides — 3. Travesties — 4. Manica — 5. from the Zeg-Zeg Postcards — The Heart of Darkness — The Songs of the PWD Man — The Death of the PWD Man; Part Three — The Nuptial Torches — Schwiegermutterlieder — The Curtain Catullus — The Bedbug — The Chopin Express — The Excursion — Sentences; Part Four — Newcastle is Peru; Part Five — Ghosts; Some Words Before Breakfast.

Note: The following poems have divisions and subtitles: Travesties: I. Distant Ophir after Hieronymi Fracastorii Syphilis sive Morbus Gallicus (Veronae, MCXXX) — II. The Ancestor — III. Rumba Manica: 1. The Origin of the Beery Way — 2. The Elephant & the Kangaroo — 3. The Foreign Body; from the Zeg-Zeg Postcards: I–XI are without titles — XII. Water Babies — XIII–XXIV are without titles —

XXV. The Mining Journal — XXV1. is without a title —
XXVII. Black Power Sentences: I. Brazil — II. Isla de la Juventud.

Note: There were an unknown number of advanced proof copies
issued in stiff vivid yellow (82) wrappers and printed on the front of
the wrapper in vivid red (11): THE LOINERS / Tony Harrison /
Uncorrected Proof / LONDON MAGAZINE EDITIONS : LONDON
1970.

A5   VOORTREKKER   1972

a. *First edition*:

Voortrekker

Collation: Poster: single sheet; 60.1 × 42 cm.

Binding: White wove paper printed in strong red (12), black, and light
gray (264); all edges trimmed.

Publication date: 2 May 1972

Price: Data unavailable from publisher

Note: The publisher reports — 'no record extant — perhaps
£1.00 (sterling)'

Number of copies: 400

Pagination: Printed on one side only: [in black on a strong red stripe
across the top of the poster]: VOORTREKKER / [4 lines of text] /
[across the top and down the right-hand side of the sheet is a rough
design of the continent of Africa with a series of five sketches of natives
in black and light gray; the lower half of the continent is a sketch of
another face in black and strong red] [to the left of the lower half of the
continent printed in black] [8 lines of text] / TONY HARRISON /
Graphics by R. Harrison — MidNAG Poster No. 17.

Contents: Voortrekker. Collected in FTSOE and SP.

A6   THE MISANTHROPE   1973

a. *First edition*:

*MOLIERE / THE / MISANTHROPE / English version by / Tony
Harrison / LONDON / REX COLLINGS / 1973*

Collation: [A]⁸ — C⁸ + D¹² = 36 leaves; 19.8 × 12.7 cm.

Binding: Glued into stiff semi-shiny white wove wrappers; white wove paper; all edges trimmed; dust wrapper of semi-shiny white wove paper printed in vivid red (11), blackish red (21), deep reddish orange (38), and black.

Note: the dust wrapper: lettered down the spine on a red rectangle which forms part of the front wrapper, spine and rear wrapper: [down the spine in white] *MOLIERE THE MISANTHROPE* [in black] *Rex Collings*; on the front wrapper at the top in blackish red: *The Misanthrope* / [to the left on a vivid red rectangle in white]: *MOLIERE / English Version / by / Tony Harrison* [to the right on a dark reddish orange rectangle in various shades of blackish red: reproduction of a photograph of the actors, Alex McCowen and Diana Rigg in silhouette; on the rear wrapper in dark reddish orange: [reproduction of a photograph of Tony Harrison in various shades of black red by Michael Childers] / [12 lines of information on Tony Harrison] / *Front cover photography by Anthony Crickmay of Diana / Rigg and Alex McCowen in the National Theatre production*; on the inside flap of the front wrapper: [22 lines of information on the play] / £1.00 net; on the inside flap of the rear wrapper: TONY HARRISON — THE LOINERS / Awarded the Geoffrey Faber Memorial Prize / 1972 / [26 lines of critical quotoations on the Loiners] / S.B.N. 9017 2036 4.

Publication Date: February 1973

Price: £1.00

Number of copies: Data unavailable from publisher

Pagination: [i] half-title; [ii] blank; [iii] title page; [iv] First published by Rex Collings Ltd. / 6 Paddington Street, London W.1 / © Rex Collings Ltd. 1973 / S.B.N. 9017 2036 4 / This pay is fully covered by copyright and all / applications for the performing rights should be / made to the publishers Rex Collings Ltd. / Printed in Great Britain by Bristol Typesetting Co. Ltd., / Barton Manor, St Philips; v–vii 'Jane Eyre's Sister': viii This version of *The Misanthrope* was first produced by the / National Theatre Company of the Old Vic on 22 February 1973 / with the following cast: / [24 lines of the cast names, director, etc.]; 1–62 text; [63–64] blank.

Contents: The Misanthrope.

b. *First American edition, hardcover issue:*

MOLIERE / THE / MISANTHROPE / Modern English Adaption by / TONY HARRISON / [publisher's logo] / THE THIRD PRESS / Joseph Okpaku Publishing Company, Inc. / 444 Central Park West, New York, N.Y. 10025 / Including photographs from the National Theatre Company premiere / production at London's Old Vic, 22

February 1973, with Diana Rigg / as Celimene and Alex McCowen as
Alceste.

Collation: [A]⁸ + B – C⁸ + ([D] + D*¹⁶) = 40 leaves; 18.6 × 12.6 cm.

Binding: Bound in black cloth and lettered down the spine in gold:
Harrison THE MISANTHROPE THE THIRD PRESS / [across the
base of the spine: publisher's logo]; white wove paper; all edges trimmed;
white wove endpapers; dust wrapper of white wove paper; shiny on the
exterior and printed in deep blue (179), and strong reddish orange (35).

Publication date: Data unavailable from publisher

Price: $5.95

Number of copies: Data unavailable from publisher

Pagination: blank endpaper; [i] half-title; [ii] [black and white
reproduction of a photograph of Diana Rigg and Alec McCowen from
the play] / [3 lines of text]; [iii] title page; [iv] copyright © 1973 Rex
Collings Ltd. / All rights reserved. / [11 lines of rights information]
/ Library of Congress Catalog Card Number: / 73-83157 / SBN:
89388-112-0 clothbound / 89388-113-9 paperback / first printing /
Designed by Bennie Arrington / Cover photo: Diana Rigg as Celimene
and Alec McCowen as Alceste / in the National Theatre Company
production; v–vii JANE EYRE'S SISTER: viii This version of *Le
Misanthrope* was first produced by the / National Theatre Company at
the Old Vic on 22 February 1973 / with the following cast: [24 lines of
the cast and crew members]; 1–38 text; [38–42]: black anid white
reproductions of the photographs from the play; 43–54 text; [55–56]:
black and white reproductions of photographs from the play; 57–68 text;
[69–72]: black and white reproduction of photographs from the play;
blank endpaper.

Contents: The Misanthrope

c. *First American edition, paperbound issue*:

[The transcription of the title page is identical with that of the hard
cover issue]

Collation: [A]⁸ + B – C⁸ + ([D] + D*¹⁶) = 40 leaves; 18.6 × 12.2 cm.

Binding: Glued into white stiff card wrappers, of which the exterior is
shiny and printed in deep blue (179), strong reddish orange (35) and
lettered down the spine: [in white] Harrison [in strong reddish orange
(35)] THE MISANTHROPE [in white] THE THIRD PRESS /
[across the base of the spine in strong reddish orange: publisher's logo] /
[across the base of the spine in white] TP 9; on the front wrapper:

[in white] MOLIERE TP-9 / [in white $2.95 / [in strong reddish orange] THE MISANTHROPE / [within a strong reddish orange rectangle: a reproduction of a photograph from the production in various shades of blue of Diana Rigg and Alec McCowen] / [within the rectangle at the lower right-hand corner] [in white] *Modern English Adaptation* / [in white] By / [in white] Tony Harrison; on the rear wrapper: [in strong reddish orange] THE MISANTHROPE / [in white] Critics Applaud Modern Translation of / [in white] Moliere's Masterpiece / [15 lines of critical opinion in white] / [publisher's logo in strong reddish orange] / [in white] THE THIRD PRESS / [in white] Joseph Okpaku Publishing Company, Inc. / [in white] 444 Central Park West, New York, N.Y. 10025 / [in white at the left-hand corner] *Jacket design by Bennie Arrington* [in white at the right-hand corner] SBN 89388-113-9; white wove paper; all edges trimmed.

Publication date: Data unavailable from publisher

Price: $2.95

Number of copies: Data unavailable from publisher

Pagination: Same as A7b

Contents: Same as A7b

d. *Second English edition, hardcover issue*:

MOLIERE / *Tony Harrison* / THE MISANTHROPE / LONDON / REX COLLINGS

Collation: $[A]^8 + B - F^8 = 48$ leaves; 21.7×13.7 cm.

Binding: Bound in light grayish olive (109) cloth and lettered down the spine in gold: Moliere / Tony Harrison The Misanthrope [in two lines] Rex / Collings; white wove paper of which pages [iii] through [xiv] are printed on shiny white wove paper; all edges trimmed; off-white wove end-papers; dust wrapper of white wove paper, of which the exterior is shiny, printed in strong reddish orange (35), and black.

Publication date: Data unavailable from publisher

Price: £3.50

Number of copies: Data unavailable from publisher

Pagination: blank endpaper; [i] half-title; [ii] *Other works by Tony Harrison* / [list of six titles]; [iii] title page; [iv] First published by Rex Collings Ltd. / 69 Marylebone High Street, London W.1 / Second edition 1975 / © Tony Harrison 1973 / S.B.N. 901720 83 6 / All applications to perform this play should be made to / Fraser & Dunlop (Scripts) Ltd., / 91 Regent Street, / London W1R 8RU /

*Plates 1, 3, 4, 6, 7, 8, photographs by Zoe Dominic. / Plates 2, 5,
photographs by Carl Samrock. / Drawings by T. Moiseiwitsch. /*
Printed in Great Britain by Bristol Typesetting Co. Ltd. /
Barton Manor, St. Philips, Bristol; v–vii JANE EYRE'S SISTER;
[viii–xiv] Plates; xv MOLIERE NATIONALIZED; xvi–xvii Drawings;
xviii–xxx [MOLIERE NATIONALIZED continued]; xxxi *For /
John Dexter*; xxxii This version of *Le Misanthrope* was first produced by
the / National Theatre Company at Old Vic on 22 February 1973 / with
the following cast: / [24 lines of cast names, director, etc.]; 1–62 text;
[63–64] blank; blank endpaper.

Contents: The Misanthrope

e. *Second English edition, paperbound issue:*

[The transcription of the title page is identical of that of the hardcover
issue]

Collation: [A]^8 – C^8 + D^4 + E^8 = 136 leaves; 19.8 × 13 cm.

Binding: Glued into stiff semi-shiny plain white wove paper wrappers;
white wove paper; all edges trimmed; dust wrapper of semi-white wove
paper printed in vivid red (11), blackish red (21), deep reddish orange
(38), and black; lettered down the spine on a vivid red (11) rectangle
which forms part of the front wrapper, spine and back wrapper: [in
white] MOLIERE THE MISANTHROPE [in black] Rex Collings; on
the front wrapper at the top in blackish red: The Misanthrope / [to the
left on a vivid red rectangle in white] MOLIERE / English Version / by
/ Tony Harrison [to the right on a dark reddish orange rectangle in
various shades of blackish red: photograph of the actor Alec McCowen];
on the rear wrapper in dark reddish orange: [photograph of Tony
Harrison] / Michael Childers / [18 lines of information on Tony
Harrison]; on the inside flap of the front wrapper: [23 lines of
information on the play] / *Front cover photograph of Alec McCowen / in.
the National Theatre Production 1973. / Photograph by Zoe Dominic /*
£1.50 net; on the inside flap of the rear wrapper: REVIEWS / [30 lines] /
S.B.N. 9017 2039 9.

Note: The S.B.N. on the verso of the title page is 901720 83 6.

Publication date: Data unavailable from publisher

Price: £1.50

Number of copies: Data unavailable from publisher

Pagination: [1] half-title; [ii] *Other works by / Tony Harrison* / [list of six
titles]; [iii] title page; [iv] First published by Rex Collings Ltd. /
6 Paddington Street, London W.1 / Second edition 1975 / © Tony

Harrison 1973 / S.B.N. 901720 83 6 / All applications to perform this
play should be made to / Fraser & Dunlop (Scripts) Ltd., / 91 Regent
Street, London W1R 8RU / Printed in Great Britain by Bristol
Typesetting Co. Ltd., / Barton Manor, St. Philips, Bristol; v–vii JANE
EYRE'S SISTER; viii This version of *Le Misanthrope* was first
produced by the / National Theatre Company at the Old Vic on
22 February 1973 / with the following cast: / [24 lines of cast names,
director, etc.]; 1–62 text; [63–64] blank.

Contents: The Misanthrope

A7   PALLADAS: POEMS   1975

a. *First edition, hardcover edition*:

PALLADAS: POEMS / *a selection* / *translated and introduced by* / Tony
Harrison / Anvil Press Poetry / *in association with* / Rex Collings.

Collation: $[1-3]^8$ = 24 leaves; 21.7 × 13.7 cm.

Binding: Bound in textured white cloth and lettered down the spine in
black: Palladas/Harrison Anvil; white laid paper; all edges trimmed;
black wove endpapers; dust wrapper of white wove paper, of which the
exterior is shiny, printed in black.

Publication date: June 1975

Price: £1.95

Number of copies: 350

Note: The publisher reports that the 350 copies is an approximate
figure.

Pagination: [1–2] blank; [3] POETICA 5 / *Palladas: Poems* / [7 lines on
the series and editors]; [4] by *Tony Harrison* / Aikin Mata (with James
Simmons) 1966 / The Loiners 1970 / Molière: The Misanthrope 1973 /
Phaedra Britannica 1975; [5] title page; [6] Published in 1975 / by Anvil
Press Poetry / 69 King George Street London SE10 8PX / Distributed
by Rex Collings Ltd / Clothbound 85646 017 6 / Paperbound 85646
0206 / Copyright © Tony Harrison 1975 / Printed in England / by
Ithaca Press London SE1; [7] [4 lines of text];
[8] ACKNOWLEDGEMENTS / [4 lines]; [9–12] Preface [Preface
signed: T.H. / *Gregynog,* / *March 1974]*; [13–43] text; [44–46] NOTES;
[47] REFERENCES; [48] blank.

Note: The text is made up of 70 individual poems. The following
numbers have titles: 41: On Gessius; 42: Maurus; 63: On a Temple of

Fortune turned into a tavern; 66: Marina's House; 67: Hypatia; 68: On Monks; 69: The Spartan Mother; 70: The Murderer & Sarapis.

Contents: Palladas: Poems

b. *First edition, paperbound issue:*

[The transcription of the title page is identical with that of the hardcover issue]

Collation: $[1-3]^8$ = 24 leaves; 21.7 × 13.7 cm.

Binding: Glued into stiff white wove paper wrappers, the exterior of which is shiny and lettered down the spine in black: PALLADAS / HARRISON ANVIL; on the front wrapper in white on a black rectangle: Palladas: Poems / a selection in versions by / Tony Harrison; on the rear wrapper printed in black: [16 lines on the text] / Cover design: Philip Bryden / Other titles in the POETICA series include; / [6 lines of titles]; white laid paper; all edges trimmed.

Note: Printed on the inside of the back wrapper are 34 lines of information on Harrison with lines of quotations from critics, and the price, 80p.

Publication date: June 1975

Price: 80p

Number of copies: 700

Note: The publisher reports that the 700 copies is an approximate figure.

Pagination: Same as A7a

Contents: Same as A7a

c. *Second edition*

Tony Harrison / *Palladas: Poems* / Anvil Press Poetry

Collation: $[1-3]^8$ = 24 leaves; 21.5 × 13.7 cm.

Binding: Glued into stiff card wrappers, shiny on the exterior and printed down the spine in black: TONY HARRISON PALLADAS: POEMS Anvil; on the front wrapper is a photograph of a Necropolis at Pompeii printed in light grey (264); on the front wrapper in black: TONY HARRISON / [single rule] / ● PALLADAS POEMS / Born naked. Buried Naked. So why fuss? / All life leads to that first nakedness; the rear wrapper is light grey; printed in black: [33 lines on Tony Harrison and his work] / *Cover: a Necropolis at Pompeii / from*

a photograph by Edwin Smith / [to the left] £2.95 [to the right]
ISBN 0 85646 127 X; white laid paper; all edges trimmed.

Publication date: 4 October 1984

Price: £2.95

Number of copies: 900

Pagination: [1] POETICA 5 / *Palladas: Poems* / [5 lines on the series and
editors]; [2] *by Tony Harrison* / POETRY / Earthworks, 1964 /
Newcastle is Peru, 1969 / The Loiners, 1970 / Palladas: Poems, 1975 /
from The School of Eloquence / *and other poems, 1978* / A Kumquat for
John Keats, 1981 / U.S. Martial, 1981 / Continuous, 1981 / Selected
Poems, 1984 / THEATRE / Aikin Mata (with James Simmons), 1966 /
The Misanthrope, 1973 / Phaedra Britannica, 1975 / Bow Down, 1977 /
The Passion, 1977 / The Bartered Bride, 1978 / The Oresteia, 1981;
[3] title page; [4] First published in 1975 / Second edition published in
1984 / by Anvil Press Poetry Ltd / 69 King George Street London
SE10 8PX / ISBN 0 85646 127 X / Copyright © Tony Harrison 1975 /
This book is published / with financial assistance from / The Arts
Council of Great Britain / Photoset in Baskerville / by Katerprint Co
Ltd, Oxford / and printed in England / at the Arc & Throstle Press /
Todmorden Lancs; [5] [4 lines of text]; [6] ACKNOWLEDGEMENTS /
[5 lines]; 7–[10] Preface [Preface signed: T.H. / *Gregynog, / March 1974*];
[11] *Palladas: Poems*; [12] blank; 13–43 text; 44–46 NOTES; 47
REFERENCES; [48] POETICA / [list of 17 authors and titles].

Contents: Palladas: Poems

A8   PHAEDRA BRITANNICA   1975

a. *First edition*

PHAEDRA / BRITANNICA / *by Tony Harrison after* / *Jean Racine* /
LONDON / REX COLLINGS / 1975

Collation: [1–4]⁸ = 32 leaves; 19.5 × 12.5 cm.

Binding: Glued in stiff, semi-shiny, white card wrappers; on the front
wrapper: [a stylized picture of the sun in strong red (12)] / PHAEDRA
/ BRITANNICA / Tony Harrison / *after Jean Racine*; on the rear
wrapper: [15 lines of information on Harrison and his work] / [at the
left-hand lower corner in strong red] £1; white wove paper; all edges
trimmed.

Publication date: September 1975

Price: £1.00

13

Number of copies: Data unavailable from publisher

Pagination: [i] half-title; [ii] *Other works by / Tony Harrison* / [6 titles];
[iii] title page; [iv] First published by Rex Collings Ltd / 69 Marylebone
High Street, London W1 / © Tony Harrison 1975 / SBN 901720 75 5
All applications to perform this play / should be made to Fraser &
Dunlop (Scripts) Ltd / 91 Regent Street, / London W1 / Printed in
Great Britain; [v] *Phaedra Britannica* was first performed by the
National Theatre Company at the Old Vic on / 9 September 1975 with
the following cast: / [29 lines giving cast and crew members] / Note: this
text does not include those / revisions made during final rehearsals. /
T.H. / In the text / means *inhale* and / X *exhale*; [vi] blank; [vii] for /
John Dexter / again; [viii] blank; 1–54 text; [55–56] blank.

Contents: Phaedra Britannica

Note: copies of the second edition could not be located

b. *Third edition, hardcover issue*:

PHAEDRA / BRITANNICA / *by Tony Harrison / after Jean Racine* /
LONDON / REX COLLINGS.

Collation: [1]⁸ + [2–3]¹⁶ + [4]⁸ = 48 leaves; 21.5 × 13.5 cm.

Binding: Glued into a yellowish grey (93) cloth wrapper and lettered
down the spine in gold: HARRISON PHAEDRA BRITANNICA Rex
Collings; white wove paper; all edges trimmed; very light yellowish grey
wove endpapers; dust wrapper of white wove paper of which the exterior
is shiny, printed in dark grayish yellow (91), vivid reddish orange (34),
and black.

Publication date: December 1976.

Price: £3.95

Number of copies: Data unavailable from publisher

Pagination: [i] half-title; [ii] *Other works by / Tony Harrison* / [6 titles];
[iii] title page; [iv] First published by Rex Collings Ltd / 69 Marylebone
High Street, London W1 / Reprinted 1975 / Second edition 1975 /
Third edition (with introductory essay / & illustrations) 1976 / © Tony
Harrison 1976 / Paper SBN 901720 75 5 / Cloth ISBN 086 036019 9 /
All Applications to perform this play / should be made to Fraser &
Dunlop (Scripts) Ltd / 91 Regent Street, London W1 / Typesetting by
Malvern Typesetting Services Ltd, / Printed in Great Britain at the /
University Printing House, Cambridge / (Euan Phillips, University
Printer); v–xxv Preface; [xxvi] *All photographs by Anthony Crickmay*;
[xxvii–xxxiv — four leaves of black and white photographs of the
production with captions]; [xxxv] [35 lines on first production, cast and

crew members and a note — (Same as A8a)]; [xxxvi] blank; [xxxvii] for / John Dexter / again; [xxxviii] blank; 1–54 text; [55–58] blank.

Contents: Phaedra Britannica.

c. *Third edition, papercover issue*:

[The transcription of the title page is identical to A8b]

Collation: Identical to A8b

Binding: Glued into plain stiff white wove paper wrappers; there are no endpapers.

Note: The dust wrapper for both the hardcover and papercover issues are identical; dust wrapper of white wove paper of which the exterior is shiny, printed in dark grayish yellow (91), vivid reddish orange (34) and black; lettered down the spine in black: Harrison/Racine Phaedra Britannica [in dark grayish yellow] Rex Collings; on the cover is an album miniature (detail); Bundi, Rajasthan: the late 18th century; at the top right-hand corner of the front wrapper printed in white: Phaedra / Britannica / by Tony Harrison / after Jean Racine; on the rear wrapper is a black and white photograph of Tony Harrison by Michael Childers and below it, a 4-line quote from *The Observer*; on the inside flap of the front wrapper: [20 lines of critical quotes] / Cover: Album miniature (detail); Bundi, Rajasthan: / late 18th century / [to the right] Hardback £3.95 / Paperback £2.25; on the inside flap of the rear wrapper: / [24 lines on Harrison and a critical quote] / Jacket designed by Richard Bird.

Publication date: December 1976

Price: £2.25

Pagination: Same as A8b

Contents: Same as A8b

A9   BOW DOWN   1977

a. *First edition*:

[To the left] BOW DOWN was devised and first / performed in the Cottesloe ·Theatre, by / members of the National Theatre / Company, 5 July 1977, as part of the / John Player Centenary Festival / © Tony Harrison 1977 / ISBN 0860 360679 / All applications to perform this piece / should be made both to / Fraser & Dunlop (Scripts) Ltd / 91 Regent Street / London W1 / and / Universal Editions (London) Ltd / 2–3 Fareham Street / London W1 / Typeset by Malvern

Typesetting / Services / Printed in Great Britain by / Sansome Printing Co, Worcester / [to the right: a long vertical rule] / [to the right] BOW DOWN / TONY HARRISON / 1977 / REX COLLINGS / LONDON

Collation: [1]¹² = 12 leaves; 25.7 × 15.2 cm.

Binding: Stapled twice into heavy white card wrappers of which the exterior is shiny and printed in black and white; on the front wrapper: *BOW DOWN* / [abstract drawing of a woman in a landscape in black and white]; on the rear wrapper: [11 lines of text on the play] / £1.95 / REX COLLINGS LTD; white wove paper; all edges trimmed.

Publication date: July 1977

Price: £1.95

Number of copies: Data unavailable from publisher

Pagination: [1] title page; [2] [25 lines on cast, director, etc.]; 3–24 text; [[xxv] text completed on the inside of rear wrapper].

Contents: Bow Down

b. *First libretto edition*:

[fancy letters] BOW DOWN / [fancy letters] Music by / [fancy letters] Harrison Birtwistle / [fancy letters] Text by / [fancy letters] Tony Harrison / [fancy letters] Playing Score / [fancy letters] UNIVERSAL EDITION

Collation [1]¹² = 24 pages; 23 × 30.5 cm.

Binding: Stapled twice into white card wrapper, semi-shiny on the exterior; on the front wrapper to the left: [fancy letters] BOW DOWN / [fancy letters] Music by / [fancy letters] Harrison Birtwistle / [fancy letters] Text by / [fancy letters] Tony Harrison / [fancy letters] Playing score / [fancy letters] UE 16180 / [fancy letters] UNIVERSAL EDITION; to the right [black and white reproduction of a photograph identical to that used on the 1977 Rex Collings edition]; on the rear wrapper in the center: UE [surrounded by a rectangle with thin lines on the inside and a rectangle with thick lines on the outside]; white wove paper; all edges trimmed.

Publication date: 12 November 1983

Price: £3.70

Number of copies: 500

Pagination: [i] title page; [ii] [within rectangle] PHOTOCOPYING PROHIBITED / [4 lines] / [within a paste-down made up of a rectangle] [2 lines of copyright information] / UNIVERSAL EDITION

/ 2/3 Fareham Street (Dean Street) / London WIV 4DU; [iii]
[information on *Bow Down*: 23 lines] / H.B./T.H. / Toronto /
21 February 1980; [iv–v] Notation / [32 lines] / Score reconstructed and
copied by Jonty Harrison; [vi] DIRECTIONS FOR PERFORMANCE;
1–17 Score; [18] blank.

Contents: Bow Down

A10   THE PASSION   1977

a. *First edition*

[To the left] First published in the United Kingdom / by Rex Collings
Ltd, 69 Marylebone / High Street, London W1M 3AQ / © Tony
Harrison 1977 / ISBN 0860 36 0717 / All applications to perform this
piece / should be made to / Fraser & Dunlop (Scripts) Ltd, / 91 Regent
Street / London W1 / Cover: / The Road to Calvary, / NT riverside
terraces / Easter Saturday, 9 April 1977 / (photo: Nobby Clark) /
Typeset by Malvern Typesetting / Services / Printed in Great Britain
by / Sansome Printing Co, Worcester / [to the right] THE PASSION /
*Selected from / the 15th century cycle of / YORK mystery plays / in a
version / by the Company with* / TONY HARRISON / 1977 / REX
COLLINGS / LONDON.

Collation: [1]^{32} = 32 leaves; 25.7 × 15.3 cm.

Binding: Stapled twice into thick white wove card wrappers, of which
the exterior is shiny; the front wrapper is a black and white reproduction
of a photograph of two figures on either side of a central figure carrying
a cross; at the upper left-hand corner of the front wrapper in black: The /
Passion; on the white rear wrapper printed in black: [22 lines of quotes
and information on the text and Tony Harrison] / £1.95 / *Cover
photography by Nobby Clark* / REX COLLINGS LTD; the inside of the
front wrapper is blank; the inside of the rear wrapper: *Work by Tony
Harrison published by Rex / Collings* / [32 lines of titles, critical quotes
and price information on the publications]; white wove paper; all edges
trimmed.

Publication date: December 1977

Price: £1.95

Number of copies: Data unavailable from publisher

Pagination: [1] title page; [2] Works by TONY HARRISON / POETRY
/ [5 titles] / THEATRE; [3] The Passion / a selection from the York
Mystery Plays / *was first performed by the National Theatre Company /
at the Cottesloe Theatre, 21 April 1977 with the / following cast*: / [40 lines

of cast, director, crew members, etc.]; [4] [Stage lay-out with notes]; [5] SCENES / [14 lines]; [6] blank; 7–64 text.

Contents: The Passion

A11   FROM THE SCHOOL OF ELOQUENCE   1978

a. *First edition*

from / THE SCHOOL OF / ELOQUENCE / and / other poems / Tony Harrison / REX COLLINGS LONDON 1978

Collation: [A]^{16} + B^{12} = 28 leaves; 21.8 × 15.8 cm.

Binding: Bound in black cloth and lettered down the spine in gold: HARRISON The School of Eloquence Rex Collings; yellow white (92) laid paper, watermarked with a crown above Old-English lettering: Abbey Mills / Greenfield; all edges trimmed; top edges stained in strong red (12); strong red endpapers; dust wrapper of white wove paper, shiny on the exterior and printed in black.

Publication date: November 1978

Price: £5.00

Number of copies: Data unavailable from publisher

Pagination: [1] half-title; [2] blank; [3] title page; [4] Acknowledgements / [15 lines] / First published by Rex Collings Ltd / 69 Marylebone High Street / London W1 / © Tony Harrison 1978 / ISBN 0 86036 0881 / Typeset and printed in Great Britain / by Ebenezer Baylis and Son Ltd / The Trinity Press, Worcester, and London; 5–6 Contents; 7–29 text; [30] blank; [31] OTHER POEMS; 32–52 text; [53] *afters*; 54–55 text; [56] blank.

Contents: Heredity — On Not Being Milton — The Rhubarbarians — Study — Me Tarzan — Wordlists — Classics Society — National Trust — Them & [uz] — Working — Cremation — Book Ends — A Close One — The Earthen Lot — History Classes — t'Ark — Social Mobility — Durham — Voortrekker — Sentences: 1. Brazil, 2. Fonte Luminosa, 3. Isla de la Juventud, 4. On The Spot — Curtain Sonnets: 1. Guava Libre, 2. The Viewless Wings, 3. Summer Garden, 4. The People's Palace, 5. Prague Spring — Doodlebugs — The Bonebard Ballads: 1. The Ballad of Babelabour, 2. The Ballad of the Geldshark, 3. 'Flying Down to Rio': A Ballad of Beverly Hills — after Rufinus — after Myrinos

A12   THE BARTERED BRIDE   1978

a. *First edition*

THE / BARTERED BRIDE / A Comic Opera in Three
Acts / Music by / BEDRICH SMETANA / Original Czech Libretto by
/ KAREL SABINA / English Libretto by / TONY HARRISON / Ed.
3170 / G SCHIRMER / New York/London.

Collation: [1]^{20} = 20 leaves; 26.3 × 17.3 cm.

Binding: Stapled three times into white card wrappers printed in vivid
red (11); on the front wrapper in white letters on a vivid red background:
Bedrich Smetana / THE BARTERED BRIDE / [fancy] *G. Schirmer's* /
[fancy] *Collection of* / [fancy] *Opera Librettos*; on the rear wrapper in
vivid red letters on a rectangular white panel: [fancy] *G. Schirmer's* /
[fancy] *Collection of* / [fancy] *Opera Librettos* / [4 lines on the librettos] /
[list of 59 librettos in two columns] / G. SCHIRMER/New York •
London / [to the left] A-1259; white wove paper; all edges trimmed.

Publication date: 1978

Price: Data unavailable from publisher

Number of copies: Data unavailable from publisher

Pagination: [i] title page; ii. for / Herbert / Dietzsch / and / his / daughter
/ Copyright © 1978 G. Schirmer, Inc. / All Rights Reserved /
International Copyright Secured / Printed in U.S.A. / 48005c / [7 lines
of information on rights]; iii ACKNOWLEDGEMENTS [Signed
TONY HARRISON / Newcastle-upon-Tyne/New York / March 1978;
iv THE BARTERED BRIDE; v–vi THE STORY; vii CAST OF
CHARACTERS; [viii] blank; 1–30, Text; [31–32] blank.

Contents: The Bartered Bride

A13   LOOKING UP   1979

a. *First edition*

[Cover title: within a thick black rectangle broken at the bottom of the
page: photograph of Tony Harrison and Philip Sharpe seated on the
tomb of Peter Mark Roget] / TONY HARRISON PHILIP SHARPE /
LOOKING UP / West Malvern 1979.

Collation: [1]^2 = 2 leaves; 20.2 × 14.4 cm.

Binding: Leaflet; heavy wove light gray (264) paper; all edges trimmed.

Publication date: 1979

Price: Data unavailable from publisher

Number of copies: Data unavailable from publisher

Note: Two copies examined were unsigned and unnumbered. Two other copies were signed by both Harrison and Sharpe and contained holograph numbers — 'B/26' and 'Q26'

Pagination: [1] title page; [2–3] text; [4] [within a black border broken at the bottom of the page: a facsimile of a manuscript] / Facsimile of the first page of the MS. classified catalogue of words completed / by Dr. P.M. Roget in 1805, which was the germ of the Thesaurus. / Migrant Press 1979.

Contents: 'Looking Up,' p. [2].

Note: The complete title and dedication reads: 'LOOKING UP / for Philip, Terry & Will Sharpe / & / the bi-centenary of the birth of / Peter Mark Roget (1779–1869) / West Malvern: May 1979.

A14   THE PASSION   1980

a. *First edition*

[fancy black letters] the / [fancy black letters] passion / [fancy black letters] part one / [fancy black letters] creation to / [fancy black letters] nativity / *Selected from the* / *YORK and WAKEFIELD mystery plays* / *in a version* / *by the Company* / REX COLLINGS LONDON 1980

Collation: [1]^{32} = 32 leaves; 21.2 × 13.6 cm.

Binding: Stapled twice into heavy white wove linen-textured wrappers, the exterior of which is printed in light gray (18); printed in fancy deep gray red (20) letters on a white rectangle on the upper portion of the front wrapper: the / passion / part one / [below the rectangle are three thick rules printed in deep gray red letters] / [across the base of the wrapper printed in deep gray red letters] creation to / nativity; on the rear wrapper at the base within a white rectangle printed in deep gray red letters: This text continues the work of the Cottesloe Company at the / National Theatre on the great medieval mystery plays, which began / in 1977 when the Company collaborated with Tony Harrison on the / Creation to the Nativity and is based on the texts of the York and / Wakefield medieval mystery plays. / [to the right] £2.50 / [in the center] REX COLLINGS LTD; white wove paper; all edges trimmed.

Publication date: Data unavailable from publisher

Price: £2.50

Number of copies: Data unavailable from publisher

Pagination: [i] half-title; [ii] blank; [1] title page; [2] First published in the United Kingdom by Rex Collings Ltd, / 6 Paddington Street, London W1 / ISBN 086036 153 5 / All applications to perform this piece should be made to / Fraser & Dunlop (Scripts) Ltd, / 91 Regent Street London W1 / Printed in Great Britain by Malvern Printers Ltd, Malvern; [3] The Passion / A selection from the York and Wakefield Mystery / Plays / *Part One: Creation to Nativity / was first performed by the National Theatre Company at the / Assembly Hall at the Edinburgh Festival, 18 August 1980 / with the following cast*: / [list of cast and production members in 31 lines]; [4] [continuation of production members in 16 lines] / [12 lines of information on the text and production] / *Bill Bryden, Director.*; 5–60 text; [61–62] blank.

Contents: The Passion. Part One. Creation to Nativity.

A15   A KUMQUAT FOR JOHN KEATS   1981

a. *First edition*

A Kumquat / for John Keats / Tony Harrison / [stylized hand-printed letters in which the two 'o's' in the two words are intertwined] BLOODAXE BOOKS

Collation: [1]^6 = 6 leaves; 21.7 × 13.7 cm.

Binding: Stapled twice into stiff strong yellowish pink (26) card wrappers of which the exterior is shiny; on the front wrapper in black is a reproduction of a painting of a kumquat extending from the lower right-hand side of the wrapper to the upper left-hand corner of the wrapper; on the lower quarter of the front wrapper in black: Tony Harrison / [a drawing of a cut kumquat] / *A Kumquat for John Keats*; on the rear wrapper in black on the lower third of the wrapper: [drawing of a cut kumquat] / [lettered as on the title page] BLOODAXE BOOKS / 0 906427 31 2 / £0.75 net in U.K.; white wove paper; all edges trimmed.

Publication date: October 1981

Price: £3.50 for the signed and numbered copies; 75p for the ordinary edition.

Number of copies: 25 signed and numbered copies; 1st printing of the ordinary edition, 725; 2nd printing, 1982 (month and day unknown), 600 copies; 3rd printing, 1984 (month and day unknown), 600 copies.

Pagination: [1] title page; [2] Copyright © Tony Harrison 1981 / All rights reserved / ISBN 0 906427 31 2 (ordinary edition) / 0 906427 32 0 (signed edition of 25 numbered copies) / First published 1981 by / Bloodaxe Books / P.O. Box 1SN / Newcastle upon Tyne NE99 1SN /

The publisher acknowledges the financial assistance / of Northern Arts. / This poem first appeared in *PN Review*, and has since been slightly revised. / Printed in Great Britain by / Tyneside Free Press Workshop Ltd, Newcastle upon Tyne. [3] A KUMQUAT FOR JOHN KEATS / [drawing in strong orange (50) of a cut kumquat]; [4] [a kumquat drawing in strong orange]; [5] text; [6] [a kumquat drawing in strong orange]; [7] text; [8] [a kumquat drawing in strong orange]; [9] text; [10] [a kumquat drawing in strong orange]; [11] text; [12] [25 lines on Harrison and a list of his works and 5 lines of information on the front cover painting].

Note: Each of the kumquat drawings within the text is different.

Contents: A Kumquat for John Keats.

Note: The signed and numbered copies have the signature in black below the author's name on the title page and a number stamped in black directly below the letters 'ISBN' on the verso of the title page.

A16   U.S. MARTIAL   1981

a. *First edition*

U.S. MARTIAL / Tony Harrison / [stylized hand-printed letters in which the two 'o's' in the two words are intertwined] BLOODAXE BOOKS.

Collation: [1]^{12} = 12 leaves; 21.7 × 13.7 cm.

Binding: Stapled twice into stiff white card wrappers, of which the exterior is shiny and printed in black; on the front wrapper is a reproduction in black and white of a photograph of a satyr's head (17.7 × 12.8 cm.); printed in white and running from top to bottom outside the lower right side of the photograph: COPYRIGHT © BETH BERGMAN 1981; below the photograph: [in white] Tony Harrison / [in vivid reddish orange (34)] U.S. MARTIAL; on the rear wrapper at the top right-hand corner printed in white: £1.00 net in U.K. / 0 906427 29 0 / [at the base of the wrapper, printed in vivid reddish orange and lettered as on the title page] BLOODAXE BOOKS] / [in white] COVER PHOTOGRAPH BY BETH BERGMAN / [in white] *Detail of the Hotel Ansonia 73rd & Broadway, New York*; white wove paper; all edges trimmed.

Publication date: October 1981

Price: £3.50 for the signed and numbered copies; £1.00 for the ordinary edition.

Number of copies: 25 signed and numbered copies; 1st printing of the ordinary edition, 975.

Pagination: [1] title page; [2] Copyright © Tony Harrison 1981 / All rights reserved / ISBN: 0 906427 29 0 (ordinary edition) / 0 906427 30 4 (signed edition of 25 numbered copies) / First published 1981 by / Bloodaxe Books / P.O. Box 1SN / Newcastle upon Tyne NE99 1SN / The publisher acknowledges the financial assistance / of Northern Arts. / Printed in Great Britain by / Tyneside Free Press Workshop Ltd, Newcastle upon Tyne; [3] [7 lines of remarks] / T.H. / [to the left] HOTEL ANSONIA, / *New York, March 1981*; [4] References; [5]–[23] text; [24] [25 lines on Harrison and a list of his works].

Contents: U.S. Martial

Note: The text is made up of 18 individual poems. The following numbers have titles: VII: Scentsong; IX: Twosum; XII: Paula; XV: To Bassara; XVI: The Joys of Separation; XVII: Sandwich Bawd Swing Song; XVIII Oh, Moon of Mahagonny!

Note: The signed and numbered copies have the signature below the author's name on the title page and a number stamped in black directly below the letters 'ISBN' on the verso of the title page.

A17   CONTINUOUS   1981

a. *First edition, limited issue*:

[strong reddish orange (35)] *CONTINUOUS* / [black] *50 Sonnets from* / The School of / Eloquence / [strong reddish orange] *TONY HARRISON* / [in black] REX COLLINGS LONDON 1981.

Collation: [1–8]⁴ = 32 leaves; 23.5 × 15.7 cm.

Binding: Bound in black cloth and lettered down the spine: [in gold] TONY HARRISON [in silver] CONTINUOUS [in gold] REX COLLINGS; on the front cover on the lower half of the cover: [in gold] C [in silver] O [in gold] N / [in gold] TINU / [in silver] O [in gold] US; the rear cover is blank; yellow white (92) laid paper, watermarked with a crown above old-English lettering: Abbey Mills / Greenfield; all edges trimmed; top edges stained in strong red (12); strong red endpapers.

Note: Issued without a dust wrapper in a plain black cloth box.

Publication date: November 1981

Price: £35

Number of copies: 100 numbered copies.

Pagination: [1] CONTINUOUS / 50 Sonnets from / *The School of Eloquence* / [10 line quote and source]; [2] *Works by Tony Harrison* / POETRY [5 titles] / THEATRE [7 titles]; [3] title page; [4] Heredity / [4 line poem by T.H.] / [single horizontal rule] / [16 line quote in italics] / John Milton (1637); [5] Contents; [6] for / mam / & / dad / *in memoriam* / F.H. 1906–1976 / H.A.H. 1903–1980; [7] ONE; [8] blank; [9–22] text; [23] TWO; [24] blank; [25–47] text; [48] blank; [49] THREE; [50] blank; [51–63] text; [64] *ACKNOWLEDGEMENTS* / [2 lines] / This edition is limited to / 100 numbered copies / and was published by Rex Collings Ltd / 6 Paddington Street, London W1 / Book design by Andrew Lamb / Text set in 11 pt Garamond / and printed by Malvern Printers, Malvern / This is copy No. [holograph number in black ink] / [holograph signature of Tony Harrison in black ink] / © Tony Harrison 1981 / ISBN 086 036 187X.

Contents: On Not Being Milton — The Rhubarbarians I, II — Study — Me Tarzan — Wordlist I, II, III — Classics Society — National Trust — Them & [uz] I, II — Working — Cremation — Book Ends I, II — Next Door I, II, III, IV — Long Distance I, II — Continuous — Clearing I, II – Illuminations I, II, III — Turns — Punchline — Marked with D — A Close One — Blocks — Bringing Up — Timer — Fire-eater — Background Material — Self Justification — Divisions I, II — Lines to my Grandfathers I, II — The Earthen Lot — Dichtung und Wahrheit — Art & Extinction — I. The Birds of America: John James Audubon (1785–1851) — II. Standards — III. Loving Memory — IV. Looking Up — V. Killing Time — VI. t'Ark.

b. *First edition, ordinary issue*:

[The transcription of the title page is identical with that of the limited issue]

Collation: 32 leaves; 23.5 × 15.5 cm.

Binding: A perfect binding glued into stiff white card wrappers of which the exterior is shiny and printed in black; lettered down the spine: [in strong reddish orange (35)] TONY HARRISON [in white] CONTINUOUS [in strong reddish orange] REX COLLINGS; on the front wrapper is a reproduction of a black and white photograph of a pillar made of cement and brick; at the top of the wrapper in crude black letters: tony / HARRISON / [on the lower half of the front wrapper: [in strong reddish orange] C [in white] O [in strong reddish orange] N / [in strong reddish orange] TINU/ [in white] O [in strong reddish orange] US; the rear wrapper is black and on the lower half the title is printed as on the front wrapper; in white at the lower left-hand side of the wrapper: £3.95; yellow white (92) laid paper, watermarked with a crown above old-English lettering: Abbey Mills / Greenfield; all edges trimmed.

Publication date: November 1981

Price: £3.95

Number of copies: Data unavailable from publisher

Pagination: Same as A17a except for a page [64]: *Acknowledgements* /
[2 lines] First published in the United Kingdom by / Rex Collings
Ltd / 6 Paddington Street, London W1 / © Tony Harrison 1981 /
ISBN 086036 159 4 / Typeset and printed in Great Britain by /
Malvern Printers Ltd, Malvern.

Contents: Same as A17a.

A18   THE ORESTEIA   1981

a. *First edition*

Aeschylus: / THE ORESTEIA / *translated by* TONY HARRISON /
REX COLLINGS LONDON 1981.

Collation: $[1-8]^8 = 64$ leaves; 21.4 × 13.7 cm.

Binding: Glued into shiny card wrappers in strong red (12), and black
and lettered down the spine in white: Harrison [The: inside the O of
Oresteia] ORESTEIA REX COLLINGS; on the front wrapper: [on the
upper half, a black and white photograph of a stylized picture of the
head of a Greek warrior in semi-profile] / [in white on a black band: The:
inside of the O of Oresteia] [fancy white letters] ORESTEIA / [a single
white rule] / [fancy white letters] The trilogy by Aeschylus in a / [fancy
white letters] version by Tony Harrison; on the rear wrapper in white
letters on a black background: TONY HARRISON's *texts for the
National Theatre* / [white] *published by Rex Collings* / [29 lines of critical
opinion] / [single rule in strong red] / [3 lines of critical opinion in
white] / [single rule in strong red] / £3.50; white wove paper; all edges
trimmed.

Publication date: December 1981

Price: £3.50

Number of copies: Data unavailable from publisher

Pagination: [i] half-title; [ii] *Other works by Tony Harrison* / POETRY /
[4 titles] / PLAYS / [6 titles]; [iii] title page; [iv] First published in Great
Britain by / Rex Collings Ltd 6 Paddington Street, London W1 / ©
Tony Harrison 1981 / ISBN 086036 178 0 / This play is fully covered
by copyright and all applications for / performing rights should be
made to Fraser & Dunlop (Scripts). Ltd, / 91 Regent Street, London

W1 / Typeset by Malvern Printers Ltd / and printed in Great Britain by / Billing & Sons Ltd, Worcester; [v] This version of *The Oresteia* was first produced by the National / Theatre of Great Britain in the Olivier Theatre on 28 November / 1981 with the following company: / [28 lines on cast, director, etc.]; [vi] [single rule] / note: / This text is written to be performed, a rhythmic libretto for masks, / music, and an all male company. / TH *October 1981* / [single rule]; [1] ONE / AGAMEMNON; [2] blank; 3–48 text; [49] TWO / CHOEPHORI; [50] blank; 51–85 text; [86] blank; [87] THREE / EUMENIDES; [88] blank; 89–120 text; [121–122] blank.

Contents: The Oresteia

A19   SELECTED POEMS   1984

a. *First edition, hardcover issue*:

Tony Harrison / [fancy] *Selected Poems* / Viking

Collation: $[1–13]^8 = 104$ leaves; 21.6×13.6 cm.

Binding: Bound in deep purple (219) cloth and lettered down the spine in silver: Tony Harrison Selected Poems [across the base of the spine] VIKING; white wove paper; all edges trimmed; white wove endpapers; pictorial dust wrapper of white wove paper, shiny on the exterior and printed in light purple (222), medium purple (223), strong yellow green (131), medium gray (265), black and white.

Publication date: 27 September 1984

Price: £9.95

Number of copies: 1,000

Pagination: [1] [Viking logo]; [2] blank; [3] title page; [4] [6 lines of Viking and Penguin addresses] / This selection first published 1984 / Published simultaneously by Penguin Books / Copyright © Tony Harrison, 1984 / The acknowledgements on pp. 11–12 constitute / an extension of this copyright page / [5 lines of rights information] / British Library Cataloguing in Publication Data / [5 lines] / Set in Monophoto Ehrhardt / Printed in Great Britain by / Richard Clay (The Chaucer Press) Ltd / Bungay, Suffolk; [5] for Teresa / '. . . son io il poeta, / essa la poesia.'; [6] blank; 7, 8, [9] Contents; [10] blank; 11–[12] Acknowledgements; 13–107 text; [108] blank; [109]–[204] text; [205–208] blank.

Contents: Thomas Campey and the Copernican System — Ginger's Friday — The Pocket Wars of Peanuts Joe — Allotments —

Doodlebugs — The White Queen: 1. Satyrae; 2. The Railroad Heroides;
3. Travesties; 4. Manica; 5. from The Zeg-Zeg Postcards — The Heart
of Darkness — The Songs of the PWD Man I, II — The Death of the
PWD Man - Schwiegermutterlieder — The Curtain Catullus — The
Bedbug — Curtain Sonnets: 1. Guava Libre; 2. The Viewless Wings;
3. Summer Garden; 4. The People's Palace; 5. Prague Spring — The
Nuptial Torches — Newcastle is Peru — Durham — Ghosts: Some
Words Before Breakfast — Palladas: Poems — Sentences: 1. Brazil;
2. Fonte Luminosa; 3. Isla de la Juventud; 4. On the Spot — Voortrekker
— The Bonebard Ballads: 1. The Ballad of Babelabour; 2. The Ballad of
the Geldshark; 3. 'Flying Down to Rio': A Ballad of Beverly Hills -
Social Mobility — On Not Being Milton — The Rhubarbarians I, II —
Study — Me Tarzan — Wordlists I, II, III — Classics Society
— National Trust — Them & [uz] I, II — Working — Cremation —
Book Ends I, II, — Confessional Poetry — Next Door I, II, III, IV —
Long Distance I, II — Flood — The Queen's English — Aqua Mortis
— Grey Matter — An Old Score — Still — A Good Read — Isolation
— Continuous — Clearing I, II, — Illuminations I, II, III — Turns
— Punchline — Currants I, II, — Marked with D. — A Piece of Cake
— A Close One — Blocks — Bringing Up — Timer — Fire-eater —
Background Material — Self Justification — Divisions I, II — History
Classes — Stately Home — Lines to my Grandfathers I, II —
The Earthen Lot — Remains — Dichtung und Wahrheit — Art &
Extinction: 1. The Birds of America: i. John James Audubon
(1785-1851); ii. Weeki Wachi; iii. Standards; 2. Loving Memory;
3. Looking Up; 4. Killing Time; 5. Dark Times; 6. t'Ark — Facing
North — A Kumquat for John Keats — Skywriting — The Call of
Nature — Giving Thanks — Oh, Moon of Mahagonny! — The Red
Lights of Plenty — The Lords of Life — Cypress & Cedar.

Note: The following poems have divisions and subtitles: Travesties:
Distant Ophir — Manica: I. The Origin of the Beery Way — II. The
Elephant & the Kangaroo — III. The Foreign Body; from The Zeg-Zeg
Postcards: I-VI are without titles — VII. Water Babies — VIII-XV are
without titles; Palladas:Poems: 1-40 are without titles — 41. On
Gessius — 42. Maurus — 43-62 are without titles — 63. On a Temple
of Fortune turned into a tavern — 64-65 are without titles — 66.
Marina's House — 67. Hypatia — 68. On Monks — 69. The Spartan
Mother — 70. The Murderer & Sarapis.

b. *First edition, paperbound issue*:

Tony Harrison / *Selected Poems* / [publisher's logo] / A King Penguin /
Published by Penguin Books

Collation: 104 leaves; 20 × 12.9 cm.

Binding: A perfect binding glued into stiff white wove paper wrappers,
of which the exterior is shiny; at the top of the spine: [publisher's logo];
lettered down the spine in black on a light gray (264) rectangle
surrounded by a white and black rule: *TONY HARRISON* •
SELECTED POEMS [lettered down the spine in two lines] ISBN
0 14 / 00.7158x; the front wrapper is composed of a photograph in
various shades of green, blue, gray, brown and yellow of Leeds with its
town hall and university from the Harrison family grave on Beeston
Hill by Graham Sykes; printed in black on the front wrapper: TONY
HARRISON / [single rule] / SELECTED POEMS / 'One of the few
modern poets who actually has the gift / of composing poetry' — James
Fenton in the *Sunday Times* / [in black on a light gray rectangle
surrounded by a white and black rule]: King Penguin; on the white rear
wrapper within a rectangle surrounded by a thick and a thin black rule:
[in black on a light gray rectangle surrounded by a white and a black
rule]: KING PENGUIN / [22 lines of opinions on Harrison] / [2 lines of
photo credits] / Poetry Book Society Recommendation / [photograph of
Tony Harrison] / [at the left-hand side of the wrapper in white on a
black rectangle with a penguin to the right]: U.K. £3.50 / AUST. $8.95
/ (recommended) / CAN. $7.95 [at the right hand-side of the wrapper]
PENGUIN POETRY / ISBN 0 14 / 00.7158x

Publication date: 27 September 1984

Price: £3.50

Number of copies: 6,000; 2nd printing of 3,000 copies on 31 January
1985; 3rd printing of 4,000 copies on 28 March 1985; 4th printing of
4,000 copies on 27 March 1986.

Pagination: [1] half-title and 17 lines of information on Harrison; [2]
blank; [3] title page; [4] [5 lines of Penguin Books addresses] / This
selection first published 1984 / Published simultaneously by Viking /
Copyright © Tony Harrison, 1984 / The acknowledgements on
pp. 11–12 constitute / an extension of this page / All rights reserved
/ Made and printed in Great Britain by / Richard Clay (The Chaucer
Press) Ltd, / Bungay, Suffolk / Set in Monophoto Ehrhardt / Except
in the United States of America, this book is sold subject / to the
condition that it shall not, by the way of trade or otherwise, be lent, /
re-sold, hired-out, or otherwise circulated without the / publisher's prior
consent in any form of binding or cover other than / that in which it is
published and without a similar condition / including this condition
being imposed on the subsequent purchaser; [5]–[204] same as A19a;
[205]–[208] 4 pages of advertisements on Penguin Books.

Contents: Same as A19a

c. *First American edition*:

Tony Harrison / *Selected Poems* / [publisher's logo] / Random House / New York.

Collation: $[1-7]^{16}$ + $[7]^8$ = 104 leaves; 20.9 × 14 cm.

Binding: Bound in light gray (264) paper-covered boards and black cloth on the spine and a quarter of the front and back boards; lettered down the spine in silver: *Selected Poems* Tony Harrison [across the base of the spine: publisher's logo] / Random / House; white wove paper; all edges trimmed; white wove endpapers; pictorial dust wrapper of white wove paper, shiny on the exterior and printed in light gray, dark gray (266) and deep red (13).

Publication date: June 29, 1987

Price: $15.95

Number of copies: Data unavailable from the publisher

Pagination: Blank endpaper; [1] half-title; [2] blank; [3] title page; [4] for Teresa / '. . . son io il poeta, / essa la poesia.' / Copyright © 1987 Tony Harrison / All rights reserved under International / and Pan-American Copyright Conventions. / Published in the United States by / Random House, Inc., New York, and / simultaneously in Canada by / Random House of Canada Limited, Toronto. / Thanks are due to the following publishers and periodicals for permission to reprint / poems in this book: / [27 lines]; [5] [7 lines of acknowledgements continued] / First published by Penguin, England in 1984 / Library of Congress Cataloging-in-Publication Data / [5 lines] / MANUFACTURED IN THE UNITED STATES OF AMERICA / 9 8 7 6 5 4 3 2 / FIRST EDITION; [6] blank; 7-9 Contents; [10] blank; [11] *Selected Poems*; [12] blank; 13-204, text; [205] ABOUT THE AUTHOR / [18 lines]; [206-208] blank; blank endpaper.

Contents: Same as A19a

A20   THE MYSTERIES   1985

a. *First edition, hardcover issue*:

[Within a rectangle composed of a thin rule on the outside and a thick rule on the inside] TONY / HARRISON / [single rule] / *The Mysteries* / [a reproduction in black and white of an engraving of the crucifixion] / [below the rectangle: publisher's logo] / *faber and faber* / LONDON • BOSTON

Collation: $[1-6]^{16}$ + $[7]^4$ + $[8]^{16}$ = 116 leaves; 19.7 × 12.7 cm.

Binding: Bound in textured vivid red (11) cloth and lettered down the

spine in gold: [a vertical thin rule] / [a vertical thick rule] TONY
HARRISON *The Mysteries* [across the base of the spine: publisher's
logo] [across the base of the spine a thick rule] / [a thin rule]; white wove
paper; all edges trimmed; white wove endpapers; dust wrapper of white
wove paper, shiny on the exterior and printed in black and vivid red.

Publication date: 5 August 1985

Price: £9.95

Number of copies: 1,462

Pagination: [1] half-title; [2] blank; [3] title page; [4] This collection first
published 1985 / by Faber and Faber limited / 3 Queen Square London
WC1N 3AU / Printed in Great Britain by / Redwood Burn Ltd,
Trowbridge, Wiltshire / All rights reserved / © Tony Harrison 1985 /
[4 lines if rights information] / British Library Cataloguing in
Publication Data / [4 lines] / ISBN 0-571-13789-X / ISBN
0-571-13790-3 Pbk; [5] CONTENTS: [6] [11 lines on the process of the
creation of the Mystery Plays] / TH / National Theatre / May 1985;
[7] From the first performance of *The Passion* on Easter Saturday /
1977, on the terraces of the National Theatre, to the re-opening / of the
entire trilogy at the Lyceum Theatre, 18 May 1985, the / Company has
included: [32 lines of cast members]; [8] [6 lines of cast members] / The
first performance of the entire trilogy was in the Cottesloe / Theatre on
19 January 1985 / [12 lines listing director, designer, etc]; [9] THE
NATIVITY; [10] CHARACTERS; 11–87 text; [88] blank; [89] THE
PASSION; [90] CHARACTERS; 91–157 text; [158] blank; [159]
DOOMSDAY; [160] CHARACTERS; 161–229 text; [230–232] blank.

Contents: The Mysteries: The Nativity; The Passion; Doomsday

b. *First edition, paperbound issue*:

[The transcription of the title page is identical to that of the first
hardcover issue]

Collation: 116 leaves; 19.7 × 12.7 cm.

Binding: A perfect binding glued into stiff white wove paper wrappers,
of which the exterior is semi-shiny and printed in black on a white
rectangle down the spine: [thin vertical rule] / [thick vertical rule] /
TONY HARRISON *The Mysteries* [across the base of the rectangle:
publisher's logo] / [a thick vertical rule] / [a thin vertical rule]; beginning
at the left of the rear wrapper and going across to the right of the upper
wrapper are rows of the publisher's logo in vivid red (11) over a black
base; on the front cover on a white rectangle and within a rectangle
composed of a thin rule on the outside and a thick rule on the inside in
black: TONY HARRISON / [single rule] / *The Mysteries* /

[a reproduction in black and white of an engraving of the crucifixion in which the body of Christ is printed in light pink (4)]; on the rear wrapper on a white rectangle and within a rectangle composed of a thin rule on the outside and a thick rule on the inside in black: [publisher's logo] / *faber and faber* / [single rule] / [20 lines of criticism on Harrison's works] / £4.95 net / ISBN 0 571 13790 3; white wove paper; all edges trimmed.

Publication date: 5 August 1985

Price: £4.95

Number of copies: 4,502; there was a second printing of 2,427 copies, but the date of the publication is not available.

Pagination: Same as A20a except on page 4 where there are an additional six lines in italics on conditions of sale listed below the ISBN numbers.

Contents: Same as A20a

A21   THE FIRE-GAP   1985

a. *First edition*:

[fancy black letters] Tony Harrison / [in dark greenish yellow (103) fancy letters] THE FIRE GAP / [in black] A POEM WITH TWO TAILS / [in dark greenish yellow stylized hand-printed letters in which the two 'o's' on the two words are intertwined] / BLOODAXE BOOKS / MCMLXXXV.

Collation: Broadsheet: single sheet printed on both sides, folded four times; 64 × 21.1 cm. (size of fully open sheet).

Binding: Glued on to the inside cover of stiff yellowish white (92) card wrappers, shiny on the exterior and printed in black; on the front wrapper: [to the left in fancy dark greenish yellow letters] THE / FIRE / GAP / [in the center of the wrapper in black, white, and dark greenish yellow: a drawing of a snake with its head near the top of the wrapper which has its tail, coming down from the top of the wrapper, in its mouth]; [at the lower right hand corner of the front wrapper in white fancy letters] Tony Harrison; on the rear wrapper at the base from left to right: [in white fancy letters] Price £1.95 [in dark greenish yellow, printed as on the title page] BLOODAXE BOOKS [in black on a white label] ISBN: 0 906427 83 5; inside the front wrapper: First published in 1985 by / Bloodaxe Books Ltd, / P.O. Box ISN, / Newcastle upon Tyne NE99 1SN / ISBN: 0 906427 83 5 / Bloodaxe Books Ltd acknowledges / the financial assistance of Northern Arts / This poem first appeared in *The Times Literary Supplement* / Copyright © Tony

Harrison 1985 / All rights reserved / Printed in Great Britain by / Tyneside Free Press Workshop Ltd, Newcastle upon Tyne / Designed and / Illustrated by / Michael Christopher Caine.

Publication date: December 1985

Price: £1.95

Number of copies: 1,400; 100 copies were issued as an unbound broadside.

Pagination: When fully open, the title page is on the verso of the fourth panel at the bottom of the broadsheet; at the top of the sheet in dark greenish letters to the left: THE FIRE-GAP / Tony Harrison [to the right in black letters, the poem extends to the bottom of the sheet in parallel columns, each containing 100 lines of text; the space between the two columns of text is in the form of a snake, with its head at the top and the tail at the base of sheet; at the base of the sheet to the left in dark greenish yellow letters: [8 last lines of text] [in the center in black a stylized drawing of Christ on the cross] [to the right in dark greenish yellow letters: 8 last lines of text].

Contents: The Fire-Gap

b. *First edition, 'deluxe issue'*

THE FIRE GAP / [grey greenish yellow (105) italics] *A POEM WITH TWO TAILS* / TONY HARRISON

Collation: Broadsheet; single sheet (two sheets pasted together) printed on one side only and folded three times; 141 × 37 cm. (size of fully open sheet)

Binding: Glued on to the right-hand inside cover of black cloth covered boards; on the front cover, inlaid in the center of the cover, an abstract design of Christ's crucifixion made up of snakeskin; the rear cover is blank; off-white laid paper; left-hand side and bottom trimmed.

Publication date: 1985

Note: The copyright date is 1985, but the copies I received were not issued until May, 1986.

Price: not for sale

Number of copies: 100

Note: There were only 20 bindings containing the inlaid snakeskin according to the publisher, Michael Caine.

Pagination: When fully open, the title appears as above; 100 lines of parallel text, the last 8 lines printed in dark greenish yellow (103); the space between the two columns of text is in the form of a snake, with its head at the top and the tail at the base of the sheet; between the last eight lines of text is an abstract drawing of Christ on the cross in black; holograph signature of Tony Harrison; in dark greenish letters at the foot of the sheet: This inscribed edition of the Fire-Gap has been designed, illustrated, printed and bound by Michael Christopher Caine. / The Monotype Garamond 14pt typeface with the Garamond display matter was set and cast by Monoset (Typesetters) Ltd of London. / The rattlesnake was caught on the land of Tony Harrison and Teresa Stratas and skinned and tanned by Jay Wood / of Wood's Wildlife Taxidermy at Gainesville, Florida, U.S.A. Copyright © Tony Harrison 1985 All rights reserved London 1985 / This book is copy number [10 in black ink] of one hundred. [holograph signature of Michael Christopher Caine in black ink] / [roman numeral X in black ink]

Note: Papers and bindings used for this edition vary greatly. Two other copies were examined. Copy number 37: THE FIRE GAP / [in hand printed light yellowish green (119) letters] a poem with two tails / TONY HARRISON; the text and edition statement are printed entirely in black; below the statement — 'This book is copy number 37 [in black pencil] of one hundred' — appear the signatures 'Michael Christopher Caine' [in pencil] and last the holograph signature of 'Tony Harrison' in black ink; the copy is bound in black cloth with a black and white cloth spine; a black label appears in the center of the front cover with 'THE FIRE GAP' in off-white letters. Copy number 49: THE FIRE GAP / [in grey greenish yellow] *A POEM WITH TWO TAILS* / TONY HARRISON; the last eight lines of the poem and the edition statement are printed in grey greenish yellow; below the edition statement: Tony Harrison [holograph in black ink] / M.C. Caine [in pencil]; the binding is a dark grey yellowish green paper with a black spine; in the center of the front cover is an abstract drawing in white of Christ on the cross; surrounding the figure as a circle in white: TONY HARRISON [top of the circle] and THE FIRE GAP [bottom of the circle]; the copy also includes two paper labels in black letters: THE FIRE GAP Tony Harrison [in one line].

A22   V.   1985

a. *First edition, hardcover issue*:

[Superimposed on a black and white photograph with a bluish cast which covers two pages] [on the left hand page] TONY [on the right-hand page] HARRISON / [in strong purplish blue (196) V. [stylized hand-printed letters in which the two 'o's' in the two words are intertwined in strong purplish blue on the right hand page]

BLOODAXE BOOKS [thick rule in strong purplish blue running across the two pages]

Collation: [1–3]⁸ = 24 leaves; 21.6 × 13.6 cm.

Binding: Bound in black cloth and lettered down the spine in gold: TONY HARRISON V. [lettered as on the title page] BLOODAXE; white wove paper; all edges trimmed; endpapers of very light blue (180) wove paper; dust wrapper of shiny white wove paper printed in light gray (264), strong purplish blue, and black.

Publication date: December 1985

Price: £8.95

Number of copies: 500

Pagination: [1] half-title; [2–3] title page; [4] Copyright © Tony Harrison 1985 / Photographs copyright © Graham Sykes 1985 / All rights reserved / ISBN: 0 906427 97 5 paperback / 0 906427 98 3 hardback / First published 1985 by / Bloodaxe Books Ltd, / P.O. Box ISN, / Newcastle upon Tyne NE99 1SN. / Bloodaxe Books Ltd acknowledges / the financial assistance of Northern Arts. / This poem first appeared in the *London Review of Books*. / Typeset by True North, Newcastle upon Tyne. Printed in Great Britain by / Tyneside Free Press Workshop Ltd, Newcastle upon Tyne; [5] [3 line quote] / ARTHUR SCARGILL / *Sunday Times, 10 January 1982*; [6–42] text and 14 photographs; [43–44] blank; [45] [37 lines of information on Tony Harrison and Graham Sykes]; [46] blank; [47–48] [2 pages of advertisements on Bloodaxe Books.

Contents: V.

b. *First edition, paperbound issue*:

[The transcription of the title pages is identical with that of the hardcover issue.]

Collation: [1–3]⁸ = 24 leaves; 21.6 × 13.6 cm.

Binding: Glued into stiff white card wrappers of which the exterior is shiny and printed down the spine: [in light gray (264) letters] TONY HARRISON [in strong purplish blue (196) V. [stylized hand-printed letters in which the two 'o's in the two words are intertwined in strong purplish blue] BLOODAXE; on the front cover a photograph of a cemetery in black, white and light gray; near the base of the cover and to the left: a light gray rectangle surrounded by a thin white border; superimposed upon the rectangle in strong purplish blue: V.; superimposed upon the 'V.' in white: TONY / HARRISON [a thick rule in strong purplish blue which goes across the spine and the back cover];

on the rear wrapper a photograph of a cemetery in black, white, and light gray; [7 lines in white on the text] / [stylized hand-printed letters in which the two 'o's' are intertwined in strong purplish blue] BLOODAXE BOOKS / [in black letters to the left] WITH PHOTOGRAPHS BY GRAHAM SYKES / [in strong purplish blue / £4.50 [to the right: ISBN stamp]; white wove paper; all edges trimmed.

Publication date: December 1985

Price: £4.50

Number of copies: 2,000; the publisher has written that there will be a 2nd edition published in April, 1989 of 2,000 copies.

Pagination: Same as A22a

Contents: V.

A23   DRAMATIC VERSE   1985

a. *First edition*

[In white on a black rectangle and within a rectangle composed of a single rule in white] DRAMATIC / VERSE / 1973–1985 / TONY HARRISON / [stylized hand-printed letters in which the two 'o's' in the two words are intertwined and printed in black] BLOODAXE BOOKS.

Collation: [1–29]⁸ = 232 leaves; 21.5 × 13.5 cm.

Binding: Bound in dark orange yellow (72) textured cloth and lettered across the spine in gold within a rectangle composed of double rules] DRAMATIC / VERSE / 1973–1985 / TONY HARRISON / [across the base of the spine in gold and lettered as on the title page] BLOODAXE; white wove paper; all edges trimmed; endpapers of light yellowish brown (76) wove paper; pictorial dust wrapper of white wove paper, shiny on the exterior, and printed in brownish orange (54), and black.

Publication date: 5 December 1985

Price: £20

Number of copies: 1,000

Pagination: [i] half-title; [ii] Also by Tony Harrison / POETRY / [11 titles] / THEATRE / [8 titles]; [iii] title page; [iv] Copyright © Tony Harrison 1985 / All rights reserved / First published 1985 by / Bloodaxe Books Ltd, / P.O. Box 1SN, / Newcastle upon Tyne NE99 1SN. / ISBN: 0 906427 81 9 / Bloodaxe Books Ltd acknowledges / the financial assistance of Northern Arts. / Typesetting by True North, Newcastle

upon Tyne. / Printed in Great Britain by / Tyneside Free Press
Workshop Ltd, Newcastle upon Tyne; [v] [22 line quote and source]; [vi]
Acknowledgements / [17 lines]; [vii] Contents; [viii] blank; [1] THE
MISANTHROPE (1973); [2]–68, cast listing and text; [69] PHAEDRA
BRITANNICA (1975); [70]–124, cast listing and text; [125] BOW
DOWN (1977) / MUSIC: Harrison Birtwistle; [126]–148, cast listing
and text; [149] THE BARTERED BRIDE (1978) / *A Comic Opera* /
MUSIC: Bedrich Smetana; [150]–184, cast listing and text; [185] THE
ORESTEIA (1981) / MUSIC: Harrison Birtwistle; [186]–292, cast
listing and text; [293] YAN TAN TETHERA (1983) / *A Mechanical
Pastoral* / MUSIC: Harrison Birtwistle; [294]–320, cast listing and text;
[321] THE BIG H (1984) / A Music Drama / MUSIC Dominic:
Muldowney; [322]–361, cast listing and text; [362] blank; [363]
MEDEA: a sex-war opera (1985) / MUSIC: Jacob Druckman; [364]–448,
cast listing and text; [449–454] blank; [455–456] advertisements for
Bloodaxe Books.

Contents: The Misanthrope — Phaedra Britannica — Bow Down —
The Bartered Bride — The Oresteia — Yan Tan Tethera — The
Big H — Medea: a sex-war opera.

Note: Yan Tan Tethera, The Big H and Medea: a sex-war opera appear
here for the first time in print.

b. *First paperbound edition:*

TONY HARRISON / [short thick rule] / [short thin rule] / THEATRE
WORKS 1973–1985 / [publisher's logo] / A KING PENGUIN /
PUBLISHED BY PENGUIN BOOKS

Collation: 232 leaves; 20 × 13 cm.

Binding: A perfect binding glued into stiff white card wrappers of which
the exterior is shiny and printed in black, light gray (264) and vivid red
(11); [across the top of the spine in black and light gray: publisher's logo]
/ [lettered down the spine in black]: TONY HARRISON • THEATRE
WORKS 1973–1985 [in two lines] ISBN 0 14 / 00.8826 1; on the front
cover in black: [the Orestes mask by Jacelyn Herbert for the National
Theatre Oresteia]; at the top of the front wrapper: [in black on a light
gray rectangle surrounded by a single black rule] KING PENGUIN /
[in vivid red fancy letters] THEATRE / [in vivid red fancy letters]
WORKS / [in white] 1973–1985 / [in white] TONY HARRISON; on
the rear wrapper: within a frame in black consisting of a thick black rule
and a thin black rule: KING PENGUIN [as on top of the front
wrapper] / [photograph of Tony Harrison in black and white
surrounded by a thin black rule] [to the right]; 28 lines of criticism and

information on Harrison] / [to the left] Drama/Theatre / U.K. £4.95 /
AUST. $14.95 / (recommended) / N.Z. $16.50 / (incl. GST) / CAN.
$10.95 [to the right: bar code label] / ISBN 0–14–008826–1; white wove
paper; all edges trimmed.

Publication date: 25 September 1986

Price: £4.95

Number of copies: 8,000

Pagination: [i] half-title and 15 lines of information on Harrison and his
work within a rectangle made up of a thick rule on the outside and a
thin rule on the inside; within the rectangle and enclosed in a rectangle
composed of a thin rule on the outside and a thin rule on the inside:
KING PENGUIN:; [ii] blank; [iii] title-page; [iv] [5 lines of Penguin
addresses] / First published as *Dramatic verse 1973–1985* by Bloodaxe
Books 1985 / Published in Penguin Books 1986 / Copyright © Tony
Harrison 1985 / All rights reserved / Made and printed in Great Britain
by / Richard Clay (The Chaucer Press) Ltd, / Bungay, Suffolk /
[9 lines of sales information]; [v] [22 line quote by Lion Feuchtwanger
and comments on Feuchtwanger]; [vi] Acknowledgements / [17 lines.
Note: the last 7 lines of information for the jacket photographs on the
Bloodaxe edition which does not pertain to the wrapper of this
paperback edition]; [vii] Contents; [viii] blank; [1] The Misanthrope
(1973); [2] [24 lines giving cast and production information]; 3–68 text;
[69] PHAEDRA BRITANNICA (1975); [70] [29 lines giving cast and
production information]; 71–124 text; [125] BOW DOWN (1977) /
MUSIC: Harrison Birtwistle; [126] [33 lines giving cast and production
information and a note on the play]; 127–148, text; [149] THE
BARTERED BRIDE (1978) / *A Comic Opera* / MUSIC: Bedrich
Smetana [150]; [32 lines giving cast and production information and a
note on pronunciation]; 151–184, text; [185] THE ORESTEIA (1981) /
MUSIC: Harrison Birtwistle; [186–187] [47 lines giving the cast and
production information and a note]; [188] blank; [189] ONE /
AGAMEMNON; 190-230, text; [231] TWO / CHOEPHORI; 232-262,
text; [263] THREE EUMENIDES; 264–292, text; [293] YAN TAN
TETHERA (1983) / *A Mechanical Pastoral* / MUSIC: Harrison
Birtwistle; [294] [13 lines giving cast, etc]; 295–320, text; [321] THE
BIG H (1984) / *A Music Drama* / MUSIC: Dominic Muldowney; [322]
[Bertolt Brecht quote]; [323–324] [56 lines giving cast and production
information]; 325–361, text; [362] blank; [363] MEDEA: a sex-war opera
(1985) / MUSIC: Jacob Druckman; [363] [7 lines of quotes]; [364]
MEDEA: A SEX-WAR OPERA / *Medea: a sex-war opera* was
commissioned by the New York / Metropolitan Opera; 366–448, text;
[449–456] 8 pages of advertisements.

Contents: The Misanthrope — Phaedra Britannica — Bow Down — The Bartered Bride — The Oresteia — Yan Tan Tethera — The Big H — Medea: a sex-war opera.

A24 TEN SONNETS FROM THE SCHOOL OF ELOQUENCE 1987

a. *First edition*:

Tony Harrison / [single rule] / TEN SONNETS FROM / *The School / of / Eloquence* / Anvil Press Poetry

Collation: [1]⁶ = 6 leaves; 18 × 14 cm.

Binding: Stapled twice into heavy medium red (15) plain paper wrappers; simulated white laid paper; all edges trimmed; dust wrapper of heavy light yellowish brown (76) paper and printed on the front: Tony Harrison / [single rule] / TEN SONNETS FROM / *The School / of / Eloquence* / Anvil Press Poetry

Publication date: 1987

Note: The publisher reports that there was no official publication date for this pamphlet. The pamphlet was 'released' in June 1987. It was to be used as part of a subscription project, but the leaflet on the pamphlet and the publisher's catalog were not issued until December 1987.

Price: £5 for the signed copies and £1.95 for the unsigned copies.

Number of copies: 600 numbered copies of which numbers 1–250 are signed by the poet.

Note: The leaflet describing this pamphlet as part of a subscription project contained the following on the front cover: TONY HARRISON / Ten Sonnets / from The School of Eloquence / [photograph of Tony Harrison in black and white] / *A signed copy completely free / with your 1988 subscription* / Anvil Press Poetry.

Pagination: [1] title-page; [2] [at the upper left-hand corner in black ink:] 413 / Published in 1987 / by Anvil Press Poetry Ltd / 69 King Street London SE10 8PX / ISBN 0 85646 180 6 (signed) / 0 85646 181 4 (unsigned) / Copyright © Tony Harrison 1987 / This edition is limited to six hundred / numbered copies of which nos. 1–250 are / signed by the poet / This booklet is published with / financial assistance from / The Arts Council of Great Britain / Typeset in Bodoni by / Juliet Grant, Bexleyheath, Kent / Printed by SBS Litho, Greenwich; [3]–[12], text.

Contents: Pain-Killers — The Morning After — Bye-Byes — 'Testing the Reality' — The Effort — Jumper — Changing at York.

A25   ANNO 42*   1987

a. *First Signed Edition*

TONY HARRISON / ANNO / FORTY / TWO / SEVEN NEW
POEMS / THE SCARGILL PRESS / [two parallel rules]

Collation: [1]⁶ = 6 leaves; 25.3 × 18.3 cm.

Binding: Sewn with silk threads into mould-made paper wrappers (Rives
mould-made 300 gsm white) and lettered on the front wrapper in vivid
red (11) letters: TONY HARRISON / ANNO / FORTY / TWO; the
rear wrapper is blank; white hand-made paper; top and side edges
trimmed; lower edge untrimmed; the bottom edge of the wrapper is
untrimmed.

Note: The publisher, Michael C. Caine, reported in a letter of
November 11, 1987 that in the total edition (A25a, b, and c) there were
115 copies on Somerset Satin Waterleaf mould-made paper, 150 gsm;
157 copies on acid-free John Purcell 'Bread & Butter' paper, 170 gsm;
12 copies on Ash Grey Khadi Indian hand-made paper, 180 gsm and
1 copy on Turquoise Mingei Japanese hand-made paper, 150 gsm
(printer's copy). The copy examined (No. 54) was printed on Somerset
Satin Waterleaf paper.

Publication date: 6 August 1987

Price: £10.00

Number of copies: 100 (out of a total 285 copies)

Note: Although the Colophon states that the edition consisted of 350
copies, the publisher reports that 65 copies were lost during production.

Pagination: [1] blank; [2] An edition of 350 copies / Typeset in 14pt
Dante Semi-Bold / Printed by Michael Caine / August 6th 1987 /
Copies numbered 1-50 [the number '50' has been crossed out in vivid
red ink and the number '100' written in, in vivid red ink] / Inscribed by
Tony Harrison / [holograph signature of Tony Harrison in vivid red
ink] / [holograph number (54) in vivid red ink] / [holograph signature of
Michael Caine in black ink]; [3] title page; [4] blank; [5–11] text; [6]
blank.

Contents: Old Soldiers — The Figure — Black & White — The Birds of
Japan — The Poetry Lesson.

Note: The Birds of Japan and The Poetry Lesson appear here for the
first time in print.

b. *First Trade Edition*

[The First Trade Edition is identical to A25a except for the following:]

Price: £3.50

Number of copies: Undetermined

Pagination: [2] An edition of 350 copies / Typeset in 14pt Dante Semi-Bold / Printed by Michael Caine / August 6th 1987 / Copies numbered 1-50 / Inscribed by Tony Harrison / [holograph number in pencil (216)] / [holograph signature of Michael Caine in pencil].

c. *First DeLuxe Edition*:

[Identical to A25a except as follows]:

Collation: 24.8–25.5 × 18.4–19.2 cm.

Binding: Sewn with silk threads into mould-made paper wrappers (Rives mould-made 300 gsm white) with an original cover design by the publisher in vivid red, brilliant blue (177) and vivid yellow (82) consisting of a white dove in flight; deckled ash grey Khadi Indian hand made paper.

Price: £30.00

Number of copies: 'Approximately twenty copies'

Note: The publisher, Michael Caine, reported in a letter of November 11, 1987 that there are 'Approximately twenty copies with decorated covers, executed in chalk pastel, some with candle smoke forming the shape of a bird.'

Pagination: [2] An edition of 350 copies / Typeset in 14pt Dante Semi-Bold / Printed by Michael Caine / August 6th 1987 / Copies numbered I-50 / Inscribed by Tony Harrison / [holograph number in black ink] / [holograph signature of Tony Harrison in black ink] / [holograph signature of Michael Caine in black ink].

*Anno 42 is comprised of a First Signed Edition, A First Trade Edition and a First Deluxe Edition. Only the First Signed Edition is described fully; only the differences are noted between the First Trade Edition and the First Deluxe Edition.

B

BOOKS AND PAMPHLETS EDITED
OR WITH CONTRIBUTIONS BY
TONY HARRISON

In this section, books and pamphlets in which a contribution by Tony Harrison appears either for the first time in a book or for the first time in print are listed in chronological order. Any material which was previously unpublished is identified by a note.

B1   OUT ON THE EDGE   1958

Out on the Edge / Edited by / A.R. Mortimer and James Simmons /
Cover by / Roger Dickinson / Department of English Literature /
Leeds, 1958.

Collation: [A]^{24} = 24 leaves; 18.5 × 12 cm.

Binding: Stapled twice into stiff light gray (264) paper pictorial wrappers
printed in very deep purple (225). On the front wrapper at the top in
rough letters in purple: out on the edge / [dilapidated building covering
front and rear wrapper]

Publication date: Data unavailable from publisher

Price: 2/6

Number of copies: Data unavailable from publisher

Contents: An Appeal to the Sybil, p. 10; Easter, p. 11; My Migratory
Bird and the Divine, p. 11; Epithalmium, p. 12; On a Rosary. To a
Catholic Poet, pp. 13–14; Spring Outings, p. 14.

Note: Harrison's name is listed as 'T. W. Harrison.'

B2   NEW POEMS   1960

[decorative floral device] / NEW POEMS / 1960 / [decorative floral
device] / *Edited by* / ANTHONY CRONIN / JON SILKIN /
TERENCE TILLER / *With a Preface by* / ALAN PRYCE-JONES /
HUTCHINSON OF LONDON

Collation: [A]^8 + B-H^8 = 64 leaves; 20.1 × 13.3 cm.

Binding: Bound in decorative paper-covered boards printed in light gray
(264), dark gray (266), vivid yellow (82), and black with the spine and
partial front and rear wrappers in strong purplish blue (196); lettered
across the spine: [in gold] New / [in gold] Poems / [decorative horizontal
rule in white] / [in gold] 1960 / [across the base of the spine in white:
publisher's logo] / [in white] HUTCHINSON; the front and rear
wrappers are covered with a series of decorative squares and rectangles
printed in the colors mentioned above; white wove paper; all edges
trimmed; white wove endpapers; dust wrapper of white wove paper
printed in light gray, vivid yellow and black.

Publication date: 10 October 1960

Price: 16s

Number of copies: Data unavailable from publisher

Contents: 'Man Against the Virus,' p. 55.

Note: The collection also includes 'My Migratory Bird and the Divine,' p. 54, which was previously collected.

Note: Both poems are signed 'T.W. Harrison.'

B3   **POETRY AND AUDIENCE 1953–60**   **1961**

poetry and audience 1953–60 / AN ANTHOLOGY / *foreword by* Professor Bonamy Dobree / *selected by* / A.R. Mortimer / and the Editorial Board / of Poetry / and Audience.

Collation: [A]⁶ + [B–F]⁸ = 46 leaves; 21.5 × 13.8 cm.

Binding: Bound in stiff white card wrappers, the exterior of which is printed in brilliant yellow (83) and lettered up the spine in black: POETRY AND AUDIENCE 1953–60 AN ANTHOLOGY; lettered in black on the front wrapper: poetry / and / audience / 1953–60 / AN ANTHOLOGY; the rear wrapper is blank; white wove paper; all edges trimmed; dust wrapper of white wove paper, of which the exterior is shiny and printed in black, vivid red (11) and brilliant yellow.

Publication date: 6 May 1961

Price: 10/6

Number of copies: Data unavailable from publisher

Contents: 'The Hybrid Growth,' p. 19; 'Ghosts: Some Words Before Breakfast,' pp. 20–21, collected in TL and SP

Note: The contents also include 'My Migratory Bird and the Divine' and 'Epithalamium' which were previously collected.

Note: All poems are signed 'T.W. Harrison.'

B4   **UNIVERSITIES' POETRY 4**   **1962**

UNIVERSITIES' POETRY / FOUR / Managing Editor / Dax MacColl *(Keele) / Literary Editors* / Anthony Tillinghast *(Nottingham)* / Clive Jordan *(Oxford)*

Collation: [1–3]⁸ = 24 leaves; 22.5 × 14 cm.

Binding: Glued into stiff, semi-shiny white card wrappers of which the front wrapper is printed in dark reddish orange (38); lettered down the spine in black: 1962 UNIVERSITIES' POETRY FOUR KEELE; on the front wrapper at the upper right-hand corner in white: KEELE /

[a large fancy '4' in black] / [in white] *UNIVERSITIES' POETRY* / [at the lower right-hand corner in white]: *two shillings / and sixpence*; white wove paper; all edges trimmed.

Publication date: April, 1962

Price: 2/6

Number of copies: Data unavailable from publisher

Contents: 'The Flat Dweller's Revolt,' pp. 18–19, collected in E.

Note: The poem is signed T.W. Harrison.

B5   NEW POEMS 1967   1968

[decorative floral device] / NEW POEMS / 1967 / A P.E.N. Anthology / of Contemporary Poetry / [decorative floral device] / *Edited by* / HAROLD PINTER / JOHN FULLER / PETER REDGROVE / HUTCHINSON OF LONDON

Collation: [A]⁸ + B–F⁸ = 48 leaves; 19.9 × 13.2 cm.

Binding: Bound in imitation black cloth and lettered down the spine in gold: NEW POEMS 1967 [vertical rule] A P.E.N. ANTHOLOGY HUTCHINSON; white wove paper; all edges trimmed; white wove endpapers; dust wrapper, shiny on the exterior, of white wove paper printed in vivid red (11), black and medium gray (265).

Publication date: 14 October 1968

Price: 25s

Number of copies: 1,750

Contents: 'The White Queen,' pp. 37–58, collected in TL and SP; 'The Heart of Darkness,' pp. 39–41, collected in TL and SP.

Note: The Contents lists Harrison's name as 'T.W. Harrison,' but on page 37, it is listed as 'Tony Harrison.'

B6   72 DRAWINGS BY JIRI JIRASEK   1969

72 drawings / by / JIRI JIRASEK / *'Even he who must submit to force, / cannot evade his duty / to show contempt for force.'* / *Literarni Listy* (Special Edition, 22nd August) 1968 / An Exposition held at the HATTON GALLERY / The University of Newcastle upon Tyne / from 16th May to 2nd June, 1969 / [single long rule] / Catalogue notes and photograph on back cover by TONY HARRISON / Published by

STAND 58 Queen's Road, Newcastle upon Tyne NE2 2PR.

Collation: [1]^{10} = 10 leaves; 16.6 × 21 cm.

Binding: Stapled twice into white card wrappers; on the front wrapper: [on the left a cartoon of a tank shooting letters] / [to the right of the bottom of the tank] *JIRI JIRASEK* / [single rule across the base of the wrapper] / PRAGUE AUGUST 1968 CARTOONS PRAGUE AUGUST 1968 PRAGUE AUGUST 1968 CARTOONS / [single rule across the wrapper]; on the rear wrapper: [photograph in black and white and light gray (264) of a stylized burning torch]; to the left in white crude letters: PRAVDA; to the right in white crude letters: VITEZI; white wove paper; all edges trimmed.

Date of publication: 16 May 1969

Price: 3/

Number of copies: Data unavailable from publisher

Contents: 'The Artist,' p. 2; [Notes] pp. 3–4, 6–7; 'The Context,' pp. 8–9; 'Filosofica Fakulta University Larlovy Katedra Anglistiky,' p. 10; [Notes] pp. 11–14, 17–19.

B7 PITH AND VINEGAR 1969

PITH / & VINEGAR / AN ANTHOLOGY OF SHORT HUMOROUS POETRY / EDITED BY / *WILLIAM COLE* / SIMON AND SCHUSTER • NEW YORK.

Collation: [1–5]^{16} = 80 leaves; 16.4 × 13 cm.

Binding: Bound in off-white linen textured cloth and lettered down the spine: [in strong reddish orange (35)] *PITH & VINEGAR* [in very dark bluish green (166) in three lines] *EDITED BY / WILLIAM COLE / SIMON AND SCHUSTER*; on the front cover at the lower left-hand corner in very dark bluish green: [a figure of a seated jester from the rear]; white wove paper; all edges trimmed; deep reddish orange (36) endpapers; dust wrapper of white wove textured paper printed in strong reddish orange, strong yellowish green (131), brownish orange (54), and black.

Publication date: November 4, 1969

Price: $3.95

Number of copies: Data unavailable from publisher

Note: The publisher reports that approximately 1,100 copies were sold.

Contents: 'The Bedbug,' p. 83, collected in TL and SP.

B8   DRYDEN'S MIND AND ART*   1970

a. *First American Edition*:

DRYDEN'S / MIND AND ART / [to the left] JOHN HEATH-STUBBS / ARTHUR W. HOFFMAN / ELIAS J. CHIASSON / JAY ARNOLD LEVINE / BONAMY DOBREE / [to the right] D.W. JEFFERSON / BRUCE KING / A.D. HOPE / T.W. HARRISON / WILLIAM FROST / Essays edited by BRUCE KING / [publisher's logo] / BARNES & NOBLE, Inc. / NEW YORK / PUBLISHERS AND BOOKSELLERS SINCE 1873.

Collation: [A]⁸–O⁸ = 112 leaves; 21.6 × 13.6 cm.

Note: The letter 'J' is not used as a signature.

Binding: Bound in dark grayish blue semi-shiny cloth and lettered on the spine in gold: [across the top of the spine] KING / [decorative device] / [down the spine in two lines] DRYDEN'S / MIND AND ART; [across the base of the spine in two lines] BARNES / & NOBLE; white wove paper; all edges trimmed; dust wrapper not seen.

Publication date: Data unavailable from publisher

Price: $7.50

Number of copies: Data unavailable from publisher

Contents: 'Dryden's *Aeneid*,' pp. 143–167.

Note: The chapter is signed 'T.W. Harrison.'

*A copy of the true first edition could not be located: King, Bruce (Ed.). *Dryden's Mind and Art*. Edinburgh: Oliver and Boyd, 1969 (Essays old and new 5). 213pp; 45/-; SBN 05 001918 3

B9   THE MISSION OR SCENES IN AFRICA   1970

THE MISSION / OR / SCENES / IN AFRICA / *Introduction by Tony Harrison* / Captain Marryat / Rex Collings / London / 1970

Collation: [1]⁸–20⁸ = 160 leaves; 21.6 × 14 cm.

Binding: Bound in light grayish olive (109) textured cloth and lettered in gold at the top of the spine on a dark bluish green (165) label with double gold rules at the top and bottom of the label: The / Mission / or / Scenes / in Africa / [single rule] / CAPTAIN / MARRYAT / [across the base of the spine] Rex / Collings; white wove paper; all edges trimmed; white wove endpapers; dust wrapper of white wove paper, of which the exterior is shiny, printed in vivid greenish yellow (97), and black.

Publication date: July 1970

Price: 45s / £2.25

Number of copies: Data unavailable from publisher

Contents: 'Introduction,' pp. v–xi.

B10   THE YOUNG BRITISH POETS   1971

a. *First edition*:

THE YOUNG / BRITISH POETS / *Edited by* / JEREMY ROBSON /
1971 / CHATTO & WINDUS / LONDON

Collation: [A]⁸ – K⁸ = 80 leaves; 19.7 × 12.9 cm.

Binding: Bound in medium purple (223) paper-covered boards and
lettered down the spine in gold: THE YOUNG BRITISH POETS
[ornament] *Edited by Jeremy Robson* / [across the base of the spine in
fancy letters] C / W; white wove paper; all edges trimmed; white wove
endpapers; pictorial dust wrapper of shiny white wove paper printed in
black.

Publication date: May 1971

Price: £1.50

Number of copies: 2,300

Contents: 'Durham,' pp. 60–62, collected in FTSOE and SP.

Note: The contents also include 'Thomas Campey and the Copernican
System,' 'A Proper Caution,' and 'The Nuptial Torches' which were
previously collected.

b. *First paperbound edition*:

THE YOUNG BRITISH / POETS / Edited by / JEREMY ROBSON /
CORGI BOOKS / A DIVISION OF TRANSWORLD PUBLISHERS
LTD / A NATIONAL GENERAL COMPANY

Collation: [A]⁸ – K⁸ = 80 leaves; 19 × 11.2 cm.

Binding: Glued into stiff white card wrappers, shiny on the exterior; at
the top of the spine: 0 / 552 / 08975 / 3 / POETRY / 0; lettered down
the spine: THE YOUNG BRITISH POETS EDITED BY JEREMY
ROBSON CORGI [in vivid red (11) and white device in the O of
CORGI]; on the front wrapper are photos in black and white of the
poets in the volume in 1 row at the top, 1 row down the edges of the
wrapper and 2 rows at the bottom of the wrapper; in the center of the

wrapper is a square in vivid red and on the square in white: THE [to the right a photo in black and white of a poet] / YOUNG / BRITISH / POETS [to the right a photo in black and white of a poet] / Edited by / JEREMY ROBSON; on the rear wrapper: [26 lines on the anthology and criticis] / UK. . . . .30p / Australia. . . . .95c / New Zealand. . . . .90c / Canada. . . . .$1.25; white wove paper; all edges trimmed.

Publication date: May 1972

Price: 30p

Number of copies: Data unavailable from the publisher

Contents: Same as B10a

B11   RESPONSES   1971

RESPONSES / The National Book League and the Poetry Society / 1971

Collation: [1]^{22} = 22 leaves; 25.2 × 19.5 cm.

Binding: Sewn loosely into semi-stiff, textured, vivid orange red wove paper wrappers and lettered on the front wrapper in black: RESPONSES; laid paper; mixture of trimmed and untrimmed edges.

Note: The colophon on page [44] reads: *Designed by Monica Schmoller and printed in Monotype Dante type by the / Westerham Press on handmade paper from Hodgkinson's Wookey Mill. / The edition consists* of [holograph in black ink] 500. [Holograph in black ink] Number . . .

Publication date: 28 May 1971

Price: £2.50

Number of copies: 500

Contents: 'On the Spot,' p. 33. Collected in FTSOE and SP.

B12   SOUTH BANK POETRY AND MUSIC   1971

[Not Seen]

[Cover title; front cover dark blue with lettering in white] SOUTH / BANK / POETRY / AND / MUSIC / Presented by / The Poetry Society and / The National Book League / with / TED HUGHES / TONY HARRISON / SEAMUS HEANEY / VERNON SCANNELL / music / JEREMY TAYLOR / and friends / [to the right: yellow crescent moon over water]

Collation: [16] pages; 21 × 14.9 cm.

Binding: Wrappers as described above.

Publication date: October 1971

Price: 20p.

Number of copies: Data unavailable from publisher.

Contents: 'On Not Being Milton.'

Note: This poem appears here for the first time in print.

B13   CORGI MODERN POETS IN FOCUS: 4   1971

Corgi Modern Poets / In Focus: 4 / Edited by / Jeremy Robson /
[publisher's logo: the head of a dog with a book in its mouth in white on
a black circle] / CORGI [in white] BOOKS / TRANSWORLD
PUBLISHERS LTD / A NATIONAL GENERAL COMPANY

Collation: 80 leaves; 17.7 × 11 cm.

Binding: A perfect binding glued into white card wrappers of which the
exterior is shiny; the outside of the wrapper (front and back and spine)
depict stylized silhouettes of a woman's head printed in strong reddish
orange (35), brilliant yellowish green (130) and black; across the top of
the spine lettered in white: 0 552 / 08844 / 7 / POETRY / [publisher's
logo in black and white]; lettered down the spine in white: CORGI
MODERN POETS IN FOCUS 4 Edited by Jeremy Robson CORGI
BOOKS; on the front wrapper on a rectangle printed in medium reddish
brown (43) surrounded on three sides by a white rule: [in white] CORGI
MODERN / [on a design resembling the top of a cross printed in dark
pink (6): half circle in brilliant yellowish green (130)] / [in black] Edited
by / [in brilliant yellowish green (130)] 4 / [in black] Jeremy Robson / [to
the left of the figure 4] Thomas Hardy / Vernon Scannell / Dannie Abse;
[to the right of the figure 4]: Tony Harrison / Daniel Hoffman / Stevie
Smith / [in white] POETS IN FOCUS; on the rear wrapper on a
rectangle printed in medium reddish brown surrounded on three sides
by a white rule and printed in white: CORGI MODERN / POETS IN
FOCUS 4 / [12 lines of information on the series] / Cover design by
Bush Hollyhead / (Nicolas Thirkell Assoc. Ltd.) / [in black at the center
at the base of the wrapper] UK . . . 30p / Australia . . . 95c /
New Zealand . . . 90c / South Africa . . . 75c / Canada . . . $1.25; white
wove paper; all edges trimmed.

Publication date: December 1971

Price: 30p

Number of copies: Data unavailable from publisher

Contents: 'Tony Harrison writes', pp. 112–116; 'Fonte Luminosa,' pp. 133–134, collected in FTSOE and SP.

Note: The contents also include 'The Hands', 'Thomas Campey and the Copernical System,' 'The Nuptial Torches,' 'Newcastle is Peru,' 'A Proper Caution', and 'Durham' which were previously collected.

Note: The prose statement appears here for the first time in print.

B14   THE GREEK ANTHOLOGY   1973

a. *First edition*:

The Greek Anthology / AND OTHER ANCIENT GREEK / EPIGRAMS / *A selection in modern verse translations,* / *edited with an* / *introduction by Peter Jay* / ALLEN LANE

Collation: [G.A. – 1]^4 + G.A.*^{12} + G.A. – 2*^{4} + G.A. – 2*^{12} – G.A. – 14*^{12} = 224 leaves; 19.3 × 12.9 cm.

Binding: Bound in semi-shiny, textured medium brown (58) cloth and lettered across the spine in gold: [single rule] / *The* / *Greek* / *Anthology* / [single rule] / Edited by / PETER JAY / [publisher's logo]; white wove paper; all edges trimmed; white wove endpapers; dust wrapper of white wove paper of which the exterior is shiny and printed in black, vivid orange yellow (66) and deep orange yellow (72).

Publication date: April 1973

Price: £3.50

Number of copies: Data unavailable from publisher

Contents: [1 poem by Alkaios], 231, p. 121; [7 poems by Antipater of Sidon], 239, 240, 243, 246, 248, 249, pp. 124–128; [1 anonymous poem], 311, p.160; [5 poems by Antipater of Thessalonika], 390, 392, 400, 404, 405, pp. 192–197; [1 poem by Myrinos], 505, p. 236; [1 poem by Ammianus], 589, p. 267; [2 poems by Strato], 604, p. 273 and 618, p. 277; [39 poems by Palladas], 637-375, pp. 284–294; [2 anonymous poems], 759, p. 327 and 771, p. 330.

b. *First American edition*:

The Greek Anthology / AND OTHER ANCIENT GREEK EPIGRAMS / *A selection in modern verse translations,* / *edited with an* / *introduction by Peter Jay* / NEW YORK OXFORD UNIVERSITY PRESS / 1973

Collation: Same as B14a

Binding: Bound in semi-shiny, textured medium brown (58) cloth and lettered across the spine in gold: [single rule] / *The / Greek / Anthology* / [single rule] / Edited by / PETER JAY / OXFORD; white wove paper; all edges trimmed; white wove endpapers; dust wrapper of white wove paper of which the exterior is shiny and printed in black, vivid yellow orange (66) and deep orange yellow (72).

Publication date: Data unavailable from publisher

Price: $12.50

Number of copies: Data unavailable from publisher

Contents: Same as B14a

c. *First English paperbound edition*:

The Greek Anthology / AND OTHER ANCIENT EPIGRAMS / *A selection in modern verse translations, / edited with an / introduction by Peter Jay* / [publisher's logo] / PENGUIN BOOKS

Collation: 224 leaves: 18 × 11 cm.

Binding: A perfect binding glued into white card wrappers printed in black and strong yellowish brown (74); printed on the spine: [across the top of the spine in white: publisher's logo] / [down the spine in white] THE GREEK ANTHOLOGY / [in 2 lines in white] ISBN 0 14 / 044.285 5; on the front wrapper: [in white] Penguin [publisher's logo] Classics / THE GREEK ANTHOLOGY / [in strong yellowish brown and black: a reproduction of a cup by Peithinos, depicting Peleus embracing Thetis]; on the rear wrapper in white: Penguin [publisher's logo] / Classics / THE GREEK ANTHOLOGY / EDITED BY PETER JAY / [22 lines on the text and the front cover illustration] / [at the left-hand corner] United Kingdom £2.50 / Australia $7.95 (recommended) / Canada $5.95 / [at the right hand corner] Poetry / ISBN 0 14 / 044.285 5; white wove paper; all edges trimmed.

Publication date: Data unavailable from publisher

Price: £2.50

Number of copies: Data unavailable from publisher

Contents: Same as B14a

Note: In one 1981 copy of this work on the verso of the title page is this statement: 'Published in Penguin Books 1981 / Revised edition published in Penguin Books 1981.'

B15   NEW POEMS 1972-73   1973

[decorative floral device] / NEW POEMS / 1972-73 / A P.E.N.
Anthology / of Contemporary Poetry / [decorative floral device] / *Edited
by* / DOUGLAS DUNN / HUTCHINSON OF LONDON

Collation: [1–4]^{16} + [5]^{12} + [6]^{16} = 92 leaves; 19.5 × 12.5 cm.

Binding: Bound in strong red (12) imitation cloth and lettered down the
spine in gold in two lines: NEW POEMS 1972-73 [vertical rule] A
P.E.N. ANTHOLOGY / Edited by Douglas Dunn / [across the base of
the spine: publisher's logo] / HUTCHINSON; white wove paper; all
edges trimmed; white wove endpapers; dust wrapper of strong orangish
yellow (68) wove paper printed in black and light brown (57).

Publication date: 19 November 1973

Price: £2.00

Number of copies: 2,000

Contents: 'Tanganyika 1940,' p. 80

Note: The contents also includes 'On the Spot' and 'On Not Being
Milton' which were previously collected.

B16   A DECADE & THEN SOME   1976

A DECADE & THEN SOME / contemporary literature — 1976 / [5
lines of fancy calligraphy] / [printed in thick italics on a diagonal from
left (high) to the right (low)] *intrepid* / [to the left] ed. Allen DeLoach /
[at the lower right hand corner of the page] ANTHOLOGY.

Collation: [1–16]^{12} = 192 leaves; 19 × 12.5 cm.

Binding: Glued into stiff wove paper pictorial wrappers (Cover
photograph: Allen DeLoach, 'Peter Orlovsky viewing Cubist art at
Albright-Knox Gallery, Buffalo, Spring, 1976') printed in black and
white; printed down the spine: INTREPID ANTHOLOGY ed. Allen
DeLoach [across the base of the spine] INTREPID / PRESS; the
printing on the front wrapper is the same as the title page; on the rear
wrapper: [3 columns of contributor's names]; white wove paper; all edges
trimmed.

Publication date: March 1976

Price: $5.00

Number of copies: 1,000

Contents: The School of Eloquence:
2. 'The School of Eloquence,' p. 140; 3. 'National Trust,' p. 140;
4. 'Working,' p. 141. All are collected in TSOE, C and SP.

Note: The title of the poem, 'The School of Eloquence,' was changed to
'The Rhubarbarians' after its appearance here.

Note: The contents also includes '1. On Not Being Milton' which was
previously collected.

B17   NEW POEMS 1977–78   1977

[decorative floral device] / NEW POEMS / 1977–78 / A P.E.N.
Anthology / of Contemporary Poetry / [decorative floral device] / *Edited
by* / GAVIN EWART / HUTCHINSON OF LONDON.

Collation: [A]¹⁶ + B–F¹⁶ = 96 leaves; 19.7 × 12.5 cm.

Binding: Bound in black textured cloth and lettered down the spine in
silver in two lines: NEW POEMS 1977–78 Edited by Gavin Ewart / A
P.E.N. Anthology of Contemporary Poetry / [across the base of the
spine: publisher's logo] / HUTCHINSON; white wove paper; all edges
trimmed; white wove endpapers; dust wrapper of brownish pink (33)
wove paper.

Publication date: 21 November 1977

Price: £4.95

Number of copies: 1,500

Contents: 'Guava Libre,' p. 84. Collected in FTSOE and SP.

B18   NEW POETRY 5   1979

New Poetry 5 / an anthology edited by Peter Redgrove / and Jon Silkin
/ Hutchinson of London / in association with the Arts Council / of
Great Britain and PEN.

Collation: [1–3]¹⁶ + [4]¹⁸ + [5]¹⁶ = 82 leaves; 21.5 × 14 cm.

Binding: Bound in black paper-covered boards and lettered down the
spine in gold in two lines: NEW POETRY 5 An Arts Council
Anthology / Edited by Peter Redgrove and Jon Silkin / [across the base
of the spine in gold: publisher's logo] / HUTCHINSON; white wove
paper; all edges trimmed; white wove endpapers; dust wrapper of shiny
white wove paper printed in strong yellowish green (117) and black.

Publication date: 19 November 1979

Price: £4.95

Number of copies: 1,500

Contents: 'Next Door,' pp. 76–77, collected in C and SP; 'Stately Home,' p. 78, collected in SP.

Note: The three divisions of 'Next Door' are published as numbers I, II, and IV in C and SP.

B19   NATIONAL POETRY COMPETITION 1980   1980
                           PRIZEWINNERS

The Poetry Society / in association with BBC Radio 3 / National Poetry Competition / 1980 Prizewinners / The Poetry Society

Collation: [1]^{14} = 14 leaves; 21 × 14.9 cm.

Binding: Stapled twice into white stiff semi-shiny card wrappers; on the front wrapper: [in vivid reddish orange (34)] National Poetry Competition 1980 / [in black letters on a white and light gray (264) reproduction of a scrabble board] [across the second line] PRIZE; [down the middle of the scrabble board] WINNERS [at the base of the wrapper all printed in vivid reddish orange] [to the left] *the Poetry Society / in association with / BBC Radio 3* [to the right] *Patricia Beer / JUDGES Douglas Dunn / George Macbeth*; on the white rear wrapper in black: [8 lines on the National Poetry Competition] / Price £1.00 ISBN 0 9505610 5 3; pale yellow (89) laid paper; all edges trimmed.

Publication date: 7 December 1980

Price: £1.00

Number of copies: 1,000

Note: The Poetry Society reports that the publication records for this pamphlet have been lost. However, a reference in an annual report stated that around 850 copies have been sold. 'Accordingly the print run is likely to have been 1,000 — certainly not more. There was only the one printing.'

Contents: 'Timer,' p. [7]. Collected in C and SP.

B20   FIREBIRD 3   1984

Editor: Robin Robertson / [stylized] *Firebird 3* / Writing Today / [publisher's logo] / Penguin Books.

Collation: 144 leaves; 19.8 × 12.9 cm.

Binding: A perfect binding glued into stiff white card wrappers of which
the exterior is shiny and lettered down the spine: [in vivid red (11)
stylized letters] *Firebird 3* [in two lines] ISBN 0 14 / 00.6797 3 / [across
the base of the spine: publisher's logo — a black and white penguin on
an oval printed in vivid reddish orange (34) surrounded by a black
outline]; on the front wrapper: [in vivid stylized letters] *Firebird 3* / [an
engraving of a phoenix printed in various shades of brown, black,
yellow, and orange] / to the left: publisher's logo] [to the right]
'*A fascinating collection of new writing . . . the most / intriguing Firebird
yet*' — *William Boyd*; on the rear wrapper at the top the title as it
appears on the front wrapper] / An annual anthology, *Firebird* reflects
the diversity of / imagination and the energy of writing today / [20 lines
on the series and contributors] / Cover engraving by Andrew Davidson
/ [to the left] U.K. £3.50 / AUST $9.95 / (recommended) / N.Z. $11.95
/ CAN $9.95 / [to the right] [publisher's logo] / Fiction /
ISBN 0 14 / 00.6797 3; white wove paper; all edges trimmed.

Publication date: 26 January 1984

Price: £3.50

Number of copies: 8,000

Contents: 'Facing North,' pp. [91]–92; 'Flood,' p. 93; 'The Birds of
America: Weeki Wachee,' p. 93; 'Cypress & Cedar,' pp. 94–98; 'Aqua
Mortis,' p. 98; 'The Lords of Life,' pp. 99–103. All of these poems are
collected in SP.

Note: 'The Lords of Life' appears here for the first time in print.

B21   YAPP BROTHERS [Wine Catalogue]   1984

[cover title] YAPP BROTHERS / Mere, Wiltshire. Telephone (0747)
860423 / [12 lines of a quotation in Greek after Hermippus] / Wine
Merchants.

Collation: [1]^{32} = 32 leaves; 21 × 14.9 cm.

Binding: Stapled twice into heavy yellowish white (92) card wrappers
printed in black and medium reddish orange (37); the front wrapper as
above; on the rear wrapper in black are the same 12 lines as printed on
the front wrapper; yellowish white wove paper; all edges trimmed.

Publication date: May 1984

Price: Issued free

Number of copies: 10,000

Contents; 'A Bourgeuil apostrophised as "sheer" '[first line of a 20-line sequence after Hermippus (5th century BC)], p. [ii]; 'Engrave on my wine-goblet, please' [first line of a 20-line sequence by an Imitator of Anacreon], p. 4; 'Sage and idiot, which is which' [first line of a 2-line sequence by Theognis (floruit 544–541 BC)], p. 9; 'Taste this wine! It comes from vines planted' [first line of an 8-line sequence from Theognis (floruit 544–551 BC)], p. 17; 'Pour wine in my beaker' [first line of a 4-line sequence by Diodoros Zonas (b. 125 BC)], p. 23; 'Drink when others celebrate. When you feel low' [first line of a 2-line sequence by Theognis (floruit 544–541 BC)], p. 25; 'Let's enjoy our wine, good conversation, laughter' [first line of a 2-line sequence by Theognis (floruit 544–541 BC)], p. 29; 'It's hailing. The sky's at it's blackest now.' [first line of an 8-line sequence by Alcaeus (b. 620 BC)], p. 30; 'Some god sends a restorative' [first line of a 23-line sequence by an Imitator of Anacreon], p. 35; 'A Gloss on a Glass' [first line of a 6-line sequence by Alcaeus (b. 620 BC)], p. 38; 'Wine to drown my sorrows and restart' [first line of a 2-line sequence: no author cited], p. 39; 'Hard drinking's bad, but wine' [first line of a 2-line sequence by Theognis (floruit 544–541 BC)], p. 50; 'Boy! Here! Kindly' [first line of a 10-line sequence by Anacreon (born 570 BC)], p. 51; 'One glass and no refill' [first line of a 4-line sequence after Amphis (4th century BC)]. p. 52; 'Don't waste time in brooding thought' [first line of a 4-line sequence by Alcaeus (b. 620 BC)], p. 62.

Note: The text also includes a sequence by Antipater of Sidon and Antipater of Thessalonika which were previously published.

Note: All the translations are from the Greek.

B22   LONDON REVIEWS   1985

London / Reviews / A selection from the London Review of Books 1983–1985 / edited by Nicholas Spice, with an introductory essay / by Karl Miller / Chatto & Windus • London.

Collation: $[1–14]^8 + [15]^4 = 116$ leaves; 19.7×12.5 cm.

Binding: Glued into stiff white card wrappers, shiny on the exterior, of which the rear wrapper and spine are in white and the front wrapper in pinkish gray (10); printed down the spine: [thick rule in vivid red (11)] / [open letters in vivid red (11)] LONDON REVIEWS / [thick rule in vivid red] / [in black and white publisher's logo]; on the front wrapper: [thick rule in vivid red] / LONDON / REVIEWS / [thick rule in vivid red] / [stylized LR printed in billiant blue (177), brilliant yellow (83) and strong reddish purple (237)] / [in black on an elongated oval in white surrounded by a black border] CHATTO / [printed diagonally at the right-hand corner of the wrapper in black on a white band bordered on the top and bottom by single rules in vivid red] A PAPERBACK / ORIGINAL; on black on the anthology] / ISBN 0 7011 2988 3 / £5.95 net / in UK only / [thick rule in vivid red]; white wove paper; all edges trimmed.

Publication date: October 1985

Price: £5.95

Number of copies: 3,000

Contents: 'V.', pp. [55]–67., Collected in V

B23   P.E.N. NEW POETRY I   1986

P.E.N. / New Poetry I / Edited by Robert Nye / [publisher's logo] / QUARTET BOOKS / London Melbourne New York

Collation: [1–7]¹⁶ = 112 leaves; 21.6 × 13.6 cm.

Binding: Bound in textured medium gray (265) cloth and printed down the spine in shiny deep blue (179) letters: new poetry I P.E.N. [in 2 lines] edited by / ROBERT NYE [across the base of the spine: publisher's logo]; white wove paper; all edges trimmed; white wove endpapers; dust wrapper of white wove paper, shiny on the exterior and printed in light greenish yellow (101), medium blue (182) and black.

Publication: February 1986

Price: £12.95

Number of copies: 1,480

Contents: 'Pain-killers,' pp. 62–63; 'Changing at York,' p. 63; 'Jumper,' p. 64.

B24   THE POETRY BOOK SOCIETY ANTHOLOGY 1986/87   1986

The / Poetry Book Society / Anthology 1986/87 / *Edited with an Introduction by* / JONATHAN BARKER / Hutchinson / London Melbourne Auckland Johannesburg.

Collation: [1–3]¹⁶ = 48 leaves; 19.8 × 12.8 cm.

Binding: Glued into stiff card wrappers printed in vivid pinkish purple (226), strong purplish blue (196) and vivid red (11); lettered down the spine in strong purplish blue: The Poetry Book Society Anthology

1986/87 [in black] Edited by Jonathan Barker HUTCHINSON [across the base of the spine: publisher's logo]; on the front wrapper: [in white on a strong purplish blue band] THE / [in strong purplish blue] Poetry Book Society / [in white on a strong purplish blue band] ANTHOLOGY / [in strong purplish blue] 1986/87 / [in white on a strong purplish blue band] Edited by Jonathan Barker / [on a white rectangle with diamonds formed by strong purplish blue lines and printed in vivid red] INCLUDING POEMS / UNPUBLISHED IN / BOOK FORM BY / Philip Larkin / Graham Greene / AND MANY / OTHERS; [on the rear wrapper in strong purplish blue: 10 lines on the anthology] / [in vivid red, in 14 lines, list of contributors in double columns] / [in black, 6 lines on the editor of the anthology] / [in black to the left] £4.95 net / IN UK ONLY / ISBN: 0 09 165961 2 / Century Hutchinson Ltd [to the right in black and white: bar code label]; white wove paper; all edges trimmed.

Publication date: Data unavailable from publisher

Price: £4.95

Number of copies: Data unavailable from publisher

Contents: 'The Morning After' (I and II), pp. 47–48; 'The Effort,' p. 48.

B25   CONTEMPORARY WRITERS   1987

[cover title] [in brilliant blue (177) letters] CONTEMPORARY WRITERS / [black and white photograph of Tony Harrison] / [holograph printed signature of Tony Harrison in black] / HEREDITY / *How you became a poet's a mystery! / Wherever did you get your talent from? / I say: I had two uncles, Joe and Harry — / one was a stammerer, the other dumb.* / TONY HARRISON

Collation: Leaflet; single card printed on both sides, folded three times to make eight unnumbered panels; 21 × 40 cm. (size of a fully opened sheet).

Binding: White card, printed in very pale blue (184) with white spotting throughout; all edges trimmed.

Publication: 1987. Details unavailable from publisher. Publication was most likely between August and December 1987. See 'Contents' below.

Price: Free

Number of copies: 7,000

Contents: Prose statement (32 lines). First line: 'Poetry is all I write, whether for book, or readings, or for . . .', panel [6]. The statement is dated August 1987.

Note: The leaflet was published by Book Trust in conjunction with the British Council.

C

CONTRIBUTIONS TO PERIODICALS
AND NEWSPAPERS BY TONY HARRISON

In this section an attempt has been made to include all of Tony Harrison's contributions, i.e. poems, prose, letters to periodicals or newspapers when they appeared there prior to publication in a book. If the poem is untitled, the first line is used for identification. The items are listed chronologically and then numerically by page number if several poems appear in one issue of a periodical or newspaper. Volume and issue numbers are given in the style of the newspaper or periodical cited. In some cases, e.g. *The Observer*, an individual issue is indicated only by the date. The place of publication of a periodical or newspaper has been listed only in the index. Titles of reviews and letters are given although in most cases the title has been assigned by the editor. Following each entry is a note that indicates where the item was published in a book or books. The term 'Uncollected' indicates that I have not been able to locate a book in which the item was reprinted. Abbreviations for Tony Harrison's books are those previously listed. B, followed by a number is a cross reference to the B section of this bibliography.

1957

C1   WHEN THE BOUGH BREAKS (Poem)
        Poetry and Audience, Vol. 4, No. 15 (22 Feb. 1957), 5

        Uncollected

C2   PLATO MIGHT HAVE SAID (Poem)
        Poetry and Audience, Vol. 4, No. 22 (24 May 1957), 4–5

        Uncollected

C3   A MAN TORMENTED BY A FOOT (Poem)
        Poetry and Audience, Vol. 4, No. 24 (7 June 1957), 2

        Uncollected

C4   SUICIDE NOTE (Poem)
        Poetry and Audience, Vol. 4, No. 24 (7 June 1957), 7

        Uncollected

C5   SPRING OUTINGS (Poem)
        Poetry and Audience, Vol. 4, No. 25 (14 June 1957), 3

        B1

C6   FROM THE CLIFFSIDE (Poem)
        Poetry and Audience, Vol. 5, No. 1 (11 October 1957), 7

        Note: Above and below the printed date is the date, 18 October
        1957, stamped in black.

        Uncollected

C7   FROM THE SUBLIME (Poem)
        Poetry and Audience, Vol. 5, No. 1 (11 October 1957), 8

        Note: Above and below the printed date is the date, 18 October
        1957, stamped in black.

        Uncollected

C8   MY MIGRATORY BIRD AND THE DIVINE (Poem)
        Poetry and Audience, Vol. 5, No. 3 (1 November 1957), 3

        E and B1, 2 and 3

C9   'WE'VE MET HIS SORT BEFORE' (Poem)
       Poetry and Audience, Vol. 5, No. 3 (1 November 1957), 3
       Uncollected

C10   TO THE EDITOR ON HIS ERRATA (Poem)
       Poetry and Audience, Vol. 5, No. 4 (8 November 1957), 2
       Uncollected

C11   NO. 63 (Poem)
       Poetry and Audience, Vol. 5, No. 6 (22 November 1957), 1
       Note: Poem by Sappho translated by Harrison
       Uncollected

C12   CROCHET 1 (Poem)
       Poetry and Audience, Vol. 5, No. 6 (22 November 1957), 5
       Uncollected

C13   AN APPEAL TO THE SYBIL ('ipsa canas oro.') (Poem)
       Poetry and Audience, Vol. 5, No. 6 (22 November 1957), 6
       B1

C14   NO. 6 (Poem)
       Poetry and Audience, Vol. 5, No. 7 (29 November 1957), [1]
       Note: Poem by Sappho translated by Harrison
       Uncollected

C15   NO. 112 (Poem)
       Poetry and Audience, Vol. 5, No. 8 (6 December 1957), [1]
       Note: Poem by Sappho translated by Harrison
       Uncollected

C16   REVIEW. BLOOD WEDDING BY LORCA (Prose)
       Poetry and Audience. Vol. 5, No. 8 (6 December 1957), 7–8
       Note: The article is signed 'John Hearsum and Tony Harrison.'
       Uncollected

1958

C17   ON A ROSARY TO A CATHOLIC POET (Poem)
Poetry and Audience, Vol. 5, No. 11 (7 February 1958), 6

B1

C18   CAVE (Poem)
Poetry and Audience, Vol. 5, No. 14 (28 February 1958), 5

Uncollected

C19   EPITHALAMIUM (Poem)
Poetry and Audience, Vol. 5, No. 15 (7 March 1958), 4

B1, 3

C20   LADIES AND GENTLEMAN A LITTLE MEDITATION
(Poem)
Poetry and Audience, Vol. 5, No. 20 (23 May 1958), 3

Uncollected

C21   THE LIGHT OF HER LIFE (For a lady taken with Plato)
(Poem)
Poetry and Audience, Vol. 6, No. 2 (17 October 1958), 2

Uncollected

C22   THE NEXT WORD BY THOMAS BLACKBURN (Prose)
Poetry and Audience, Vol. 6, No. 10 (12 December 1958), 3–6

Uncollected

1959

C23   THE HYBRID GROWTH (Poem)
Poetry and Audience, Vol. 6, No. 12 (30 January 1959), [1]

E and B3

C24   G.W. IRELAND: HIS POETRY (Prose)
Poetry and Audience, Vol. 6, No. 13 (6 February 1959), 1–3

Uncollected

C25   MAN AGAINST THE VIRUS (Poem)
Poetry and Audience, Vol. 6, No. 24 (29 May 1959), 4

B2

C26   EDITORIAL (Prose)
Poetry and Audience, Vol. 7, No. 1 (1959), 1–2

Unsigned (Harrison was Editor of *Poetry and Audience*)

Uncollected

C27   THE MAN ALONE (Poem)
Poetry and Audience, Vol. 7, No. 4 (1959), 4

Uncollected

C28   NARCISSUS COMPLEX (Poem)
Poetry and Audience, Vol. 7, No. 6 (20 November 1959), 1

Uncollected

C29   KING KINUNDERSKIN (Poem)
Poetry and Audience, Vol. 7, No. 9 (11 December 1959), 7

Uncollected

1960

C30   EDITORIAL (Prose)
Poetry and Audience, Vol. 7, No. 13 (5 February 1960), 4–6

Unsigned (Harrison was Editor of *Poetry and Audience*)

Uncollected

C31   THE PROMISED LAND (Poem)
Poetry and Audience, Vol. 7, No. 14 (1960), 1–2

E

C32   THE LAST TESTAMENT OF T.W. HARRISON (Poem)
Poetry and Audience, Vol. 7, No. 22 (20 May 1960), 1–2

Uncollected

C33   GHOSTS: SOME WORDS BEFORE BREAKFAST (Poem)
Poetry and Audience, Vol. 7, No. 22 (20 May 1960), 6–7

TL, SP and B3

C34   HYMN FOR A POSTEARD (Poem)
Poetry and Audience, Vol. 8, No. 4 (28 October 1960), 7

Uncollected

C35   EMANUEL LITVINOFF. THE LOST EUROPEANS
(Prose)
Stand, Vol. 4, No. 4 [1960–1961], 45–47

     Uncollected

C36   SOME MEN ARE BROTHERS. D.J. ENRIGHT (Prose)
Stand, Vol. 4, No. 4 [1960-1961], 49-51

     Uncollected

     1961

C37   THE PIT OF PERCEPTION (Poem)
Stand, Vol. 5, No. 1 (1961), 40

     E

C38   THE FLAT DWELLER'S REVOLT (Poem)
Poetry and Audience, Vol. 8, No. 19 (10 March 1961), 6–7

     E

C39   THE HANDS (Poem)
Poetry and Audience, Vol. 9, No. 10 (8 December 1961), 1

     E and B13

C40   THE TOOTHACHE (Prose)
Stand, Vol. 5, No. 2 (1961), 41–45

     Uncollected

C41   IAIN CRICHTON SMITH — THISTLES AND ROSES
(Prose)
Stand, Vol. 5, No. 2 (1961), 58-60

     Uncollected

     1967

C42   THE CURTAIN CATULLUS (Poem)
London Magazine, New Series, Vol. 7, No. 4 (July 1967),
[63]–64

     TL, SP

C43   THE WHITE QUEEN (Poem)
       London Magazine, New Series, Vol. 7, No. 4 (July 1967), 64–66

       Note: Part I only

       B5, TL, SP

C44   THOMAS CAMPEY AND THE COPERNICAN SYSTEM
       (Poem)
       London Magazine, New Series, Vol. 7, No. 4 (July 1967), 66–7

       TL, SP

C45   ENGLISH VIRGIL: THE AENEID IN THE XVIII
       CENTURY (Prose)
       Philologica Pragensia, X, (1967), 1–11, 80–91.

       Uncollected

       1968

C46   GINGER'S FRIDAY (Poem)
       Phoenix 3, Spring 1968, 31–32.

       TL, SP

C47   THE HEART OF DARKNESS (Poem)
       Phoenix 3, Spring 1968, 32–34

       TL, SP

C48   BEDBUG (Poem)
       The New Statesman, Vol. 75, No. 1933 (29 March 1968), 419

       TL, SP

C49   PROPER CAUTION (Poem)
       The New Statesman, Vol. 75, No. 1943 (7 June 1968), 767

       TL

C50   THE THIRD SONG OF THE P.W.D. MAN (Poem)
       The Honest Ulsterman, No. 2 (June 1968), 35–36

       Uncollected

C51   EMIGRE (Poem)
       The Honest Ulsterman, No. 2 (June 1968), 36–37.

       Uncollected

C52 SCHWIEGERMUTTERLIEDER (Poem)
The Honest Ulsterman, No. 2 (June 1968), 37–38.

TL, SP

C53 THE SONGS OF THE P.W.D. MAN (Poem)
London Magazine, New Series, Vol. 8, No. 3 (June 1968),
[83]–85

TL, SP

C54 REVIVAL SONG (Poem)
The Honest Ulsterman, No. 5 (September 1968), 6

Uncollected

C55 THE CHOPIN EXPRESS (Poem)
The Honest Ulsterman, No. 5 (September 1968), 7–8

TL

C56 NEWCASTLE IS PERU (Poem)
London Magazine, New Series, Vol. 8, No. 7 (October 1968),
[36]–41

NIP, TL, SP

C57 THE NUPTIAL TORCHES (Poem)
Stand, Vol. 9, No. 3 (1968), 51–52

TL, SP

C58 THE WHITE QUEEN (Poem)
The Lesser Known Shagg, [n.d.: 1968?] [21–23]

Note: Part I and II

TL, SP

1969

C59 THE POCKET WARS OF PEANUTS JOE (Poem)
The Honest Ulsterman, No. 13 (May 1969), 24–25

TL, SP

C60 THE EXCURSION (Poem)
London Magazine, New Series, Vol. 9, No. 7 (October 1969),
9–11

TL

C61   AUGUST GRAFITTI (Prose)
        Stand, Vol. 10, No. 2 (1969), 21

        (Collected and translated by Vera Blackwell, Tony Harrison, John Hearsum and Jiri Jirasek)

        Uncollected

        1970

C62   DOODLEBUGS (Poem)
        The Honest Ulsterman, No. 21 (Jan,/Feb. 1970), 18

        SP

C63   MORE ZEG-ZEG POSTCARDS (Poems)
        London Magazine, New Series, Vol. 9, No. 11 (February 1970), [22]–25.

        Note: Poems are numbered I through XIV; I – V, VII and XIII are collected in TL and I – V are collected in SP

C64   NORTHERN ARTS ASSOCIATION (Prose)
        The Times Literary Supplement, No. 3556 (23 April 1970), 454

        Uncollected

C65   SHANGO THE SHAKY FAIRY (Prose)
        London Magazine, New Series, Vol. 10, No. 1, (April 1970), [5]–27.

        Uncollected

C66   NORTHERN ARTS ASSOCIATION (Prose)
        The Times Literary Supplement, No. 3559 (14 May 1970), 539.

        Uncollected

C67   THE WHITE QUEEN (Poem)
        London Magazine, New Series, Vol. 10, No. 3 (June 1970), [5]–6. [Section of poem with title, "The Railroad Heroids"]

        TL, SP

C68   BRAZIL (Poem)
        The Times Literary Supplement, No. 3567 (9 July 1970), 752.

        FTSOE, SP

C69   ISLA DE LA JUVENTUD (Poem)
         The Times Literary Supplement, No. 3567 (9 July 1970), 752.

         FTSOE, SP

C70   THE DEATH OF THE PWD MAN (Poem)
         The Honest Ulsterman, No. 24 (July/August 1970), 7–9.

         TL, SP

C71   NEW WORLDS FOR OLD (Prose)
         London Magazine, New Series, Vol. 10, No. 5 (September
         1970), 81–85

         Reviews of: Neruda, Pablo. *Selected Poems*. Jonathan Cape;
         Anthology of Mexican Poetry. Calder & Boyars; Ahern, Maureen
         and David Tipton, Eds. *Peru, the New Poetry*. London
         Magazine Editions; Cisneros, Antonio. *The Spider Hangs Too
         Far From the Ground*. Cap Goliaro.

         Uncollected

C72   POEMS FROM THE GREEK ANTHOLOGY (Poems)
         The Honest Ulsterman, No. 25 (September/October 1970), 31.

         B14

C73   BEATING THE RETREAT (Prose)
         London Magazine, New Series, Vol. 10, No. 8 (November
         1970), 91–96.

         Reviews of: Dyment, Clifford. *Collected Poems*. J.M. Dent;
         Kavanagh, P.J. *About Time*. Chatto & Windus: The Hogarth
         Press; MacBeth, George. *The Burning Cone*. Macmillan;
         MacDiarmid, Hugh. *More Collected Poems*. MacGibbon & Kee.
         Davie, Donald. *Six Epistles to Eva Hesse*. London Magazine
         Editions.

         Uncollected

         1971

C74   CROW MAGNON (Prose)
         London Magazine, New Series, Vol. 10, No. 10 (January 1971),
         86–88.

         Review of: Hughes, Ted. *Crow*. Faber & Faber

         Uncollected

C75   ALL OUT (Prose)
London Magazine, New Series, Vol. 10, No. 12 (March 1971),
87–91.

Review of: Bold, Alan, Ed. *The Penguin Book of Socialist Verse*.
Penguin.

Uncollected

C76   WONDERLAND (Prose)
London Magazine, New Series, Vol. 11, No. 1 (April/May
1971), 163–168.

Review of: Bishop, Elizabeth. *The Complete Poems*. Chatto &
Windus; Levertov, Denise. *Relearning the Alphabet*. Jonathan
Cape; Niedecker, Lorine. *Collected Poems 1968*. Fulcrum Press;
Dugan, Alan. *Collected Poems*. Faber & Faber; Hoffman, Daniel.
Broken Laws. Oxford Univ. Press; Merrill, James. *The Fire
Screen*. Chatto & Windus. The Hogarth Press; Rich, Adrienne.
Snapshots of a Daughter-in-Law. Chatto & Windus. The
Hogarth Press.

Uncollected

C77   TANGANYIKA 1940 (Poem)
The New Statesman, Vol. 82, No. 2117 (15 October 1971), 511

B15

C78   ADRIAN HENRI (Letter-Poem)
The Times Literary Supplement, No. 3636 (5 November 1971),
1392.

Uncollected

C79   ANTIPATER OF SIDON (Poem)
Stand, Vol. 12, No. 4 (1971), 9

B14

C80   FONTE LUMINOSA (Poem)
Stand, Vol. 12, No. 5 (1971), 5

FTSOE, SP

1972

C81   ON NOT BEING MILTON (Poem)

The Times Literary Supplement, No. 3673 (21 July 1972), 839

FTSOE, C, SP

C82 BLACK AND WHITE AND RED ALL OVER: THE
FICTION OF EMPIRE (Prose)
London Magazine, New Series, Vol. 12, No. 3 (August/
September 1972), 90–103

Uncollected

1973

C83 STUDY (Poem)
London Magazine, New Series, Vol. 12, No. 5 (December
1972/January 1973), [70]

FTSOE, C, SP

C84 FANTASIA–ASIA (Prose)
London Magazine, New Series, Vol. 12, No. 5 (December
1972/January 1973), 135–140.

Review of: Naipaul, V.S. *The Overcrowded Barracoon*, Andre
Deutsch; Theroux, Paul. *V.S. Naipaul: an Introduction to his
work*. Andre Deutsch

Uncollected

C85 ME TARZAN (Poem)
London Magazine, New Series, Vol. 12, No. 5 (December
1972/January 1973), [70]–71

FTSOE, C, SP

C86 WORDLISTS (Poem)
London Magazine, New Series, Vol. 12, No. 5 (December 1972/
January 1973), 71. Part I only

FTSOE, C, SP

C87 SPEAKING FOR THE INARTICULATE (Prose)
Index, Vol. 2, No. 4, (Winter 1973), 105–107.

Review of: Soyinka, Wole. *The Man Died*. Rex Collings.

Uncollected

C88   MOLIERE NATIONALIZED (Prose)
       Gambit, International Theatre Review, Vol.6, No.23, (1973),
       67–82.

       A6d

C89   NATIONAL TRUST (Poem)
       Stand, Vol.14, No.2 (1973), 4

       FTSOE, C, SP

C90   WORKING (Poem)
       Stand, Vol.14, No.4 (1973), 65

       FTSOE, C, SP

       1974

C91   t'ARK (Poem)
       The Times Literary Supplement, No.3770 (7 June 1974), 604.

       FTSOE, C, SP

C92   FROM 'THE SCHOOL OF ELOQUENCE' (Poems)
       Planet, Nos.24/25 (August 1974), 18–20.

       On Not Being Milton, 18
       The School of Eloquence, 19
       Them and Us, 20

       FTSOE, C, SP

       1975

C93   AFTER RUFINUS (Poem)
       The Honest Ulsterman, Nos.46/47 (November 1974-February
       1975), 7

       FTSOE

C94   WORKSHEETS FROM NEWCASTLE IS PERU (Poem)
       Phoenix 13 (Spring 1975), Final Issue, 52–54.

       Uncollected

C95   FROM THE GREEK OF PALLADAS (Poem)
       Phoenix 13 (Spring 1975), Final Issue, 85,

       PP, SP

       1976

C96   HEREDITY (Poem)
       The New Statesman, Vol. 92, No. 2385 (3 December 1976),
       806.

       FTSOE

       1977

C97   SOCIAL MOBILITY (Poem)
       Stand, Vol. 18, No. 2 (1977), 16

       SP

C98   CREMATION (Poem)
       Stand, Vol. 18, No. 2, (1977), 16.

       FTSOE, C, SP

C99   THE BALLAD OF BABELABOUR (Poem)
       Stand, Vol. 18, No. 2 (1977), 17

       FTSOE, SP

       1978

C100   GUAVA LIBRE (Poem)
       London Magazine, New Series, Vol. 17, No. 17 (January 1978),
       41

       FTSOE, SP

C101   CLASSICS SOCIETY (Poem)
       Poetry Review, Vol. 68, No. 2 (June 1978), 16.

       FTSOE, C, SP

C102   THE EARTHEN LOT (Poem)
       Poetry Review, Vol. 68, No. 2 (June 1978), 16–17.

       FTSOE, C, SP

C103   PRAGUE SPRING (Poem)
        Poetry Review, Vol. 68, No. 2 (June 1978), 17.
        FTSOE, SP

C104   THE PEOPLE'S PALACE (Poem)
        Poetry Review, Vol. 68, No. 2 (June 1978), 18
        FTSOE, SP

C105   DANSE MACABRE. A BALLAD OF BEVERLY HILLS
        (Poem)
        Poetry Review, Vol. 68, No. 2 (June 1978), 18–20.
        FTSOE, SP ('Flying down to Rio': A Ballad of Beverly Hills.)

C106   SUSPENSIONS (Poem)
        Poetry Review, Vol. 68, No. 2 (June 1978), 20–21.
        Uncollected

C107   WORDLISTS (Poem)
        Stand, Vol. 19, No. 2 (1978), 64.
        FTSOE, C, SP Parts I & II
        Note: Section II has title: In Memoriam F.H. 1906–1976

C108   RHUBARBARIANS (Poem)
        Stand, Vol. 19, No. 2, (1978), 65.
        FTSOE, C, SP

C109   BOOK ENDS (Poem)
        Stand, Vol. 19, No. 2 (1978), 66
        FTSOE, C, SP

C110   A CLOSE ONE (Poem)
        Stand, Vol. 19, No. 2 (1978), 66
        FTSOE, C, SP

        1979

C111   NEXT DOOR (Poem)
        Stand, Vol. 20, No. 2 (1979), 2–3
        C, SP
        B18

C112   A QUESTION OF SENTENCES (Poem)
Stand, Vol. 20, No. 2 (1979), 3

Uncollected

C113   STATELY HOME (Poem)
Stand, Vol. 20, No. 2 (1979), 4.

SP

B18

C114   THE PROGRESS OF POESY (Poem)
Iron, No. 28 (April-June 1979), 20.

Uncollcted

C115   WHEN THE SAINTS . . . (Poem)
Iron, No. 28 (April-June 1979), 20.

C, SP (under title DICHTUNG UND WAHRHEIT)

C116   DIVISIONS (Poem)
Iron, No. 28 (April-June 1979), 21.

C, SP

Note: Poem number 'I' only

1980

C117   MALVERN MEMORIALS: I. LOVING MEMORY
The Times Literary Supplement, No. 4015 (7 March 1980),
260

C, SP

C118   MALVERN MEMORIALS: II. LOOKING UP (Poem)
The Times Literary Supplement, No. 4015 (7 March 1980),
260

C, SP

C119   CONTINUOUS (Poem)
The Times Literary Supplement, No. 4054 (12 December 1980),
1410

C, SP

C120   ILLUMINATIONS (Poem)
        The Times Literary Supplement, No.4054 (12 December 1980),
        1410

        C, SP

C121   TURNS (Poem)
        The Times Literary Supplement, No.4054 (12 December 1980),
        1410

        C, SP

C122   COLLECT (Poem)
        The Times Literary Supplement, No.4054 (12 December 1980),
        1410

        C, SP

C123   CLEARING (Poem)
        The Times Literary Supplement, No.4054 (12 December 1980),
        1410

        C, SP

C124   LINES TO MY GRANDFATHERS (Poem)
        Stand, Vol.21, No.3 (1980), 4

        C, SP

        1981

C125   GREY MATTER (Poem)
        The Times Literary Supplement, No.4087 (31 July 1981), 879

        SP

C126   AN OLD SCORE (Poem)
        The Times Literary Supplement, No.4090 (21 August 1981),
        947

        SP

C127   A GOOD READ (Poem)
        The Times Literary Supplement, No.4091 (28 August 1981),
        986.

        SP

C128 SCENTSONG (Poem)
The Times Literary Supplement, No.4097 (9 October 1981),
1166.

Uncollected

C129 STILL (Poem)
The Times Literary Supplement, No.4102 (13 November 1981),
1330.

SP

C130 GIVING THANKS (Poem)
The Times Literary Supplement, No.4105 (4 December 1981),
1425.

SP

C131 ORESTEIA GLOSS-SONGS (Poem)
Quarto, No.24 (24 December 1981), 6.

Uncollected

C132 ART AND EXTINCTION (Poem)
PN Review 22, Vol.8, No.2 (1981), 25–26.

C, SP

C133 SKYWRITING (Poem)
PN Review 23, Vol.8, No.3 (1981), 17–18.

SP

C134 DARK TIMES (Poem)
PN Review 23, Vol.8, No.3 (1981), 18.

SP

1982

C135 REMAINS (Poem)
Aquarius, No.13/14 (1981/1982), 117.

SP

C136 THE FALL OF THE BOLD SLASHER (Poem)
PN Review 27, Vol.7, No.1 (1982), 38.

Uncollected

C137   THE CALL OF NATURE (Poem)
        The New Statesman, Vol. 103, No. 2652 (15 January 1982),
        17.

        SP

C138   AQUA MORTIS (Poem)
        Encounter, LVIII, No. 5 (May 1982), [40].

        SP

C139   THE QUEEN'S ENGLISH (Poem)
        Encounter, LVIII, No. 5 (May 1982), [40]

        SP

C140   CONFESSIONAL POETRY (Poem)
        Encounter, LVIII, No. 5 (May 1982), [41]

        SP

C141   FLOOD (Poem)
        Encounter, LVIII, No. 5 (May 1982), [41]

        SP

C142   A PIECE OF CAKE (Poem)
        Quarto, No. 28 (May 1982), 7.

        SP

        1983

C143   THE BIRDS OF AMERICA: WEEKI WACHEE (Poem)
        051 Art/Poetry, No. 3 (1982–1983), [4]

        C, SP

C144   LEAVINGS (Poem)
        Encounter, LX, No. 2 (February 1983), 86.

        Uncollected

C145   FACING NORTH (Poem)
        The Times Literary Supplement, No. 4174 (11 March 1983),
        237.

        SP

C146   ISOLATION (Poem)
        The Observer, 10 April 1983, 31.

        SP

C147   CYPRESS & CEDAR (Poem)
        The Times Literary Supplement, No.4188 (8 July 1983), 724.

        SP

C148   THE RED LIGHTS OF PLENTY (Poem)
        The Times Literary Supplement, No.4188 (8 July 1983), 724.

        SP

C149   LOSING TOUCH (Poem)
        London Magazine, New Series, Vol.23, Nos.5 & 6 (August/
        September 1983), 64.

        Uncollected

        1984

C150   PAIN-KILLERS (Poem)
        The Observer, 12 February 1984, 53.

        B23

C151   RUBBISH (Poem)
        The New Statesman, Vol.107, No.2763 (2 March 1984), 26.

        Uncollected

C152   TESTING THE REALITY (Poem)
        The Times Literary Supplement, No. 4230 (27 April 1984), 456.

        Uncollected

C153   THE MORNING AFTER (Poem)
        The Times Literary Supplement, No. 4232 (11 May 1984), 513.

        B24

C154   JUMPER (Poem)
        Critical Quarterly, Vol. 26, Nos. 1 & 2 (Spring & Summer
        1984), 155.

        B23

C155   CHANGING AT YORK (Poem)
Critical Quarterly, Vol. 26, Nos. 1 & 2 (Spring & Summer 1984), 155.

B23

C156   A 'SCANTY PLOT OF GROUND' (Poem)
Critical Quarterly, Vol. 26, Nos. 1 & 2 (Spring & Summer 1984), 156.

Uncollected

C157   BREAKING THE CHAIN (Poem)
The Observer, 23 September 1984, 22.

Uncollected

C158   BYE-BYES (Poem)
Poetry Review, Vol. 74, No. 3 (September 1984), 36.

Uncollected

C159   THE FIRE-GAP (Poem)
The Times Literary Supplement, No. 4253 (5 October 1984), 1141–1142.

TFG

1985

C160   V [Versus] (Poem)
The London Review of Books, Vol. 7, No. 1 (24 January 1985), 12–13

V

1986

C161   FOLLOWING PINE (Poem)
London Review of Books, Vol. 8, No. 2 (6 February 1986), 5

Uncollected

C162   THE HEARTLESS ART (In Memoriam S.T., died 4th April, 1985) (Poem)

The Times Literary Supplement, No. 4334 (25 April 1985), 450.

Uncollected

C163   THE ACT (Poem)
Critical Quarterly, Vol. 28, Nos. 1–2 (Spring, Summer 1986),
32–34.

Uncollected

C164   PROLOGUE (Poem)
Critical Quarterly, Vol. 28, No. 3 (Autumn 1986), 69–70.

Uncollected

C165   Y (Poem)
Verse, Issue 6 (1986), 3–4.

Uncollected

C166   OLD SOLDIERS (Poem)
The Observer, 16 November 1986, 27.

A25

1987

C167   ANNO 32 (Poems)
The Observer, 2 August 1987, 21.

Note: The poems are 'The Figure' and 'Black & White.'

A25

C168   ANNO 42 (Poems)
Poetry Review, Vol. 77, No. 3 (Autumn 1987), 4–6.

Contains: 1. The Figure; 2. Black & White; 3. Snap; 4. First Aid
in English; 5. The Birds of Japan; 6. The Poetry Lesson

A25

ADDENDUM

C169   THE WHITE QUEEN'S ZAZZAU MSS (Poems)
London Magazine, New Series, Vol. 9, No. 2 (May 1969),
[27]–30.
Includes 'From the Zeg-Zeg Postcards' and 'Water Babies'.

TL, SP

D
MISCELLANY

This section lists interviews, radio and television appearances, and a translation. There are also listings of poems which appear subsequent to either first periodical or first book appearances. In many instances, for example in television appearances, details were not available from the producers.

INTERVIEWS

D1   Gardner, Raymond. 'Scanning a one man map of the world,'
        The Guardian, 14 June 1971, p. 8.

D2   Stringer, Robin. 'The Yorkshire lad,' *Daily Telegraph*, 16 April
        1977, p. 16.

D3   Burton, Rosemary. 'Tony Harrison,' *Quarto*, No. 28 (May
        1982), pp. 6–7.

D4   Lennon, Peter. 'Taking people to poetry,' *The Times*,
        21 December 1984, p. 14.

D5   'The metre reader,' *The Guardian*, 18 January 1985, p. 13.

RADIO AND TELEVISION APPEARANCES

D6   Arts Magazine, BBC Home Service (Acknowledged in
        Earthworks; details unavailable from BBC)

D7   New Poetry, BBC Third Programme (Acknowledged in
        Earthworks; details unavailable from BBC)

D8   Northern Poetry, BBC Home Service (Acknowledged in
        Earthworks; details unavailable from BBC)

D9   Today Poetry, BBC Radio 4, 14 August 1968, 7:15 A.M.
        (details unavailable from BBC)

D10   Poetry Now, BBC Third Programme, 15 December 1968, 9:30
        P.M. (Acknowledged in *The Loiners*; details unavailable from
        BBC)

D11   A Word In Edgeways, BBC Radio 4, 29 March 1975, 10:15
        P.M. (details unavailable from BBC)

D12   BBC Radio 3 (Acknowledged in *From The School of Eloquence*;
        details unavailable from BBC)

D13   Poetry 80, BBC Radio 3, June 24, 1980, 19:00 (details
        unavailable from the BBC)

D14   Loving Memory, BBC 2 (television). Four television
       programmes on the subject of death, written and presented by
       Tony Harrison. 'Letters in the Rock' (16 July 1987); 'Mimmo
       Perella non e plu' (23 July 1987); 'The Muffled Bells' (30 July
       1987); 'Cheating the Void' (6 August 1987).

D15   V, Channel 4 Television, 4 November 1987, 11–11:40 P.M.
       Written and presented by Tony Harrison. Printed versions of
       this poem were published previously.

TRANSLATION

D16   Sommer, Piotr, Ed. *Antologia Nowej poezji brytyjskiej*.
       Warszawa: Czytelnik, 1983.

       Z cyklu: Szkola elokwencji (The School of Eloquence).
       Arka (t'Ark), p. 116
       Podporki do ksiazek (Book Ends), pp. 116–117
       Gabinet (Study), pp. 118–119
       Praca (Working), p. 119
       Zajecia z historii (History Classes), p. 120
       Durham, pp. 120–123
       Z cyklu: Zdania (Sentences)
       I. Brazylia (Brazil), pp. 123–124
       II. Fonte Luminosa, pp. 124–125
       III. Isla de la Juventud, p. 126
       IV. W miejscu (On the Spot), pp. 127–128
       Z cyklu: Sonety Zza Kurtyny (Curtain Sonnets)
       I. Guava Libre, p. 128
       II. Niewidzialne skrzydla (The Viewless Wings), p. 129
       III. Letni ogrod (Summer Garden), pp. 129–130
       Pluskwa (The Bedbug), p. 130
       Ballada o wykastrowanym rekinie (Ballad of the Geldshark),
       pp. 130–131
       Rece (The Hands), pp. 131–132

*BOOK APPEARANCES SUBSEQUENT TO FIRST BOOK
APPEARANCE*

D17   Wedgwood, C.V., Ed. *New Poems 1965. A P.E.N. Anthology of
       Contemporary Poetry*. London: Hutchinson, 1966.

       'The Hands,' p. 81.

D18   Brownjohn, Alan, Seamus Heaney, Jon Stallworthy, Eds.
       *New Poems 1970-71. A P.E.N. Anthology of Contemporary
       Poetry*. London: Hutchinson, 1971.

       'The Nuptial Torches,' pp. 44–46.

D19   Robson, Jeremy, Ed. *Poetry Dimension 1*. London: Robson
       Books, [1973].

       'Fonte Luminosa,' pp. 117–118.

D20   Silkin, Jon, Ed. *Poetry of the Committed Individual. A Stand
       Anthology of Poetry*. Harmondsworth: Penguin Books in
       association with Victor Gollanz, 1973.

       'The Nuptial Torches,' pp. 105–107.

D21   Abse, Dannie, Ed. *Poetry Dimension 2*. London: Robson
       Books, [1974].

       'Allotments,' pp. 197–198.

D22   Heath-Stubbs, John and Davis Wright, Eds. *The Faber Book of
       Twentieth-Century Verse*. London: Faber and Faber, 1975, 3rd
       ed.

       'The Hands,' p. 139.

D23   Hanson, Neil. Ed. *Presences of Nature. Words and Images of the
       Lake District*. Carlisle: Carlisle Museum & Art Gallery, 1982.

       'Lines to my Grandfathers,' p. 114.

D24   Schmidt, Michael, *Some Contemporary Poets of Great Britain
       and Ireland. An Anthology*. Manchester: Carcanet Press, 1983.

       'Thomas Campey and the Copernican System,' pp. 15–16.
       'The Nuptial Torches,' pp. 16–17.
       'On Not Being Milton,' p. 18.
       'Classics Society,' pp. 18–19.
       'National Trust,' p. 19.
       'Book Ends,' pp. 19–20.
       'Continuous,' p. 20
       'Timer,' p. 21.
       'Art & Extinction,' pp. 21–26.
       'A Kumquat for John Keats,' pp. 26–29.

       Note: Also issued as *PN Review 36* (1983)

D25   Lucie-Smith, Edward. *British Poetry Since 1945*.
        Harmondsworth: Penguin Books, 1985.

        'Voortrekker,' p. 241.
        'Study,' pp. 241–242.
        'Long Distance II,' p. 242.
        'Clearing I,' p. 243.

D26   Paulin, Tom, Ed. *The Faber Book of Political Verse*. London,
        Boston: Faber & Faber, 1986.

        'On Not Being Milton,' p. 456.

D27   Crossley-Holland, Kevin, Ed. *The Oxford Book of Travel Verse*.
        Oxford, New York: Oxford University Press, 1986.

        'Prague Spring,' p. 221.
        'From Sentences (Brazil),' pp. 361–362.

PERIODICAL APPEARANCES SUBSEQUENT TO FIRST PERIODICAL APPEARANCE

D28   *Translantic Review*, Winter 1959–60.

        'Epithalamium,' pp. 70–71.
        'The Light of Her Life,' pp. 71–72.
        'The Hybrid Growth,' pp. 72–73.

D29   *Stand*, Vol. 4, No. 1 (1960).

        'My Migratory Bird and the Divine,' p. 28.

D30   *Stand*, Vol. 5, No. 1 (1961).

        'The Flat Dweller's Revolt,' p. 41.

D31   *Phoenix*, Nos. 6 and 7 (Summer 1970).

        'Ghosts: Some Words Before Breakfast,' pp. 33–37.

D32   *Antaeus*, No. 12 (Winter 1973).

        'Allotments,' pp. 54–55.

D33   *Encounter*, LIX, No. 2 (August 1982).

        'Remains,' p. 61.

D34   *The Agni Review*, No. 18 (1983).

'On Not Being Milton,' p. 18.
'Study,' p. 19.
'National Trust,' p. 20.
'Aqua Mortis,' p. 21.
'The Call of Nature,' p. 22.
'Long Distance,' pp. 23–24.
'Remains,' p. 25.

D35   *Hubbub*, Vol. 3, No. 1 (Spring 1985).

'Pain-Killers,' pp. 23–24.

D36   *Critical Quarterly*, Vol. 28, No. 3 (Autumn 1986).

'The Morning After,' p. 68.

D37   *Fortnight*, April 1987.

'The Act,' p. [30].

D38   *Poetry Review*, Vol. 77, No. 4 (Winter 1987/88).

'Y,' p. 26.

E
CRITICISM

This section lists selected critical articles on Tony Harrison's work. In addition, references to his work in books are also cited.

BOOKS

E1   Buckley, Peter. 'Top Banana?' in Morley, Sheridan, Ed.
            Theatre 73. London: Hutchinson, 1973. pp. 77–79.

            On *The Misanthrope*

E2   Simon, John. 'Translation or adaptation,' in *From Parnassus.*
            Essays in Honor of Jacques Barzun. New York: Harper & Row,
            [1976]. pp. 147–157.

            On *The Misanthrope*

E3   Booth, Martin. *British Poetry 1964 to 1984. Driving Through the*
            Barricades. London, Boston, Melbourne and Henley: Routledge
            & Kegan Paul, 1985. pp. 55, 218.

E4   Lamb, C.E. 'Tony Harrison' in Sherry, Vincent B., Jr., Ed.
            Poets of Great Britain and Ireland Since 1960, Part 1: A-L
            (Dictionary of Literary Biography, Vol. 40). Detroit: Gale
            Research Company, 1985. pp. 157–166.

JOURNALS

E5   Laidlaw R.P. 'Earthworks,' *Poetry and Audience*, Vol. 12, No. 5
            (6 November 1964), 5–6.

E6   Bryom, B. 'Earthworks,' *Agenda*, Vol. 4, No. 1 (April-May
            1965), 58–59.

E7   Hecht, Roger. 'Earthworks,' *Poetry*, Vol. 110, No. 2 (May
            1967), [112]–119.

E8   Chambers, Harry. 'Shorter Notices,' *Phoenix 6 and 7*
            (Summer 1970), 178.

            On *The Loiners*

E9   Simmons, James. 'National Geographic Poetry,' *The Honest*
            Ulsterman, No. 25 (Sept./Oct. 1970), 24–30.

            On *The Loiners*

E10   'Iambic attitudes,' *The Times Literary Supplement*, No. 3576
            (11 September 1970), 994.

            On *The Loiners*

E11   Wall, Stephen. 'Letting It happen,' *The Review*, No. 23
        (September/November 1970), 61–65.

        On *The Loiners*

E12   Cluysenaar, Anne. 'New Poetry,' *Stand*, Vol. 12, No. 1
        (1970–71) 72–76.

        On *The Loiners*

E13   Mills, Ralph J., Jr. 'Newcastle is Peru,' *Poetry*, Vol. 117, No. 5
        (February 1971), 331–338.

E14   Pritchard, W.H. 'Comment,' *Poetry*, CXIX, No. 3 (December
        1971), 161.

        On *The Loiners*

E15   Murphy, Peter. 'Odd and Even,' *Agenda*, Vol. 9, No. 1 (Winter
        1971), 64 66.

        On *The Loiners*

E16   Pybus, Rodney. 'The Greek Anthology,' *Stand*, Vol. 14, No. 4,
        (1973), 57–58.

E17   'Commentary,' *The Times Literary Supplement*, No. 3706 (16
        March 1973), 297.

        On *The Misanthrope*

E18   Macinerney, John. 'The Floating's,' *The Times Literary
        Supplement*, No. 3709 (6 April 1973), 395

        On *The Misanthrope*

E19   Weightman, John. 'Molière à la mode,' *Encounter*, XL, No. 5
        (May 1973), 50–52.

        On *The Misanthrope*

E20   Weightman, John. 'Phaedra Victorian,' *Encounter*, XLV, No. 6
        (December 1975), 46–48.

        On *Phaedra Britannica*

E21   Levi, Peter. 'Pagan idioms,' *The Times Literary Supplement*,
        No. 3856 (6 February 1976), 149.

        On *Palladas: Poems*

E22   Graham, Desmond. 'New Poetry,' *Stand*, Vol. 17, No. 3 (1976), 75–79.

On *Palladas: Poems*

E23   Fisher, Emma. 'Dead ends,' *Spectator*, Vol. 241, No. 7849 (9 December 1978), 24–25.

On *From the School of Eloquence*

E24   Clucas, Humphrey. 'The Luck of Palladas,' *Agenda*, Vol. 16, Nos. 3–4 (Autumn-Winter 1978/79), 170–171.

On *Palladas: Poems*

E25   Porter, Peter. 'Conflicting loyalties,' *The Observer*, 7 January 1979, 34.

On *From the School of Eloquence*

E26   Brownjohn, Alan. 'Fascination of What's Difficult. Recent Poetry,' *Encounter*, LII, No. 3 (March 1979), 61–65.

On *From the School of Eloquence*

E27   Bakewell, John. 'Tony Harrison,' [Profile]. *The Illustrated London News*, Vol. 267, No. 6968 (March 1979), 32–33.

E28   Motion, Andrew. 'Self's the Man,' *The New Statesman*, Vol. 97, No. 2509 (20 April 1979), 562–563.

On *From the School of Eloquence*

E29   Wainwright, Jeffrey. 'The Silence Round All Poetry,' *Poetry Review*, Vol. 69, No. 1 (July 1979), 57–59.

On *From the School of Eloquence*

E30   Graham, Desmond. 'The Evidence of Poetry: Recent Poetry,' *Stand*, Vol. 20, No. 4 (1979), 75–80.

On *From the School of Eloquence*

E31   Swarbrick, A.P. 'Scholars and Poets,' *P[oetry] N[ation] Review*, 15 (Vol. 7, No. 1, 1980), 57–58.

On *From the School of Eloquence*

E32   Fisher, Maria. 'The 1980 National Poetry Competition,' *The Poetry Society Newsletter*, January, 1981, 1.

Tony Harrison won first prize for 'Timer.'

E33   Fay, Stephen and Philip Oakes. 'Mystery Behind the Mask,' *The Sunday Times*, No. 8213 (29 November 1981), 33.

On *The Oresteia*

E34   Nye, Robert. 'Poetry,' *The Times*, No. 61104 (10 December 1981), 11.

On *Continuous*

E35   Hamilton, Ian. 'Poet and Parent,' *The Sunday Times*, No. 8216 (20 December 1981), 33.

On *Continuous*

E36   Lucas, John. 'Opening prisons,' *The New Statesman*, Vol. 103, No. 2650 (1 January 1982), 18–19.

On *Continuous*

E37   Reid, Christopher. 'Articulating the awkwardness,' *The Times Literary Supplement*, No. 4111 (15 January 1982), 49.

On *Continuous, U.S. Martial* and *A Kumquat for John Keats*.

E38   Porter, Peter. 'The Latinist of Leeds,' *The Observer*, 17 January 1982, 31.

On *Continuous, A Kumquat for John Keats, U.S. Martial* and *The Oresteia of Aeschylus*.

E39   Nye, Robert. 'Poetry,' *The Times*, No. 61149 (4 February 1982), 10.

On *The Oresteia, U.S. Martial* and *A Kumquat for John Keats*.

E40   Dunn, Douglas. 'Acute accent,' *Quarto*, No. 26 (March 1982), 11–12.

On *Continuous, A Kumquat for John Keats* and *U.S. Martial*.

E41   O'Neill, Michael. 'Thinking Hearts,' *Poetry Review*, Vol. 72, No. 1 (April 1982). 62–64.

On *Continuous, 50 Sonnets from the School of Eloquence, A Kumquat for John Keats* and *U.S. Martial*.

E42   Morrison, Blake. 'Labouring,' *London Review of Books*, Vol. 4, No. 6 (1–14 April 1982), 10–11.

On *Continuous, The Oresteia, U.S. Martial* and *A Kumquat for John Keats*.

E43   Davis, Dick. 'Vision and anger,' *The Listener*, Vol. 107, No. 2759, (6 May 1982), 26–27.

On *Continuous*

E44   'Letters. Tony Harrison,' *London Review of Books*, Vol. 4, No. 8 (6–19 May 1982), 4.

Four letters on *The Oresteia*

E45   Spender, Stephen. 'Changeling,' *The New York Review of Books*, XXIX, No. 12 (July 15, 1982), 26–28.

On *Continuous*

E46   Jenkins, Alan. 'A Barbarous Eloquence. Recent Poetry,' *Encounter*, LIX, No. 2, (August 1982), 55–57.

On *Continuous*

E47   Cox, C.B. 'Editorial,' *Critical Quarterly*, Vol. 24, No. 4 (Winter 1982), 3–4.

On *Continuous*

E48   Lomas, Herbert. 'Reviews,' *Ambit* 90 (1982), 73–74.

On *Continuous, U.S. Martial* and *A Kumquat for John Keats*.

E49   Pybus, Rodney. 'Recent Poetry,' *Stand*, Vol. 24, No. 2 (1983), 73–74.

On *Continuous* and *U.S. Martial*.

E50   Young, Alan. 'Weeds and white roses: the poetry of Tony Harrison,' *Critical Quarterly*, Vol. 26, Nos. 1 & 2 (Spring & Summer 1984), 157–163.

E51   Schmidt, Michael. 'Speaking for the voiceless,' *The Sunday Times*, No. 8362 (11 November 1984), 42.

On *Selected Poems*

E52   Britton, Jeremy. 'Books,' *Isis*, No. 1753 (November 30th 1984),
        22.

        On *Selected Poems*

E53   Nye, Robert. 'American Dionysus: Shelley of his age,' *The
        Times*, No. 62005 (6 December 1984), 11.

        On *Selected Poems* and *Palladas: Poems*

E54   Lucas, John. 'Prodigal son,' *The New Statesman*, Vol. 108,
        No. 2803 (7 December 1984), 32, 34.

        On *Selected Poems*

E55   Morrison, Blake. 'Backstreet Hamlet,' *The Observer*, 16
        December 1984, 18.

        On *Selected Poems*

E56   Davis, Dick. 'All over Europe,' *PN Review*, 37 (Vol. 10, No. 5,
        1984), 55–57.

        On *U.S. Martial*

E57   Cook, Jon. 'Books,' *The New Statesman*, Vol. 108,
        No. 2805/2806 (21/28 December 1984), 45.

        On *Selected Poems*

E58   Davis, Dick. 'Prosy childhoods,' *The Listener*, Vol. 113,
        No. 2890 (3 January 1985), 26–27.

        On *Selected Poems*

E59   Rawson, Claude. 'Family voices,' *The Times Literary
        Supplement*, No. 4266 (4 January 1985), 10.

        On *Selected Poems* and *Palladas: Poems*

E60   Nightingale, Benedict. 'Resurrection,' *The New Statesman*,
        Vol. 109, No. 2810 (25 January 1985), 36–38.

        On *The Mysteries*

E61   Peter, John. 'Magical mystery tour de force,' *The Sunday
        Times*, No. 8373 (27 January 1985), 43

        On *Doomsday*

E62 Donoghue, Denis. 'Venisti tandem,' *The London Review of Books*, Vol. 7, No. 2 (7 February 1985), 18–19.

On *Selected Poems* and *Palladas: Poems*

E63 Perkin, Michael. 'Reviews,' *Outposts Poetry Quarterly*, No. 144 (Spring 1985), 27–28.

On *Selected Poems*

E64 Brugière, Bernard. 'Esquisse d'un panorama de la poésie Britannique contemporaine,' *Etudes Anglaises*, XXXVIIIᵉ annee, No. 2 (avril-juin 1985), 129–143.

E65 Grant, Damian. 'The Voice of History in British Poetry, 1970–84,' *Etudes Anglaises*, XXXVIIIᵉ annee, No. 2 (avril-juin 1985), 158–179.

E66 Simmons, James. 'Out of the Sandbagged Nets,' *The Honest Ulsterman*, No. 78 (Summer 1985), 49–53.

On *Selected Poems*

E67 Worpole, Ken. 'Scholarship Boy: The Poetry of Tony Harrison,' *New Left Review*, No. 153 (September/October 1985), 63–74.

E68 O'Donoghue, Bernard. 'Local Deity,' *Poetry Review*, Vol. 75, No. 3 (October 1985), 61–63.

On *The Mysteries*

E69 Morrison, Blake. 'Dialect does it,' *London Review of Books*, Vol. 7, No. 21 (5 December 1985), 14.

On *The Mysteries*

E70 Tunnicliffe, Stephen. 'Reviews,' *The Anglo-Welsh Review*, No. 79 (1985), 98–102.

On *Selected Poems*

E71 McDuff, David. 'New Poetry,' *Stand Magazine*. Vol. 27, No. 1 (Winter 1985–86), [72]–80.

On *Selected Poems*

E72 Burton, Rosemary. 'V. Good,' *Punch*, January 8, 1986, 39.

On *Dramatic Verse 1973-1985, The Mysteries, V* and *The Fire-Gap*

E73 Reid, Christopher. 'Here Comes Amy,' *London Review of Books*, Vol. 8, No. 7 (17 April 1986), 20

On *V* and *Dramatic Verse 1973-1985*

E74 Murray, Oswyn. 'Poetry in public,' *The Times Literary Supplement*, No. 4340 (6 June 1986), 615–616

On *Dramatic Verse 1973-1985*

E75 Eagleton, Terry. 'Antagonisms,' *Poetry Review*, Vol. 76, No. 1/2 (June 1986), 20–22.

On *V*

E76 Thorpe, Adam. 'The Tut Factor,' *Literary Review*, September 1986, 58–59.

On *V*

E77 Young, A. 'Short Notices,' *Critical Quarterly*, Vol. 28, No. 3, (Autumn 1986), 119.

On *V*

E78 Casterton, Julia. 'Reviews,' *Ambit* 105 (1986), 83–84.

On *V*

E79 Easton, David. 'Reviews,' *Anglo-Welsh Review*, No. 83 (1986), 126–128.

On *The Fire-Gap* and *V*

E80 Kerrigan, John. 'Knowing the Dead . . . ,' *Essays in Criticism*, XXXVII, No. 1 (January 1987). 11–42.

E81 'Book Review,' *Library Journal*, Vol. 112, No. 12 (July 1987), 81.

On *Selected Poems*

E82 Richman, Robert. 'Them, Uz and Annie,' *The New York Times Book Review*, November 29, 1987, 25–26.

On *Selected Poems*

E83   Morrison, Blake. 'The Filial Art: A Reading of Comteporary British Poetry,' *The Yearbook of English Studies*, Vol. 17 (1987), [179]–217.

E84   Burton, Rosemary. 'On the loose with an aerosol,' *The Catalogue* (1987), Bloodaxe Books, 6–7.

INDEX

References in this index are to item numbers in the bibliography. The titles of all works written by Tony Harrison are capitalized. The titles of books and pamphlets by Harrison and all other books, periodicals and newspapers are in italics. Untitled poems are indexed by first lines enclosed by quotation marks, with the note that the reference is a first line. The titles of books reviewed by Tony Harrison and the authors of books reviewed have not been indexed; however, the titles of these reviews are given reference numbers. Publisher's of books and persons listed in the introduction or acknowledgements sections of this book are not indexed.